A RAVEN'S HEART

K. C. BATEMAN

Copyright © 2016 by Kate Bateman

Ebook ISBN: 978-1-7326378-8-7

Print ISBN: 978-1-7326378-9-4

Excerpt from A Counterfeit Heart by K. C. Bateman © 2016 by Kate Bateman

© 2020 Cover Art by Cora Graphics

© Periodimages.com

❀ Created with Vellum

"Prison walls cannot confine him who loves."

—Antoine de Saint Exupéry

CHAPTER 1

*E*ngland, June 1816

"I'm a spy, not a bloody nursemaid!"

William de l'Isle, Viscount Ravenwood, glared across the desk at his mentor, Lord Castlereagh.

The older man shook his head, supremely unmoved by his outburst. "Miss Hampden needs immediate protection. Someone's targeting my code breakers and whoever killed Edward could also have discovered her identity. I can't afford to lose her, too."

Raven narrowed his eyes. "Use another agent."

Castlereagh gave him one of those level, penetrating looks he so excelled at. "Who? Neither of her brothers are here; Nic's in Paris, and Richard's following a lead on that French forger he's been after for months. Who else is left?" He pinched the bridge of his nose. "We've lost too many good men. First Tony got himself killed in France, then Kit disappeared. There's been no news of him for months."

Raven frowned. He refused to consider the distasteful probability that his friend was dead. Kit was like him, a master of survival. He could be deep undercover. But with every week that went by with no word it became harder and harder to stay positive.

"And now another good man, Edward Lamb, had been murdered," Castlereagh sighed. "I don't want Miss Hampden to be next."

The older man was a master of applying just the right amount of pressure and guilt. He hadn't made it to head of the Foreign Office without knowing how to manipulate people.

"You think I should entrust her to a less competent operative?" Castlereagh mused softly. "You're not burdened by false modesty, Ravenwood. You know you're the best I have. I was hoping you'd use your exceptional talent for survival to keep Miss Hampden alive, too."

Raven sighed, well aware he was being backed into a corner. If it had been anyone else he wouldn't have hesitated. But Heloise Hampden was the fly in his ointment. The spoke in his wheel.

A total bloody menace.

Hellcat Hampden had been the subject of his guilty daydreams for years. What had started out as adolescent musings had matured into fevered erotic fantasies that showed absolutely no sign of abating. He'd told himself the attraction was because she was forbidden, tried to lose himself in other, far more available women. Nothing had worked. And while he'd rarely paid much attention to the monotonous sermons preached by the clergy, he was fairly sure there was something in the bible that said "thou shalt not covet thy best friend's little sister." Or words to that effect.

He was the last person she should be entrusted to. He'd sworn to stay away from her. Had avoided her quite successfully—give or take a few blessedly brief skirmishes—for the past six years.

Hell, he'd traveled to the far corners of war torn Europe to try to forget her.

And now here he was, drawn back to her by some malevolent twist of fate.

As if his life wasn't cursed enough already.

Over the past few years they'd settled into an uneasy, albeit barbed, truce; it was a sad reflection on his twisted nature that he preferred sparring with her to holding a reasonable conversation with anyone else.

His blood thrummed at the prospect of seeing her again and he smiled in self-directed mockery. Few things increased his heartbeat anymore. In combat he was a master of his emotions, sleek and deadly and efficient. Fighting barely elevated his pulse. He could kill a man without breaking a sweat. But put him ten paces away from that slip of a girl and a furious drummer took up residence in his chest, battering away against his ribs.

He shook his head. Being near her was a torture he both craved and abhorred, but he had a duty to keep her safe. A duty to her family, to Castlereagh, to the whole damn country. Much as he'd like someone else to deal with her, he didn't trust anyone else. She was his to torment.

Castlereagh, the old devil, smiled, as if he already sensed Raven's grudging acceptance. "That's settled, then. She's safe at home right now. You can go over and get her in the morning."

He rose and strode to the door of the study, then flashed an amused glance at Raven's immaculate evening attire and the mask resting on the desk. "I apologize for interrupting your evening, Ravenwood. I'll leave you to your entertainments."

SHE WAS IN.

Heloise smiled in triumph as she trailed a group of masked revelers toward Lord Ravenwood's infamous ballroom.

She'd never been invited to one of these masquerades. Raven and her brothers had always excluded her from anything remotely interesting as a child, and the situation hadn't improved now she was twenty-two and perfectly capable of looking after herself. Tonight, however, she had a valid reason for sneaking in; the crumpled translation she'd stuffed down the front of her bodice. Raven would forgive her when he heard what she'd discovered.

The extravagant debauchery of his annual gathering was the stuff of legend. Even the most sophisticated members of the ton discussed it in scandalized whispers, behind twitching fans. She was finally going to discover whether its reputation was justified.

Heloise reached the entrance to the ballroom, glanced up, and stopped dead. Her lips formed a soundless O of astonishment. The gilt-edged invitation she'd "borrowed" from Richard's study had promised "An Evening of Heaven and Hell." The rumors had not been exaggerated.

She blinked. The guests had embraced the suggestion of depraved licentiousness with enthusiasm. Scantily-clad gods and goddesses mingled with angels and devils in a dizzying sea of color. Grotesque masks, all curved beaks and twisting horns, swirled above acres of exposed flesh. A hundred perfumes entwined with the smell of warm bodies, hair powder, and wine, while the string quartet in the corner was almost inaudible over the boisterous hum of conversation.

Heloise glanced down at her own comparatively simple costume. She'd pilfered an authentic second-dynasty Egyptian beadwork collar from her father's collection of Ancient jewelry and improved a black silk half-mask with whiskers and a pair of papier mâché ears. There: Bastet, the Ancient Egyptian cat goddess. Not that anyone here would have any idea who she was supposed to be.

Her stomach gave an excited flip. She didn't need to find Raven immediately. A few extra minutes wouldn't make any difference. There was such a delicious freedom in being masked and anonymous. No one was who they appeared. That gilded lady over there could be a duchess or courtesan, actress or spy. That silver-masked satyr could be a diplomat or a prince.

Heloise shivered, despite the stifling heat. The possibilities of the evening shimmered in the air like a summer haze, magical and dangerous. She could be anyone she wanted. Not someone's unmarriageable little sister. Not the bookish code breaker. She could be flighty and irresponsible, the secret, daring girl she'd been before her face was scarred. The beautiful one, for once, instead of the clever one. Anticipation tingled through her body as if she were poised at the top of a steep, smooth slope. Just one small nudge would send her hurtling down, toward adventure.

She grabbed a glass of champagne from a passing servant and took a few fortifying sips as her skin prickled with the unpleasant conviction that she was being watched. That was foolish. Neither of her brothers was here to curtail her enjoyment and the only other person who could potentially unmask her—tonight's host, their neighbor and most irritating man on the planet, William Ravenwood—wouldn't be expecting to see her. She was going to have the devil of a time finding him in this crowd.

As if the very thought had summoned him, all the fine hairs on her arms lifted in warning and Heloise glanced around with a sense of impending doom. The crowd parted obligingly, and there he was. The god of the Underworld, staring at her.

Oh, hell and damnation.

He stood motionless, a pillar of darkness amid the colored gaiety, his tall frame somehow managing to radiate a barely leashed tension, as if he was poised to attack. Heloise repressed the instinct to cross herself.

His mask was black like hers, only far more elaborate. The long muzzle of a jackal, ears pricked and alert, eyes rimmed with thick lines of gold, covered the top half of his face. Only his jaw was visible; hard and male, with unfashionably tanned skin shadowed by the hint of a beard. Dark hair curled out from beneath the mask to brush his snowy cravat and pitch-black evening jacket.

The tiny part of her brain not frozen into immobility—and inexplicably concerned with historical accuracy—whispered that to be *totally* authentic, Anubis should be bare-chested. Her mouth went dry as she imagined the broad shoulders and well-defined chest concealed beneath all that black silk.

The role of Anubis fitted him to perfection. The jackal guardian of the Underworld, a creature of the night, perfectly at home in darkness and shadows. She shivered as he turned and looked directly at her. He tilted his head to one side, the mannerism exactly like that of a dog—a hint of interest, a silent question.

Her first instinct was to run, but her feet seemed glued to the floor. She took another gulp of champagne and when she looked up again he'd disappeared, swallowed up by the swirling mass of dancers. Her heart hammered unpleasantly against her rib cage. Surely he hadn't recognized her from all the way across the room?

You recognized him.

She shook herself. It didn't matter. She'd run from William Ravenwood far too often. Tonight she would stand her ground.

Speak of the devil.

Raven narrowed his eyes at the slim, white-clad figure slinking around his ballroom, and cursed. She was supposed to be tucked up safe in bed. What the hell was she doing here? The debauched, cynical world he inhabited was no place for someone like her.

His heart pounded in anticipation as he weaved through the

excited throng, keeping to the shadows out of habit. There. Black mask near the door. It was definitely her. He'd know her from half the world away, in a crowd of a hundred thousand. It was a simple enough matter to spot her in a room of two hundred. She alone made his blood sing in his veins, made his body vibrate with awareness, as if he were a tuning fork that responded only to her pitch.

Bloody woman.

She was dressed as a cat. He almost laughed at the irony. And here he was, a dog. How utterly appropriate. Bastet and Anubis. Both Egyptian gods of the Underworld. Both black as midnight. As different as night from day. Opposite, and yet at the same time oddly connected. It had been like this between them since they were children. It was a bloody curse.

At this distance the tilted cutout eyes of her mask hid her face but he already knew the astonishing color of her eyes; lavender-gray, the exact hue of a thunderstorm-ready sky.

He circled the room and approached her from the back. She turned, an elegant sweep of shoulder and throat, and he clenched his fists against the insanely erotic urge to press his mouth to her nape and bite her. He shook his head. Such a perverse attraction. She was light. He was darkness. Not for him. Never for him.

She'd tried to tame her dark blond hair into some kind of elaborate twist, but stray tendrils curled down the graceful line of her neck, refusing to conform. He leaned one shoulder against a marble pillar. To all outward appearances the creature in front of him was a respectable member of the ton; cool and poised and infinitely alluring. It was a lie. The rebellious nature she tried so hard to suppress was like those little wisps of hair — always trying to escape.

It amazed him that no one else could see it, even her own brothers. They thought she'd outgrown her childish yearnings for excitement and equality, but he knew better. No doubt that was why she'd come here tonight; she simply could not resist an adventure.

The devil in him relished the idea of coaxing all that repressed mayhem into breaking free. Heloise Hampden needed to let her hair down, both literally and figuratively. Except God only knew what would happen if she did.

She placed her empty glass on the tray offered by a passing servant. She was so small he could tuck the top of her head under his chin and pull her into his side. His hip would fit neatly into the curve of her waist. Her breasts would press perfectly into his chest. His mouth would fit precisely—

Raven banged his head against the pillar. Insane. Which was ironic, really. He'd managed to remain *compos mentis* despite spending eight weeks of his life locked up in a cell expecting to be executed. He'd witnessed some of the worst sights a decade of warfare could inflict upon a man and stayed sane. Yet Hellcat Hampden made him crazy. And, idiot that he was, he enjoyed it.

He stepped up behind her and caught a hint of her midnight-and-roses scent. It tightened his gut and turned his knees to water, but he composed his features into their usual expression of cynical boredom. The day she discovered the effect she had on him was the day he'd cut his own wrists. Not. For. Him.

"All alone, mademoiselle?" he murmured dryly. "Who are you waiting for?"

CHAPTER 2

*H*eloise jumped at that low, achingly familiar voice. "Oh no, I—"

She stopped and frowned. Why had Raven called her "mademoiselle" instead of "Hellcat"? He never missed the chance to use his taunting nickname for her. The fact that he hadn't was . . . odd. Her heart stuttered. Perhaps he really hadn't recognized her?

A sudden, reckless urge took hold of her. He didn't know who she was! Which meant she'd been granted a completely unexpected opportunity to break out of their usual cycle of petty insults and studied avoidance. A flush of hot excitement skittered over her skin. Why not pretend? Just for a few minutes. Pretend she was a woman he'd flirt with. A woman he'd desire.

He was scandalously close behind her. She glanced over her shoulder and caught a brief glimpse of his perfect lips hovering beneath the snarling muzzle of his mask.

"Don't turn around," he murmured. "I'm enjoying the view."

She stilled.

"You're very beautiful, mademoiselle cat."

Heloise curled her lips at the irony. No one who saw her face ever claimed that. "How can you tell? For all you know I could be hideously scarred beneath this mask."

"No," he mused, quietly confident. "You're definitely beautiful."

Heloise closed her eyes as pleasure and pain curled together in her chest. A few years ago she'd have done anything to hear him say those words. She managed a creditable shrug. "What's that saying? 'All cats are gray in the dark.'"

His breath warmed her shoulder, the curve of her neck. "Let's just say I have an unerring instinct in such matters."

She opened her mouth to refute him, but he spoke again.

"So why a cat? Cats are haughty and cruel. Is that a fair reading of your character?"

"Why a dog, sir?" she countered archly. "Are you loyal? Faithful? Devoted?"

He chuckled. "Hardly. But don't worry—I'm not about to mark my territory against one of these elegant pillars. I'm considered relatively domesticated."

Heloise repressed an unladylike snort. After the past decade working as a spy alongside her brothers, Raven was about as tame as a jackal. And she shouldn't be finding such puerile humor amusing. "If you're hoping I'll throw you a stick, I'm afraid you're doomed to disappointment."

His lips quirked as if at some private joke. "How true. You realize, of course, that as cat and dog we can never be friends. I think the best we can hope for is friendly enemies."

She made a moue with her mouth. "That is disappointing."

His lips curved upward. "Ah, but then, I've always found enemies extremely . . . stimulating."

Her heart thumped at his suggestive tone. The fiend could make even the most innocuous conversation fraught with innuendo. Or maybe it was just her overactive imagination.

"Can I get you a drink?" he asked smoothly before she could form an appropriate response. "A saucer of milk?" His voice held the ghost of a laugh. "Or perhaps you'd prefer champagne?" A servant appeared at his elbow and he took two glasses of the sparkling liquid. "Drink up," he urged gently.

"I really shouldn't." She wasn't used to drinking spirits. Almack's only served tea and lemonade. And she'd already had one glass.

He curled his fingers around hers and raised the glass to her lips. "You really should."

The champagne burned down her throat, blissfully cool. No doubt the vintage was hideously expensive; money was no object for Raven. Her fingers burned where he touched her and she sucked in a relieved breath when he released her hand. His nearness was having the most unsettling effect on her nerves. She glanced around the room, trying to appear no more than innocently curious. "I wish I knew which of these people was our host."

She waited for him to take the cue and reveal himself.

"You mean Ravenwood?"

Heloise raised her brows under her mask. Apparently he wanted to remain incognito, too. Interesting. "Yes, I'd like to congratulate him. He's certainly achieved what was promised on the invitation—an evening of heaven and hell."

Raven's shoulder brushed hers as he moved to stand beside her, and she risked another sideways glance at him. His coat was exquisite, perfectly molded to his body as if someone had poured liquid silk over him and simply waited for it to dry. It was a miracle it didn't rip when he moved. The stark contrast of black and white enhanced the lean perfection of his features. Heloise took another long sip of champagne.

He glanced around, a slight, cynical smile on his lips. "Yes, someone should tell Ravenwood this is an excellent party. The brandy's contraband, the rooms are so overcrowded one can barely breathe, and I can see at least five—no, six—of the seven deadly sins being committed as we speak."

That was true. Examples of pride, envy, greed, gluttony, and lust were everywhere she turned. Tables groaned with food, solid silver platters piled high with exotic fruits and cheeses. A rumble of chatter emanated from the card room next door, the chink of glasses mingling with occasional exclamations of delight or groans of despair.

There were other groans, too. Heloise hastily averted her eyes from a couple huddled in a darkened corner. The man's hand seemed to be disappearing into the scandalously low bodice of his partner's gown.

"I trust the evening's sufficiently uninhibited for your taste?" Raven inquired politely.

She swallowed. "Yes indeed. Although there seems to be far more of hell here tonight than heaven."

"A quirk of society, is it not? We adore the wicked and loathe the good. Our host is the perfect example. They say he's blackened beyond redemption, yet those same hypocrites fall over themselves for an invitation to this very ball."

"Your choice of mask is very apt," she laughed. "The word 'cynic' derives from the Greek word 'kynikos,' meaning doglike."

As soon as she'd said it, Heloise wished she'd held her tongue. Such bookish knowledge was sure to betray her. How many other women in the room had an interest in Ancient Greek, for heaven's sake? She held her breath, expecting exposure, but Raven merely inclined his head.

"It's not cynical if it's true. Everyone reads Dante's Inferno and skips his Paradiso. It's because paradise is boring. Hell is far more interesting."

A throaty laugh from nearby drew her attention.

"Ah, the divine Lady Brooke," Raven murmured, following her gaze. "London's favorite merry widow."

And your most recent mistress, Heloise added silently. Her heart sank as she studied the voluptuous woman, whose impossibly curvy body seemed to defy the laws of gravity. Heloise glanced down at her own sadly average chest and sighed wistfully. If she'd been born with a body like that, in addition to her brains, the world would have been hers for the taking. "A marble statue with those proportions would fall flat on its face," she muttered darkly.

"Maybe she has enormous feet to act as counterbalance?" Raven offered blandly.

Heloise bit her lip. No doubt he knew the precise dimensions of Lady Brooke's feet. Along with every other part of her. She cleared her throat and attempted to inject just the right amount of casual speculation into her tone. "Perhaps our mysterious host is her companion. Rumor has it she's Ravenwood's latest paramour."

Raven tilted his head. "Is that what rumor says?"

Heloise shrugged. "She certainly has all the necessary attributes he seems to require in a mistress. Namely, an ample pair of breasts and an inability to speak coherent English."

He chuckled. "You seem remarkably well informed of Lord Ravenwood's taste in women."

Heloise waved her hand in a vague, airy gesture. "Oh, you know how it is. There are no secrets in the ton. Especially when it concerns an eligible bachelor like Lord Ravenwood. His previous mistress was French. And the one before that was an Italian opera singer. I suppose only taking up with foreigners saves him from having to exert himself to actually *talk* to them."

He slanted her a wicked sideways glance. "I'm fairly sure he doesn't engage them for conversation."

Heat rushed into her face as her skin prickled with awareness. Raven invariably managed to veer every conversation off onto a distinctly racy tangent. She gave an unconcerned lift of the shoulder and ignored the ache in her chest at the idea of him with another woman. "Well, I expect she'll be replaced soon enough. Ravenwood seems to be able to snap his fingers and have any woman he wants."

"Not all of them," he murmured. "A select few have remained frustratingly elusive."

Her heart stuttered. He absolutely wasn't talking about her.

"Still, it's true Ravenwood's never had a problem attracting most women," he continued, as if they were discussing nothing more innocuous than the weather. "Nothing elicits desire in a female more than the promise of a ducal title and an outrageously large . . ." he paused teasingly ". . . house."

Heloise's mood lightened at his self-deprecating humor. A face like a fallen angel and the body of a Greek god probably don't hurt, either. She glanced up at the arched ceiling and pretended to admire the soaring architecture. "It's certainly impressive," she said, straight-faced. "Very . . . imposing."

"Ravenwood would be delighted to hear it. A man never tires of women praising the size of his endowments."

Heloise bit back an unladylike snort as the quartet in the corner struck up a waltz. Couples began to form on the dance floor and she stiffened in surprise when Raven slipped an arm around her waist and pulled her onto their midst before she could object.

"Dance with me."

She shouldn't. It would only make things worse. She should reveal who she was and tell him about the message. But the crowd pushed them together and her face pressed up against his chest and she made the tactical error of inhaling. Oh Lord, he smelled delicious, like a forest after rain. She placed her hands on his lapels and pushed backward. Raven's hand slid down her back and came to rest at the very bottom of her spine, scandalously low. Heloise drew in an unsteady breath as his touch burned through the fabric of her dress. They fitted together perfectly.

"I don't think—"

"Good," he countered softly. He removed her hand from his chest and repositioned it on his shoulder. "In situations like this, thinking is highly overrated." He captured her other hand, brought it up to shoulder level, and whirled her away into the dance.

Heloise gasped. Such magic. Her body knew the secret, even if it hadn't informed her brain. The confidence of his steps, the surety of his grip, transferred themselves to her and she was flying over the floor as if they'd done this a thousand times before. Which they had, of course, but only in her fanciful childhood dreams.

Raven splayed the fingers of his left hand and tugged her closer still. The muscles of his arm flexed beneath the fabric of his jacket. Her breasts pressed against the hard contours of his chest and the blood heated in her veins. He was almost a full head taller—her cheek only reached his shoulder—so his size should have been intimidating, but instead she felt oddly protected.

When the music ended they swirled to a giddy stop. Heloise pulled back, breathless as the couples around them began to disband, but instead of releasing her, Raven tightened his grip. She glanced up and his sudden intent stillness made her skin prickle with alarm. She watched, mesmerized, as he slowly tilted his head and lowered his mouth toward hers.

Good Lord, he was going to kiss her! Right here—in the middle of the crowded dance floor!

Disbelief and reckless anticipation sizzled through her veins. Why not? She'd promised herself some forbidden fun, and kissing Raven definitely came under that category. This might be her only chance—ever—and besides, he'd never need to know it was her.

She angled her head and parted her lips. Closed her eyes in breathless anticipation. Raven's warm breath skimmed over her cheek and she almost groaned in frustration when he paused a hairbreadth away from her lips in deliberate restraint, drawing out the moment until every cell in her body was screaming for him to make contact.

Heloise strained upward on tiptoe. His mouth grazed the very corner of hers in a tantalizing butterfly kiss that sent fizzles of excitement racing over her skin. She turned her head, blindly seeking his lips, but he pulled back with a chiding sound, his fingers tightening their grip on her upper arms.

Heloise opened her eyes and frowned behind her mask. What on earth was he waiting for, the dolt? An engraved invitation?

And then those perfect lips curved into the smug, self-satisfied smile she knew only too well, and her stomach plummeted in dread.

Raven's chin brushed her temple as he casually tucked a strand of her hair behind her ear. "Hellcat Hampden," he scolded softly. "What in God's name are you doing in my ballroom?"

CHAPTER 3

*F*or one moment of awful, icy realization, Heloise couldn't move. And then she whacked him on the arm. Hard.

"Ravenwood! You beast! Get off me!" She placed both palms flat on his chest and shoved as hard as she could. The deceitful swine didn't budge an inch. "You knew it was me the whole time! Why did you carry on?"

He stepped back, that wicked mouth curving into his usual irritating grin. "Why did you?" he countered. "And don't tell me you thought I was someone else. You knew it was me, too."

"I did not," she lied indignantly, certain she was blushing to the roots of her hair. Thank God she was wearing a mask.

He still didn't let her go; his hands gripped her elbows, keeping her close against his chest. "I must say, that was a very interesting experiment. How far would you have gone if I hadn't called you out? Could I have steered you into the games room for a bit of indiscretion? Could I be seducing you right now on that billiard table in there?"

Heloise gasped in outrage, even as his scorching mental images sent a shameful wave of heat through her body.

"Admit it. You were enjoying it."

"I was not!" she said, very aware of what Shakespeare had to say about ladies who protested too much. But if she didn't protest, she'd throw her arms around his neck and beg him to kiss her properly, and she had far too much self-respect for that. She would not become another of his faceless conquests. His paramours were as interchangeable as his cravats. And about as intelligent.

"Come on, you've fancied me since you were sixteen," he goaded mercilessly.

"It was a temporary aberration. I'm cured of it now."

Raven released one of her arms and steered her effortlessly through the crowd. "So to what do I owe the pleasure of your company, Hellcat? Because I *know* you weren't on the guest list. And don't tell me your brothers are here. Richard's in London with your parents and Nic's still on his honeymoon."

"You seem remarkably well informed of my family's where-abouts," she snapped, unsuccessfully trying to disengage her elbow from his grip.

"I'm a spy," he whispered. "I know lots of things about lots of people. Why aren't you up in London with the rest of your family?"

She affected a shrug. "There's something I've been working on here and I wanted to get it finished."

His mouth tightened. "Another scholarly translation?"

"Sort of," she hedged. "In fact, that's what I need to talk to you about."

His lips flattened into a disapproving line. "You shouldn't be locked away studying dusty old tomes. You should be out, enjoying yourself."

"Yes, well, I don't get invited to that many ton functions," she said pointedly.

He ignored the barb. "You know what I think? I think you're hiding. Even without that mask."

She crossed her arms. "I don't know what you mean."

"You bury yourself in books and research because you'd rather deal with Ancient civilizations than interact with real, live people."

Heloise felt a spark of anger, mainly because there was a grain of truth in what he said.

"What are you so afraid of?"

Of letting go, she almost said. *Of opening myself up. Because I did that once and look what happened; you rejected me.*

Luckily Raven didn't seem to require a response. "I expect it's too much to hope you're chaperoned," he said bleakly. Her stubborn silence was answer enough. He sighed. "Some things never change. You, Miss Hampden, are a magnet for disaster. Don't try to deny it. You may have fooled the ton with your bookish airs and demure ways, but I know you. You've a penchant for trouble."

"I do not!"

He raised a disbelieving brow. "If there's ever a plume of smoke on the horizon, I'll stake my life you'll be at the bottom of it with a tinderbox, an out-of-control bonfire, and a guilty expression."

She glared at him. "That is not true!"

"You were such a scruffy little urchin. Always traipsing around the estate and getting into scrapes." He shook his head, chuckling. "You never could refuse a challenge, either."

Heloise ground her teeth. She hated the way he constantly reminded her of her childish exploits. Would he never see her as a woman? He treated her with the same affectionate disdain as her brothers did. She half expected him to ruffle her hair. If he tried it now she'd kick him in the shins.

"You try to hide your true nature but you can't fool me."

She huffed inelegantly.

He adopted a mock-pitying tone. "It's sad, really, to see you so repressed."

She rolled her eyes, both horrified and amused.

He chuckled. "Yes, I see it as my earthly duty to bring you out of hiding."

She almost choked. "It is not your duty. You're neither my relative nor my husband. You have no responsibility for me whatsoever."

"For which I thank God on a daily basis," he muttered fervently. He took two more glasses from a servant. "Here, drink this."

She accepted it without thinking. A drunken reveler jostled her arm and a cold wash of champagne splashed onto her chest and trickled down between her breasts. "Oh, bugger-and-arse!" she muttered.

"That's what I love about you, Hellcat. Always so ladylike. Just when I despair that the impulsive hellion I grew up with has vanished, you say something like that and the world rights itself again."

She growled at him. Actually growled.

"You shouldn't do that, either," he admonished gently. "It makes little wrinkles in your nose." He ran a forefinger over the tip of her nose left uncovered by the cat mask. Heloise's stomach flipped. She quelled the impulse to snap her head around and bite him.

Why was he the only one who could make her abandon six years of hard-won decorum with nothing more than a few sly comments and childish jibes?

"That's what I love about you, Ravenwood," she echoed sweetly. "You're so unfailingly ungentlemanly. I don't feel the slightest need to act with propriety when I'm with you."

His smile turned wolfish, and she realized belatedly how her words could be misconstrued. He didn't disappoint. "I'm considered an expert at making prim young ladies abandon propriety. I'm glad I have the same effect on you."

Heloise suddenly recognized the champagne-spilling culprit

behind them; Lord Collingham. She instinctively ducked her head and hunched her shoulders. Ravenwood chuckled.

"Avoiding Collingham, are you? Is he still proposing once a season?"

Heloise nodded. "The drunken idiot's surprisingly persistent. And he's so stupid he's immune to my usual strategy for dissuading suitors."

"What's that?"

"I discuss etymology," she said. "At great length."

"Insects?"

Heloise clucked her tongue. Raven was many things, but stupid wasn't one of them. His air of languid insouciance disguised the fact that he was almost as well-read as herself. "You know it's not. That's entomology. I'm talking about words. Their meanings, where they come from."

"Of course."

"It usually only takes a few minutes for their eyes to glaze over."

"I can't think why," Raven's tone was drier than the Sahara. "It sounds fascinating."

"The word 'sarcasm,' for example," she continued, warming to her theme, "comes from the Greek word 'sarcophagus,' which literally means to tear the flesh. As in to cut someone with your verbal barbs."

"Have I drawn your blood, Hellcat?"

"Hardly," she snorted. "I'd have to care about your opinion for it to hurt me."

He feigned a wince. "Ouch. But I heard you've had other offers, despite that cutting tongue of yours. What about Wilton?"

Heloise stilled. How did he know about that? Lord Wilton had only proposed last week.

Raven cleared his throat. "He's a good man."

"Yes. He is."

There were a hundred reasons why she should accept Lord

Wilton's suit. He was a good man. Kind, wealthy, even-tempered, only slightly older than herself. He even shared her interest in Egyptology. She'd been trying to get an invitation to study his collection of New Kingdom papyri for years.

Unfortunately, the one reason she couldn't marry Lord Wilton was standing right next to her; six foot two inches of pure heartache. Heloise suppressed a sigh. Unrequited love was so aggravating.

She'd actually researched the definition of "requited" once. It should, logically, mean the opposite of "unrequited"—namely, returned. Not so. "Requited" meant revenged or retaliated. That summed up their strange, quarrelsome relationship perfectly; a simmering attraction tinged with mutual animosity. A war of attrition neither could win.

"I suppose I should be grateful to get any offers at all," she said, focusing her attention on the dancers. "Most of my suitors cried off after my accident. But Collingham's so desperate for my dowry, he's willing to overlook my scarred face. Wilton, on the other hand, thinks that because I avoid society I won't bankrupt him by buying the latest fashions and hosting lavish parties."

The strange thing was, she'd long ago stopped resenting her scar for curtailing her marriage prospects. She had no desire for a husband—unless it was Raven—and she was glad to avoid a society that revered the frivolous and distained her scholarly pursuits as freakish and unfashionable.

"Speaking of marriage proposals, what about you?" she said. "Haven't you ever thought about taking a wife?"

"Constantly," he drawled. "Whose did you have in mind?"

She elbowed him in the ribs. "You know what I mean."

He'd probably already had half the married women in here, she thought morosely. The man was a menace. He just crooked his finger and they came running, lured by all that lazy, dangerous charm. She really ought to stop flirting and tell him about the message. "Come to think of it, forget I asked. You'd make an appalling husband."

"My thoughts exactly. Which is why I've no intention of ever entering the married state. Marriage is a prison. And speaking as someone who's had intimate knowledge of imprisonment, I can say with authority that anything that endangers one's personal liberty is to be strictly avoided."

Heloise stilled. Raven rarely volunteered information about his time as a captive. Six years ago he'd been abducted by a London gang seeking to blackmail his grandfather, the Duke of Avondale. While the duke had stalled and negotiated, Raven had escaped, but only after weeks of imprisonment. The experience had changed him. Now his eyes held a fathomless, haunted look, as if he'd faced the darkest levels of hell and emerged . . . if not unscathed, at least wiser and more cynical. And he still refused to forgive his grandfather.

Heloise tossed her head. She was determined to enjoy herself, and nothing was more fun than baiting Raven. It was rather like poking a wolf with a stick; dangerous, but undeniably thrilling. She cast around for some way to taunt him, as he'd teased her earlier with that ridiculous almost-kiss, and hit on the very thing.

"You asked what I'm doing here. If you must know, I'm using you."

"Oh, really?" his tone was highly skeptical.

"Yes. I thought I'd take the opportunity to show my suitors a little healthy competition."

He snorted. "You'll need a better plan, then. Nobody knows who you are under that mask except me."

Drat. She'd forgotten about that. Still, she couldn't resist trying to needle him. She racked her brains for something suitably shocking. "All right, then. The truth is, I thought I might take a lover."

She prayed he'd choke on his champagne, but he merely lifted an intrigued eyebrow.

"Anyone I know?"

"I'm considering you."

He didn't even bat an eyelid, the swine. "Me? Interesting."

She hated it when he used that word. He managed to imbue it with a hundred shades of inferred meaning, none of them good.

"Why?" he asked.

"Why do I want a lover? Or why am I considering you, specifically?"

"Both."

"Well, I've had several offers of marriage, and I suppose I'll have to accept one of them sooner or later. I can't live with my parents forever. Unlike you men, single women don't have the luxury of setting up their own establishments. So, before I'm immured in a loveless marriage of convenience with someone like Wilton, I've decided to live a little."

Ha. She'd never accept Wilton, not even to gain a modicum of independence.

"Hmm," Raven said.

"I made a list."

"Of course you did. Women are forever writing lists. What of?"

"All the things I wish to achieve before I marry. Or die. Whichever comes first."

"Death would be infinitely preferable," he drawled. "This list includes taking a lover, does it?"

"Indeed. Why should you men get all the fun?" Heloise hid her smile. She really *did* have a list, although taking a lover wasn't on it. At least, not officially. "As to why I'm considering you, I'm being practical. Your reputation with women is well known. I can only assume you must be an accomplished lover. I might as well learn from someone who knows what they're doing." Her heart was racing. She couldn't believe she was having such a risqué conversation.

His lips twitched. "You flatter me."

Heloise studied her nails. "At first I considered going to a professional, but I'm not entirely clear on how I'd go about finding one."

"Your brothers would be extremely relieved to hear that," he murmured.

"And then I thought of you. The next best thing, so to speak. After all, we do have a certain amount of shared history. I think I might be able to relax and enjoy it more if it's not with a complete stranger. Although again, you men seem to have no trouble with that, from what I've heard."

Heloise bit the inside of her cheek to banish the mischievous smile from her lips. "Of course, there's always the danger you might not find me attractive enough. You've turned me down before, let's not forget. And that was before I was scarred."

He made a noise that was very close to a snort. She ignored it.

"From listening to my brothers I've received the impression that when faced with a naked female most men manage to muster up some enthusiasm. Especially after a period of abstinence. Which for someone as . . . ah . . . active as yourself, I imagine must count as a few days, at best."

Raven cleared his throat. "It sounds like a decidedly one-sided arrangement. I fail to see what's in it for me. Why should I waste my time with a tiresome virgin?"

"The novelty?" she hazarded. "I thought men liked virgins."

"On the contrary. It's rarely pleasurable when one's partner has no experience whatsoever. On the other hand, some men prefer virgins because they're like a blank piece of paper. Untouched by human hand, so to speak. They've had no time to pick up nasty habits." He raised his brows. "Or diseases," he added, straight-faced.

"Charming," she said. "I'm insulted on behalf of virgins everywhere."

He grinned, showing straight, white teeth. "You started it. And though it pains me to point out a flaw in your otherwise perfect plan, won't your husband-to-be expect you to be untouched on your wedding night?"

There wasn't going to be a wedding, or a wedding night, so it was moot point. Having seen the love between her parents and, more recently, that between her brother Nic and his new wife, Marianne, Heloise was firmly of the opinion that marrying for anything less than love was unthinkable. Since the only man she'd ever wanted had made his views on marriage quite clear, she'd undoubtedly end up as an eccentric spinster aunt to her brother's children, living in one wing of her parents' house forever.

She suppressed a sigh. "Never mind. Forget I asked. I need to talk to you about something important."

"More important than your virginity?" he teased.

"You'll think so. Is there somewhere we can be private?"

Raven's intrigued smile made her stomach knot with desire. "Of course. This way."

CHAPTER 4

*H*e steered her through the open French doors and out onto the terrace. The strains of a quadrille followed them as he drew her around the corner of the house. Heloise's skin tingled as he pulled her down the steps from the terrace and into the shadowy garden beyond. Her heart skipped, even though he wasn't escorting her anywhere for nefarious purposes. Sadly, the only time men tried to lure her into dark corners was to get her opinion on the latest translation of Ovid.

Glowing lanterns suspended on shepherd's crooks, like those at Vauxhall, lit the intersecting pathways that snaked off into the gardens. At the far end of the lawn a shadowy team of groundsmen were making final preparations for the fireworks display that would signal the midnight unmasking.

Her stomach tightened in anticipation as she imagined how happy Raven would be when she told him what she'd discovered.

Raven drew her toward a long, low building set at right angles to the main house. Huge floor-to-ceiling windows made up almost the whole front facade. "The orangery," he murmured grandly, "although previous dukes—my grandfather included— used the place as a statue gallery."

A blast of dense, warm air engulfed them as he opened the door, like the exhalation of some giant beast. Heloise half expected to hear the thud of a dragon's heartbeat, slow and steady in the darkness, the dragging scrape of scales sliding against the stone floor.

Alternate strips of shadow and illumination crossed the flagstones. Rows of orange trees, each one set in a terra-cotta planter, flanked the central path, and the pleasant scent of citrus mingled with the moist, rich aroma of dirt. Raven closed the door with a faint click, enclosing them in the tiger-striped darkness.

As Heloise's eyes became accustomed to the gloom she saw that the trees were interspersed with huge lumps of stone. Statues plundered from Ancient empires of the past loomed up out of the shadows. A giant Roman foot in a sandal. A Hellenistic female in a pleated gown, lacking her arms and head. She stopped in front of a gorgeously defined Greek warrior. In the half-light it was easy to imagine him living flesh instead of cold stone. Each perfectly attenuated muscle and bulging sinew of his torso looked ready to spring to life. Her fingers itched to touch it.

"My father's always been jealous of your grandfather's collection," she said wryly. "He'd give his right arm to buy some of these."

Raven bowed his head. "I thought you'd appreciate them."

"I do. Thank you for bringing me here." Heloise sighed inwardly. It was hard to remember he was a heartless, amoral brute when he did sweet things like this.

Raven snapped a dead leaf from the tree next to him. "They don't belong here. These should be back in their home countries, not moldering in an English hothouse. I much prefer seeing such things in situ."

Heloise gave a wistful sigh. "Well, I for one am glad they're here. At least here I can see them. You have no idea how lucky you are, being born a man, with money. You can travel to Italy or Greece or Egypt and see wonders like this anytime you want."

He had a freedom she could only dream about. He'd been to the far-flung places she'd only ever read about in books and visited in her dreams. She was twenty-two years old and she'd never had an adventure.

Raven's footfall crunched on the path behind her. "There are some Egyptian pieces over here. I know how mad you are about all that picture writing." He pointed to a large stone sarcophagus case, about the same height as a kitchen table, and Heloise rushed forward to get a closer look. Carvings in low relief covered the entire surface; stylized figures, both animal and human, were surrounded by neat rows of mysterious hieroglyphic text. She stared at the symbols, lured as ever by their foreignness, their exotic beauty.

The stone was cool to the touch, despite the humid air. This was one code that still eluded her, despite her considerable skills. Her fingers traced the dips and grooves scratched into the hard surface. The tantalizing little devils taunted her with their silence. They were a challenge, calling to her, as elusive and frustrating as the man behind her.

Raven's presence produced that same feeling of heightened anticipation she experienced when faced with a new linguistic challenge. Except with Raven, she wasn't sure she wanted to know his hidden depths. She cleared her throat. What had they been talking about? Oh, yes. Egypt. Hieroglyphics. Right. She glanced at him over her shoulder.

"Father took me to see the Rosetta Stone at the British Museum when it first arrived. I was eight. That's when I fell in love with Egypt. I've dreamed of cracking the hieroglyphic code ever since."

"But you've had no luck?"

She shook her head. "Despite my best efforts, it remains a total mystery."

"That's a long time to be denied something you desire." Raven's voice was smooth, almost mocking. "It must be very frustrating."

Heloise hesitated, suddenly unsure whether he was talking about hieroglyphics or something else entirely. She had the oddest feeling he was laughing at her. Or at himself.

"Well, yes. It's like understanding's just out of reach." She traced the pleated skirt of a figure holding a sheaf of wheat. "Still, I'm certain it can be done. It was written by humans, after all, so it must be translatable. It's extremely vexing."

* * *

RAVEN FROWNED as Heloise turned back to the sarcophagus, effectively dismissing him from her mind. A shiver passed through him as he watched her trace her fingers over the surface of the stone. Delicate fingertips, pretty oval nails. He wished she'd touch him with the same amount of reverence, the same thirst for knowledge. Desire sent a rush of blood straight to his groin. God, he was jealous of a big lump of rock.

She bent to get a closer look at the carvings and his gaze went to the rounded lines of her pert derriere. He stepped up behind her with a flash of irritation. The foolish girl was so absorbed in what she was doing she was oblivious to his approach. She'd make a useless spy. Guarding her was going to be a nightmare. She had no appreciation of danger. She saw the best in everything, everyone, whereas he always saw the worst.

He glared at the vulnerable curve of her nape. The tiny bumps of her spine disappeared into the back of her white dress like a delicate string of pearls, beckoning him to trace them all the way to the base of her spine. His stomach clenched as he inhaled the faint perfume of her skin. What was it about her that always had him looking for the nearest horizontal surface?

Losing his patience, he placed his hands on either side of her, trapping her within the cage of his body, and felt a surge of satisfaction when she gasped in surprise. She tried to twist around then stiffened, clearly realizing he'd left her no room to maneuver.

"What are you doing?" she hissed over her shoulder.

He eased back a fraction and allowed her to turn within the confines of his arms, but didn't release her. Instead he raised one hand and toyed with the black ribbon that secured her mask.

"Time to dispense with this, don't you think?"

* * *

HELOISE JERKED her head as Raven tugged on the ribbon.

"Stand still," he ordered.

She tilted her head the opposite way, evading his fingers.

"Coward," he said.

She pressed herself back against the cold stone.

"Come on, Hellcat. I already know what you look like."

That was true. He'd seen her only a few weeks after her accident, when her face had been far worse than it was now. But her pulse beat erratically in her throat and she forced a light laugh to hide her sudden unease.

"You can't hide all the time," he whispered.

She cleared her throat as the ribbon loosened. "I know that. Wearing a mask on a daily basis is very impractical. The only people who can get away with it are highwaymen and executioners, and I don't have the stomach for either."

The bow came undone. As the mask dropped, she lowered her chin so her hair fell forward over her temple, hiding her scar.

Raven put his finger beneath her chin and forced her face upward. She squeezed her eyes shut. She knew what he would see: a thin, pale line that ran from her hairline down her forehead and into the edge of one eyebrow. It curved at the end like a sickle moon, ending just to the right of her eye.

Heloise forced herself to stand still for his verdict as the silence stretched taut. She felt utterly exposed. People rarely stared at her so intently. They usually averted their gaze out of politeness. Or disgust. But Raven had faced the worst devils in hell and lived to tell the tale. Surely if anyone could stomach her ravaged visage, it would be him?

His cool fingers skimmed her cheek as he brushed a curl back behind her ear.

"I know it shouldn't bother me," she breathed, giving in to the overwhelming need to fill the silence. "I never was going to be a great beauty. But honestly, when was the last time you read a fairy tale that started, 'Once upon a time there lived an ugly princess . . .'? I mean, it's perfectly acceptable for heroes to be scarred, at least until they're transformed into a handsome prince at the end. Their ugliness is usually a punishment for being selfish . . ." She trailed off, uncomfortably aware that she was babbling.

"You think your scar is a punishment?"

She snapped her eyes open, startled by the anger in his tone.

"Of course not. I got it saving Tony's life. How could I regret it?"

His mask made it impossible to see his expression. Was it pity? Indifference? She exhaled a shaky breath. "Does it bother you?"

His fingers traced the line of her jaw. Heloise fought the treacherous warmth that slid through her, urging her to lean into his touch, to bury her head against his chest.

"No. It doesn't bother me."

The warmth of his breath slid across her temple and she suppressed a little shiver of awareness. The heat of his body seeped into her through the layers of clothes. Her heart pumped furiously against her breastbone.

"You were pretty before," he whispered. "Pretty and perfect."

His thumb brushed her scar in the briefest of caresses. "That's so boring. This makes you interesting."

He stepped back and Heloise experienced a foolish wave of disappointment. She cleared her throat and gestured at his head. "Your turn."

He lifted the snarling Anubis mask. Dark hair fell around his shoulders as he placed the mask on the stone slab beside her. She could barely see him in the shadows, but she knew the contours of his face as well as she knew her own, knew the startling effect of those green eyes against suntanned skin, the thick, black lashes that were wasted on a man. In her more fanciful moments she'd called the color of his hair "obsidian," mainly because it was such a lovely word.

"So now we're both naked," he whispered wickedly. He stepped close again and her heart somersaulted as his eyes met hers. "Just admit it. Hellcat."

"Admit what?" she stammered.

His lazy gaze dropped to her lips. "The reason you came here tonight. You don't have anything to tell me. You just wanted an adventure. You want me to kiss you."

She jerked back. "I do not!"

"Afraid you'll like it?" he taunted softly.

"Hardly," she scoffed.

"Afraid you'll never want me to stop?"

God, yes. That was exactly what she was afraid of. She pursed her lips and adopted a faintly bored expression. "Those legions of women panting after you must have warped your brain, William Ravenwood. Contrary to popular belief, you are not irresistible."

"That's true. You've resisted me for years. Why is that?"

She fought the seductive pull of him. "Because unlike so many of your conquests, I possess a working brain?"

He chuckled.

"I don't know why you're bothering to flirt with me," she said irritably. "You don't want me. You just can't resist a challenge."

"Is that what you are?"

"Of course. It's human nature to want what you can't have."

He raised a brow and pressed closer, full length against her, chest to chest, thigh to thigh. Her heart stuttered. "You think I can't have you?"

Her stomach knotted with a strange, curling tension and she laughed to cover her nerves, suddenly acutely aware of the fact that they were alone. In the dark. Far from the house. "Of course not. My brothers would kill you."

"Do you honestly think that would deter me?"

Everything inside her stilled at the predatory intensity of his look.

"If I truly wanted you, Hellcat, nothing—not your brothers, not your father, not Napoleon himself—would stop me."

CHAPTER 5

*A*h, there it was, Heloise thought with a bittersweet pang. That big, modifying *IF*.

She pushed ineffectively against his chest. "I don't want you to lay a finger on me."

He didn't move. "Don't lie. You've been watching me for years. I feel your gaze on the side of my face. It makes the hairs on my arms prickle."

She shook her head.

"Deny it all you want, but deep down you know it. You want me."

"No!"

He crowded her back against the sarcophagus, stealing the air from her lungs. "Yes."

Heloise stiffened in shock as he bent and pressed his lips to her throat, just below her ear.

"This is the real you," he whispered against her skin. "This wildness. Let it out. Embrace it."

Oh, he was a devil. Taunting her with possibilities she hadn't dared voice, only dream. She'd spent years suppressing her hoydenish ways, avoiding moats and fires. She no longer shinned up trees, rode bareback, stole pistols. Letting go would be the height of folly.

But dear God, it was tempting.

She drew in a shuddering breath and stared blindly at the ceiling as he kissed a trail of fire down the side of her neck. He didn't want her. He was only doing this to prove a point. Although it was becoming difficult to imagine what his point was, exactly. . .

He pushed aside the beaded choker at her collarbone and pressed his mouth there, too. Butterflies somersaulted in her stomach.

She told herself she was unmoved. As stony as that marbled athlete. She was absolutely *not* going to grab hold of his head to hold him in place. This wasn't why she'd come out here. She needed to tell him about the message, but as soon as she did that he'd leave, and the selfish part of her wanted to steal just a little more time with him.

Raven kissed the top swell of her breast and Heloise nearly passed out. She clutched the edge of the sarcophagus, a solid anchor when the rest of the world was rapidly spinning out of control. *That's quite enough. And* yet her treacherous chin tilted upward to give him more room to maneuver.

She almost jumped out of her skin when the first firework screamed through the sky, illuminating the interior of the orangery like midday. She caught a brief, clear glimpse of Raven's face as he straightened, all sharp angles and harsh planes, before the room was plunged into darkness again. She opened her mouth to say something—anything—but his lips found hers. And stayed.

Heloise closed her eyes in stunned disbelief. She'd kissed William Ravenwood a thousand times in her mind, caressed every last inch of his body in her dreams. Reality—the lush, wicked feel of his lips on hers—was infinitely better. His tongue stroked the corner of her mouth and when she gave a startled gasp he slid inside, taking full advantage. Heat bloomed in her veins as everything inside her went on a slow boil.

He didn't give her chance to pull away. His hands cupped her face and he kissed her with thrilling urgency, as if she was as vital to him as oxygen.

Heloise had no intention of pulling back. She let go of the stone, grabbed hold of his lapels, and returned the kiss with equal fervor, instinctively mimicking his movements.

Properly. He was finally kissing her properly!

This wasn't the chaste, knightly kiss she'd always imagined. It was something hotter, darker, forbidden. The culmination of six long years of yearning.

She wanted more.

Heloise groaned as his hand slid down and covered her breast, but before she could assimilate the incredible sensation, his fingers slipped inside her bodice and cupped her, bare skin to bare skin.

All the breath left her lungs in a rush. She arched up into his touch with an incoherent gasp as her nipple pebbled against his palm.

"Jesus," Raven murmured against her lips. "Hellcat—"

Another firework screamed up into the sky and burned away in a blaze of glittering sparks. With a supreme effort Heloise dragged her mouth away from his. Her lips were wet, tingling.

"We can't!" she protested.

He shut her off with another demanding kiss that made her blood sing and her head whirl.

"This is—" she panted.

"—long overdue," he finished roughly.

In one swift movement he caught her hips and lifted her up, onto the edge of the sarcophagus. Heloise gasped in mixed arousal and alarm as he pushed himself between her open thighs. She could feel him, his stomach, his hips, and oh God, *him*, hard and thick and demanding, through the fabric of her dress and layers of petticoat. She wanted this, wanted him, with a sudden desperation that was terrifying.

"Wrap your legs around me," he ordered, and she complied without thought. And then his hand was at the hem of her skirts, dragging them up, past stocking and garter and knee. His fingers slid over the heated skin of her outer thigh and he caught her whimper of protest with his mouth.

She should not be doing this. Absolutely not. *But it felt so good.*

With another muffled curse, Raven pushed her backward so she was half lying on the stone. Another firework burst overhead, fizzing and crackling downward like sparks from a celestial anvil.

Heloise threw her arms around his neck. God alone knew why he'd suddenly decided to touch her now, after all this time. He probably had some fiendish, ulterior motive, but right now she didn't care what it was. She kissed him again, deeply, desperately, drowning in the wicked red-blackness, raking her fingers through his thick hair, reveling in the silky texture of it. God, the taste of him, like—

The shatter of glass broke her concentration. Raven swore, and her first, confused thought was that someone had dropped a wineglass. And then he shoved her roughly onto the floor. One second she was in his arms, the next she was sprawled inelegantly on her stomach behind an orange tree.

Heloise yelped as her elbows made painful contact with the flagstones. She started to get up, to berate him, but Raven covered her with his body, squashing all the breath from her lungs. His arms curved protectively around her head.

A second explosion came, like someone clapping their hands right next to her ear, and chips of terra-cotta exploded from the planter next to her. She tried to lift her head but Raven pushed her back down.

"Stay down," he hissed.

Her heart was racing. Raven's dizzying shift from passionate lover to ice-cold professional was disorienting. Her hands were trapped beneath her body and the stone was cold against her cheek. She felt him tense; his weight increased, then suddenly eased as he sprang to his feet and bolted into the garden.

"Don't move!"

And then he was gone.

Heloise became aware of her own panting breath, choppy and panicked. She pulled herself onto hands and knees and stared dazedly at the glass shards littering the floor around her. They glittered like ice crystals in the moonlight, tinkling like dropped hairpins as they fell from her clothing. She glanced up at the two broken panes in the tall window opposite. Each had an intricate spiderweb of fractures surrounding an ominous central hole. Cold air was blowing in, and she shivered as her brain struggled to accept the evidence in front of her eyes. Every thought seemed slow, like treacle.

Someone had shot at them.

Raven had left her.

She had to move, get back to the house. Warn people.

Where the hell had he gone?

Her legs were shaking but she staggered to the door just as a shadow loomed out of the darkness. Her squeal of terror was stifled by a hand across her mouth and a strong forearm that snaked around her ribs and robbed her of breath.

"Keep still," Raven ordered gruffly, and Heloise sagged against him in relief, stilling her struggles. He bent to her ear but didn't release her. "Are you hurt?"

She managed to shake her head.

He released her mouth and she took a deep breath in. "What on earth is going on?"

"No talking until we're inside." He grabbed her hand and started pulling her toward the house, his pace so brisk she had to run to keep up with him, two strides for every one of his.

"Someone tried to shoot you!" Heloise panted, frantically

scanning the undergrowth. "What if they come back? What if they try to shoot someone else?"

Raven frowned at her over his shoulder. "They're gone. And I said no talking."

A crowd had gathered on the terrace to watch the fireworks; a collective murmur of "ooh" and "aah" accompanied each pyrotechnic burst. No one appeared to have heard the shots. Even if they had, Heloise thought wildly, the sound of a pistol discharging probably wasn't unusual enough to warrant comment at one of Raven's unholy gatherings.

"This way." Raven located a door beneath the curving terrace stairs and bundled her into the dark interior. Without letting go of her hand he marched along a corridor in what was clearly the servants' domain. Heloise ducked her head as they encountered two liveried footmen bearing trays of champagne, but they merely nodded and continued as if there was nothing unusual about their master dragging a terrified woman behind him.

A narrow set of stairs and another dim corridor. Heloise could hear the muffled noise of the party from behind the wooden panels as they passed a series of closed doors. More stairs, then Raven pulled her into a richly decorated hallway.

The change from undecorated service area to opulent main house was disorienting. All was luxury, as befitted the residence of his grandfather, a duke. Heloise caught a brief glimpse of her own startled reflection in a gilt-framed mirror as they strode along, all huge eyes and disordered hair.

Raven finally halted. Without relinquishing his hold on her wrist he thrust open a door and pulled her into the room beyond. Heloise took one glance at the giant four-poster bed and distinctly masculine furnishings and spun on him with renewed alarm.

"Good God, is this your bedroom?"

CHAPTER 6

"*O*f course it's my bedroom," Raven closed the door and dropped her wrist as if she were hot coals.

Heloise rubbed the red mark he'd left and glared at him, then lurched back against the door as he planted his hands on either side of her head and leaned in close.

"Don't pretend you haven't been desperate to see it for years."

Blood rushed to her face at his insolent challenge. She could hardly look at him, considering what they'd just been doing. God, if they hadn't been interrupted—

He smiled that maddeningly perceptive smile of his—the one that suggested he knew her every secret and found her mildly amusing. She wanted to throw something at him.

He pushed away and strode over to the fireplace and she dragged in an unsteady breath. The flare of a taper briefly illuminated his face as he lit an oil lamp on a side table then turned and crossed his arms over his chest. "Now, why don't you explain why someone just tried to blow my head off?"

Heloise stared at him in astonishment. "I have no idea."

He raked a hand through his dark hair. "Wherever you go, disaster follows."

She gasped at that blatantly unfair accusation. "Why would it have anything to do with me? You're the spy. This is your house. Of the two of us, you're far more likely to have incited someone to murder."

He shook his head.

"Did you see whoever it was?" she asked.

"No. It was a man, but he rode off before I could get a good look."

Heloise frowned. "But you must have been the target. Other than my family and a few close friends, hardly anyone's aware I even exist. Why would someone try to shoot me?"

He leveled her with a piercing glance. "I have some bad news, I'm afraid. Castlereagh was here earlier. Your colleague, Edward Lamb, was murdered last night."

All the blood leeched out of her face in a cold wash. She clapped a hand over her mouth. "What? No."

Her legs buckled and she leaned back against the door for support, afraid she was going to pass out. "Edward can't be dead. I only saw him a week ago and—"

The image of Edward's earnest, bespectacled face with its broad, scholarly forehead filled her mind. She clutched her stomach as a tight ball of grief assailed her. Dead? Edward was like a brother to her, a kindred spirit. They talked for hours whenever she visited Castlereagh in London, engrossed in codes, arguing over possible solutions. Theirs was a friendship based on mutual respect.

A sob rose in her throat. Oh God. It was like losing Tony all over again.

Raven poured a glass of water from a pitcher and held it out to her wordlessly. She took it, but her hand was shaking so much the rim of the glass chinked against her front teeth when she tried to drink.

She took a deep breath. "But why would someone want to kill him? Or me, for that matter?"

He regarded her as if she were dim-witted. "God, Heloise. Don't you realize how valuable you are?" He rubbed his forehead. "Any British asset's an automatic target for the French. You think England's problems have disappeared just because Bonaparte's been exiled again?" He leaned back against the corner of a desk. "We're still at war, Hellcat, even if it's not official. Believe me, there are always people prepared to do whatever it takes to ensure sensitive information stays secret."

Heloise gulped as the full implications of that sunk in.

"Why did you come here tonight?"

Heloise reached into her bodice and blushed at the impropriety of her hiding place. The translation had been the furthest thing from her mind when Raven's hand had been there a few minutes ago. She half turned away and extracted the crumpled paper—slightly damp with spilled champagne—with a flourish.

"What's that?" he asked.

"A message that, until a few hours ago, was undecipherable."

"And now?"

"I've cracked it." Heloise savored the rush of elation. She'd been so excited about her breakthrough, but there had been no one at home with whom to share her success. As a woman, she'd been ineligible to fight on the front lines against Napoleon, or even behind them, like Raven and her brothers, but her skill at code-breaking had given her an unexpected opportunity to serve her country.

"The French change their codes about every six months or so. They created this one just after Napoleon was defeated, and it's proved far more complicated than usual. I've been working on it for months. Tonight I finally had a breakthrough." She waved the paper at him. "I think this message is about your friend Kit Carlisle."

Raven straightened, instantly alert. "Kit? Why, what does it say?"

Heloise glanced down at her hastily scribbled translation then back up at him. "It's dated three weeks ago, addressed to Rovigo."

Raven nodded. "That's Anne Jean Marie René Savary, Duc of Rovigo. He was Napoleon's top spymaster, along with Fouché, but he managed to retain his position despite the French defeat. The man's as slippery as an eel. Who's it from?"

"It's signed Alvarez."

He frowned. "I don't know who that is. What does it say?"

" 'The prisoner is in poor health and gives us no new information. I urge you to consider completing the exchange you suggest quickly. The Baker will be of more use returned to us than this English Apollo. I can bring him to the church at Endarlatsa with notice of a few days.' "

Raven's eyebrows rose in disbelief. "Apollo? Are you sure?"

"Yes. That's Kit's code name isn't it?"

Castlereagh's spies all had code names based on the Greek and Roman gods. Her brother Nic was Mercury, god of messengers and thieves, and Richard, being the eldest sibling, was Jupiter. She'd yet to discover Raven's code name.

Raven exhaled slowly. "Yes. And this suggests he's still alive. Or, at least, he was three weeks ago." He ran a hand through his hair. "Bloody hell. Do you know where this message was intercepted?"

Heloise shook her head.

"Is there nothing else? A seal? A watermark? Anything that might determine where it came from?"

"No, but I looked at an atlas. There's a village called Endarlatsa; it's in northern Spain, near the border with France." She glanced up at him. "Who's the Baker?"

Raven's jaw tightened. "The French give their agents code names based on trades or professions. The Doctor, the Farmer, the Shoemaker. The Baker is a man called Marc Breton. He's currently our guest in Newgate. Richard and I are the ones who brought him in for questioning."

The way he intoned the word "questioning" held a world of dark menace. Heloise shivered.

Raven pushed off the desk and started pacing. "I have to go and get Kit."

It was no more than she'd expected. Raven was insanely loyal to his brothers in arms. "Do you think the French have already approached Castlereagh and indicated that they're willing to swap Kit for this Baker?"

"No. Castlereagh would have told me if he'd heard Kit was alive."

"What if Savary's changed his mind?"

He made a dismissive gesture with his hand. "It doesn't matter if he has. We know where Kit is now—it must be somewhere within range of this church."

"What if they haven't offered because Kit's already dead?" She hated to voice the question, but it needed to be said.

Raven fixed her with a piercing look. "If there's even a chance he's still alive, I'm going after him."

Heloise nodded. She'd do the same, in his place. "Well, the good news is, now I've cracked this code, I'll be able to read all the other messages we've intercepted. One of them might reveal something more about his location. I can go to London immediately and show Edward how to—" She stopped on a pained gasp. Edward wouldn't be there to tell.

Raven stopped pacing. "No. London's too dangerous. Someone's already taken a shot at you."

Heloise bit her lip. "I suppose Castlereagh could send the remaining messages here by courier. Or I could go to one of the safe houses, until all this blows over."

Raven nodded absently, as if his mind was already on something else. "Could you write a message in this code?"

"I suppose so."

He strode back to the desk, pulled forward paper and ink, and waved her over with an impatient hand. Heloise crossed to the chair he pulled out for her and sank into it. "What do you want me to write?"

"Date it for last week. Say, 'Still in hospital. Expect to make a full recovery.' Encoded French, of course."

Heloise shot him a how-stupid-do-you-think-I-am glare, pulled the sheet toward her, and flattened the translated message on the desk. She ignored the inward curl of pleasure that being so close to Raven produced. Her whole body hummed in awareness. "I have all my notes and workings at home. This would be a lot easier if I could just—"

Raven shook his head. She frowned as he hovered over her shoulder. "I'll need a while to work this out, you know. Go glower somewhere else, at least."

He stepped back and she began to reverse-engineer the code into its individual letter components. Muffled sounds of revelry from the party downstairs joined the scratch of her pen as she first wrote out the message in French, then started to encode it, letter by letter. "What does it mean, anyway?"

"It's a French spy code. 'Still in hospital' means still a prisoner. 'Expect to make a full recovery,' means he'll await rescue or further instructions. Sign it Baker."

Heloise nodded. So this was supposed to be a note from the Frenchman in custody. At least the name was easy—it was already encoded in the original message. "There." She turned to Raven and handed him the note then glanced at the ormolu clock on the mantel. "So now what?"

He folded the note and slipped it inside his jacket. "I'll send this to Castlereagh. He can get it into French hands without arousing suspicion."

Heloise stood, smoothed down her skirts. Raven sidestepped, blocking her escape. He was half-smiling again, a look that made her instantly apprehensive. His dark gaze dropped to her mouth and a traitorous warmth curled through her. "I haven't thanked you properly."

He leaned forward and pressed a gentle kiss on her lips. Heloise frowned. Was this a goodbye kiss, because he'd be going to Spain? He kissed her again, and everything went a little hazy.

When the back of her knees hit something hard she realized, dimly, that he'd maneuvered her to the side of the bed. She shivered when he entwined their fingers and drew her arms behind her back, angling his head to press kisses along her jaw, her ear, her temple.

"Hellcat . . ." he murmured against her lips. "I'm sorry about this."

Heloise frowned. Sorry? Why would he be—?

A terrible suspicion formed the exact moment something cold closed around her wrist with an ominous metallic click. She felt her arm jerk sideways and glanced down as Raven reared back. Disbelief quickly gave way to fury.

The pig-swiving bastard had handcuffed her to the bed.

CHAPTER 7

*H*eloise took a deep, calming breath.

Raven, sensible devil, took a few more steps back —well out of kicking range—and regarded her with a distinctly self-satisfied air, arms crossed, legs apart like a pirate surveying a ship full of treasure.

She gave her wrist an experimental tug. The cuff rattled against the wooden bedpost and scraped uncomfortably against her skin but didn't give an inch.

"No point struggling." Raven grinned cheerfully. "That post is best Cuban mahogany." He held up a small metal key and made great show of tucking it into the breast pocket of his waistcoat, and patting it.

Heloise strove for a reasonable tone. "This is completely unnecessary. Let me go."

His obnoxious smile widened. "Can't, I'm afraid." He leaned back against the wall, all long and lean and supremely relaxed. Bastard.

He shrugged. "I can't let you go home. I promised Castlereagh I'd keep an eye on you until we find out who killed Edward. Don't glare at me like that, Hellcat. I care more about your safety than your good opinion."

She rattled her wrist. "It never occurred to you to simply explain and ask me to stay? No, of course not. You boys always prefer the dramatic physical gesture over intelligent diplomacy. This is kidnapping!"

"Tsk. 'Kidnapping' is such a strong word. Let's call it 'protective custody.'"

"Calling it something else doesn't alter the facts."

The corners of his eyes crinkled.

"You think this is amusing?" She hissed. "Let me tell you, Ravenwood, you're as funny as toothache."

"It's for your own good. Think of me as your bodyguard."

She folded her arms across her chest. At least she tried to, but her right arm was pulled up short by the handcuffs. She gave a frustrated growl. "I'm perfectly capable of guarding my own body, thank you very much."

His gaze turned wicked and his eyes flickered down the length of her in a leisurely perusal that somehow seemed more intimate than a caress. Heat rose in her cheeks.

"Ah, but I'll do a much better job."

She didn't even want to think about how the man had such easy access to a pair of handcuffs. In his bedroom, of all places. Her skin prickled. As if he'd read her mind, his eyes took on a devilish glint. "You know, some people like to be restrained."

"Do *you*?" she fumed, then bit her tongue. Antagonizing him was not going to help matters.

He laughed. "God no, I've had more than enough imprisonment for one lifetime, thank you. No one will ever control me like that again."

"Yet now you're the one imprisoning someone."

Raven inclined his head. "The irony's not lost on me. But I've always found it easier to ask for forgiveness than permission."

He sent her a mock-evil leer. "Having you so completely in

my power, Miss Hampden, is a heady prospect. You should be glad I'm such a gentleman."

"Really?" Heloise allowed her sarcasm full reign. "I should thank you for shackling me to a bed?"

"No. But you should be grateful I'm not taking advantage of the situation. A more unscrupulous man might."

"Ha! You have the scruples of an alley cat. My brothers will kill you when they find out about this."

"I doubt it. They'll probably applaud. What do you think I'm going to do? Molest you?"

Heloise flushed. Of course he wouldn't. He didn't truly desire her, despite what had happened in the orangery. He'd simply been trying to embarrass her, or frighten her off, and she . . . well, she'd chalk it up to a champagne-fueled aberration. One she had absolutely no intention of repeating.

She gave an inward sigh. If she were any other woman, he'd probably be seducing her into exhausted acquiescence right now. And curse it, even as annoyed with him as she was, a part of her —the very stupid, brainless, part—wished she were one of those other women.

Raven must have interpreted her silence as uncertainty, however, because his expression darkened. "Don't worry, you're perfectly safe with me," he growled. "Christ, you don't really think I'd hurt you, do you?"

Heloise shrugged. "So what do you propose to do now?"

"Tonight's attempt to kill you failed, but I can guarantee that whoever it was will try again."

A cold wash of fear skittered down her spine as the truth of what he was saying began to register, but she shook her head.

"You disagree?" he said silkily.

"Of course I disagree. If I ever find myself agreeing with you, Ravenwood, I'll need a moment to sit down and recover. We don't know I was definitely the target. What if you're wrong?

What if you were the target? If that's the case, I'll be in more danger with you than if I leave."

"You're staying with me." He forestalled her argument with a raised hand and glanced over at the clock. "How many languages do you speak?"

She narrowed her eyes. "A few. Why?" His expression immediately made her want to defend herself. "What? Maman is French and Father's English, so I learned those two from the cradle."

"Which others?"

"Greek, Latin, Italian."

"Can you be pleasant in any of them?"

"You are such a—"

"Apparently not," he sighed wistfully. "Any Spanish?"

"No."

"Pity. Because you're coming to Spain with me. We'll leave at high tide."

CHAPTER 8

*H*eloise's heart slammed against her ribs. "I'm sorry, did you say Spain? Have you hit your head?"

He set his mouth into a tight, stubborn line and shot an ironic glance at her wrist. "You don't have a choice. If you haven't noticed, you're in no position to argue."

She could hardly breathe. The thought of going anywhere with Raven was a heady prospect, but for pride's sake she ought to make at least a token protest. "I understand your desire to go and help your friend, but you have to consider things from my perspective. I can't go haring all over Europe with you. I'll be ruined."

"A good man's life is worth more than your reputation. Besides, I thought you wanted to get rid of your suitors. This is the perfect opportunity."

"People will think we've eloped."

"Not if they know either one of us," he replied succinctly. "If we both disappear they're more likely to assume I've murdered you and fled the country."

Heloise scowled. He was right. Raven's well-known aversion to marriage would work in his favor. People really *would* believe he'd kill someone rather than get married. "It's all right for you. You don't have a reputation to lose."

He wasn't shackled by his gender and the suffocating restrictions of society. The flagrant double standards between behavior acceptable for men and that permitted to women was one of the things that irritated her most about the ton. Yes, she'd been fortunate enough to be born into a wealthy family, but money hadn't been able to buy her the equality she craved. Or the freedom.

Raven tilted his head as he approached her. "Argue all you want, but I'm not going to change my mind. You're staying with me."

Heloise sighed. She couldn't go home. With her family away, the house was staffed with only a handful of servants and she undoubtedly needed protection. Raven might tease her, but she had absolutely no qualms about his ability to keep her safe.

The idea of being ruined socially didn't particularly concern her. Maybe Collingham and Wilton would think twice about her as a suitable bride if she disappeared with Raven.

She sat down on the edge of the bed. "You'll need to let my family know where we've gone. They'll be worried sick if I just disappear."

He recognized her acceptance with a nod. "I'll write to Castlereagh and your brother Richard and tell them where we're going." He undid his cravat and slipped it from his neck in a slow slide. Heloise watched the movement with deep suspicion.

"What are you doing?" The way he drew the silk through his left hand was both menacing and a caress. Suddenly uneasy, she edged backward. "I've said I'll come with you. Don't touch me," she warned as he came closer.

His smile was not reassuring. The mattress dipped as he placed one knee beside her. Heloise shrank back against the bolster.

"I doubt any of the party guests would investigate if they

heard you shouting," he murmured, "and the servants are too well trained to interrupt, but just in case . . ."

Quick as a flash he slipped the silk across her mouth and tied it behind her head. Heloise punched him with her free hand but he warded off her blows with a chuckle and stepped back to survey his impromptu gag. The beast had got it between her teeth, like a horse's bit. She tried to pull it down with her free hand but the knot at the back of her head was too tight.

Thoroughly incensed, she kicked out at him with her foot. She had a moment's satisfaction when she connected with his thigh, but realized her mistake when he caught her ankle and her skirts rode high up her legs, giving him a scandalous view of stockings, garter, and thigh.

His brows shot up in surprise. She jerked her leg, but instead of releasing her the devil traced a maddening circle around her ankle bone with his thumb. Heloise stilled, mortified by the hum of awareness his touch generated.

"You're so well educated, I always assumed you wore blue stockings under there," he said, grinning. "But no. Who'd have thought such a demure outer garment would hide such exotic underclothes?"

Her face burned. Her one sinful extravagance was an abiding love of beautiful underwear, a passion for silk and lace inherited from her very French mother. She rebelled against the staid, conventional exterior ordained by society by wearing the most decadent and inappropriately colorful underwear she could buy. And she'd imagined herself to be safe because, really, who would ever see?

"Peach is one of my very favorite colors," Raven drawled. He released her foot and Heloise scrambled to rearrange herself into a more demure position, then glared at him over the gag. His smile widened at her impotent fury.

Determined not to rise to the bait, she held perfectly still as he caught her chin. She thought about trying to kick him again but her body seemed paralyzed by the hot, wicked look in his eyes. His breath tickled over her skin as he leaned forward and kissed the very tip of her nose.

Chuckling, he stepped away and crossed to the door and Heloise realized incredulously that he was going to leave her, like this, gagged and handcuffed to his bed. She made a muffled sound of protest and he turned, his eyes glittering with amusement.

"Stay where you are, sweetheart. I've got a few things to do, but I'll be back soon. I promise."

The furious, ironic look she shot him needed no translation. Just to prove she wasn't cowed, Heloise pulled off her slipper and threw it at his head. Unfortunately, her aim with her left hand was poor. The bastard didn't even have the grace to duck. It bounced harmlessly off the doorframe next to his head.

* * *

RAVEN LEANED back against his bedroom door with a sigh. Kissing Heloise again had been beyond stupid. He'd done it partly to annoy her—he loved her tousled and furious—and partly because he'd needed her flustered enough to get her over to the bed so he could secure her.

Taking her to Spain with him was insane. It would be hard enough trying to track down Kit without having Little Miss Hampden trailing along, driving him to distraction. The terrain of the Peninsula was harsh and unforgiving. She had no field experience at all. She'd probably never been farther afield than London.

But what other choice did he have? She'd barely escaped with her life tonight. The danger to her here, from some unnamed French assassin, was surely greater than if she came with him. If their enemies had managed to discover where she lived, they might also have discovered the location of Castlereagh's numerous safe houses. He couldn't risk sending her to one of those, and it would be almost impossible for anyone to track them once they left the country.

Keeping her with him would be dangerous, but the simple truth was he didn't trust anyone else. She'd be safe with him. Despite his teasing and threats, he respected her too much to treat her like all the other women in his life—as a brief, shallow amusement. Her brothers, Richard and Nic, trusted him implicitly and he'd never risk losing their friendship by dishonoring her. They'd not only expect him to keep their precious little sister alive, but to return her in exactly the same state she left in. Unhurt. Untouched. *Unkissed.*

The woman was a walking temptation, but he didn't doubt his ability to resist her. He'd been doing precisely that for the last six years. But she didn't make it easy, and proximity would only make it worse.

The unexpected sight of her courtesan's underwear had nearly sent him to his knees. A too-clever scholar had no right to wear silk and lace nothings. Underwear like that was a visual promise to sin—one Miss Heloise Hampden had absolutely no intention of keeping. It was damned false advertising.

How was he going to concentrate now that he knew what she had on underneath her pure-as-the-driven-snow dress? It had been bad enough when he'd only had his imagination to deal with. Reality surpassed even his lascivious imaginings.

Bloody hell.

Raven pushed off the door and strode back toward the party. His lack of cravat and general dishabille would occasion no comment. A certain state of undress was expected of him by this time in the proceedings, although he doubted many of his guests would be sober enough to notice.

At the head of the great staircase he glanced up. Some Raven-wood ancestor had commissioned a famous Italian to paint the ceiling. The riotous scenes complemented the evening's entertainments perfectly; the writhing celestial debauchery of the assembled Olympian gods mirrored the acres of heaving bare flesh in the ballroom below.

Raven felt a brief, childish stab of satisfaction. His grandfather, the starchy old bastard, would have another apoplexy if he could see the stately seat of the Dukes of Avondale now, filled with iniquity and sin. The disrespect, though petty, was still remarkably enjoyable.

The old miser's belated attempts to make amends after Raven's kidnapping had been too little, too late. He'd shown where his priorities lay when he'd refused to pay the ransom. Raven hadn't taken a penny of his grandfather's money, nor the titles that were due to him after his father's death. He'd told his grandfather to bequeath the marquisate to a distant relative.

The only thing he had accepted was this house, though he hated the place. Not the building itself, but the accumulation of things it represented. It weighed him down with a sense of noble responsibility, when he wanted his life to be as simple and unencumbered as possible. But the remote coastal location had been perfect for wartime subterfuge and it bordered the Hampden's estate, home of the best friends and only family he'd ever truly known. Little Miss Hellcat included.

His practiced gaze picked out the dark figure of Hades abducting a protesting Persephone and he hissed in silent commiseration. Poor sod, driven to such desperate measures. Raven knew exactly how that felt. Heloise Hampden was everything he wanted, and everything he couldn't have.

He avoided the ballroom and entered his study, where he scrawled a hasty message to Richard and another to Castlereagh, enclosing Heloise's encoded note, then sat back in his chair with a sigh.

God, what a mess. He stared moodily across the room at the crest carved into the mantel and grimaced at the irony of his family motto. The Latin phrase came from Virgil's Aeneid; "Sic itur ad astra." Thus you shall go to the stars.

What was that supposed to mean, anyway? The stars were as remote and untouchable as the girl currently cuffed to his bedpost. A man like him could never reach them.

Raven frowned in sudden recollection. He'd had a signet ring with that crest on it, once. It had been his father's. The bastards who'd kidnapped him had sent it as proof of life to his grandfather. He wondered where it was now.

Raven rang for a servant and handed him the notes. "I want these delivered to Lord Castlereagh immediately."

"Yes, my lord."

"And have someone saddle my horse."

CHAPTER 9

*H*eloise glared at the clock as it chimed two. Raven had been gone for over an hour. An initial burst of fevered activity had resulted in nothing more than a bruised wrist and an increasingly frayed temper. From what she could hear, the party was still going strong; carriages would arrive at dawn for the last straggling revelers. He'd better not have left her to rejoin the party—

The door swung open and her head snapped up.

Raven bent and retrieved her slipper, then held it out to her like a peace offering. She accepted it with as haughty a look as she could manage while handcuffed to his bed and gagged.

"I'll let you go if you promise you won't try to escape."

Heloise nodded enthusiastically. She held still as he released her wrist, judging the distance to the door as he removed the gag. Worth a go. She leaped forward.

He caught her around the waist with humiliating ease and lifted her off her feet while she kicked and thrashed. Her heel made contact with his shin and he growled, tightening his grip.

"Stop it!"

"No!"

"Stop it or I'll throw you on that bed and show you just how much stronger I am."

It was a good threat. Heloise stilled, breathing heavily. He loosened his grip slowly and lowered her to the floor.

"That's better. Now, are you going to be sensible?"

She nodded meekly.

"Good. Come on." He caught her hand.

"Don't you need to pack?"

He shook his head. "My ship's still at anchor in the cove, always ready to go at a moment's notice."

"How convenient," she murmured sarcastically.

She'd forgotten that he kept his own ship in the bay. During the war he'd regularly posed as a smuggler to slip unnoticed into France, and only a few months ago he'd rescued her eldest brother Nic; his now-wife, Marianne; and the French aristocrat Louis-Charles de Bourbon, in a daring nighttime raid from Brittany.

The only people they encountered in the hall were an amorous couple entwined in a doorway. The man ushered his giggling partner backward with an audible "Shhh!" and the door clicked closed. Heloise felt her face flame and glanced up to catch the slow, mocking curl of Raven's mouth.

Instead of using the main stairs, he led her to another service staircase and through an enormous, and deserted, reception room.

Heloise gasped. Whereas the hallway depicted gods and goddesses in joyful abandon, this room depicted hell, all red, black, and orange. All four walls enclosed one huge battle scene —with rearing horses, and soldiers in billowing capes with slashing swords. Above, on the ceiling, a grotesque catlike animal with a yawning mouth depicted the entrance to the Underworld itself. Gruesome souls writhing in torment were wreathed in smoke and flames, surrounded by more battling gods and goddesses. The trompe l'oeil effect was so well executed that the real green marble pillars of the room were almost impossible to differentiate from those that had been merely painted on. The whole effect was uncomfortably disorienting.

There was the Grim Reaper, with his sickle and hood. And Hades, thundering up from the Underworld in his chariot. The tale of Hades and Persephone had been one of her favorite Greek myths as a girl. Her younger self had thought it breathtakingly romantic; imagine having a man desire you so much that he'd defy the gods to have you.

Heloise suppressed a snort. Ha! It was just another kidnapping. And there was nothing romantic about *that*. Raven wasn't stealing her away because he loved her. He was only doing it out of duty and friendship.

Raven shot her a teasing look over his shoulder as they crossed the marble floor. "I'll be honest, Hellcat. I expected more histrionics."

"I haven't seen where it would help," she said bluntly. "If you'd like me to start screeching like a banshee, you have only to say."

They reached a side door without encountering another soul, not even a servant. Raven retrieved a dark leather satchel waiting on a hall chair, slung it over his shoulder, and drew her out into the kitchen garden.

The slap of the cool night air brought the reality of the situation home with a jolt. This wasn't a joke or a nightmare. Raven really was planning to put her on his ship and sail away. He was completely mad.

Clouds covered the moon, but he led her unerringly through the shadows, apparently unconcerned that whoever had shot at them earlier could still be loitering in the darkness. Heloise was about to point this out, but she found she needed all her breath to keep up with his brisk pace. She flinched at every snapped twig and looming bush but they navigated the gardens without incident and plunged into a bank of huge rhododendrons. When they emerged on the other side, the moon slid out from behind the clouds and Heloise stopped dead.

They were standing at the top of a cliff. A gust of wind flattened her dress against her legs, bringing with it the bracing tang of seaweed and brine. Below them, in a rocky inlet, the dark outline of Raven's ship bobbed on the tide.

A set of rough steps had been cut into the side of the cliff. Raven let go of her wrist and took her hand and Heloise was glad of the reassuring strength of his fingers. Her legs seemed to be alarmingly shaky. He helped her down onto a wooden jetty attached to the rocks and she suppressed a shiver. The ship creaked and groaned like an invalid and the waves sucking at the rocks sounded like a monster smacking its lips in anticipation of a good meal.

Raven hailed a shadowy figure on the deck with a shout. "We're here. Prepare to weigh anchor."

Heloise's feeling of doom persisted as her feet left the solidity of the dock and she ventured up the swaying gangplank; she glanced down at the dark, unfriendly waves and shuddered. Raven ushered her across the unsteady deck and down a set of steep wooden steps. The area below was extremely cramped. A number of small wooden cots had been set in rows on one side, presumably where the crew slept, and the air was warm and close.

"They double as coffins if anyone dies at sea," he said cheerfully, noting the direction of her gaze. "Not an inch of space in a place like this." He led her to a narrow door and opened it with a flourish. "Only one cabin, in fact. Mine."

And with that, he shoved her inside.

CHAPTER 10

$\mathcal{H}$eloise glared over her shoulder at him and straightened. So this was what a smuggler's cabin looked like.

She stifled a spurt of disappointment. It looked like an ordinary, rather cramped study. A chair and leather-topped desk competed for space with a large bed, apparently built into one wall. There was a set of shelves with odd, low brass railings running along the edges—presumably to prevent items from falling off—and a couple of wooden trunks. Small, glazed portholes provided little illumination.

She gestured at the ceiling and summoned her most imperious tone. Raven might have bullied her onto his ship, but he was not going to order her about. "Don't you have to be up there, captaining or something?"

"Trying to get rid of me?"

"Yes."

Raven opened a cupboard set into wall. She heard the chink of glasses, the splash of liquid, and he turned, holding two tumblers. "I'm going. But first, drink this." He handed her a glass filled with liquid the color of a sunset.

She eyed it with deep suspicion. "What's that?"

"Pink gin to combat seasickness. It's just a precaution. Don't want you ruining my nice clean cabin." He glanced down at his feet. "This is an extremely expensive rug."

Heloise took a tentative sniff. Her eyes watered and she blinked rapidly. "Is the idea to get me so drunk I pass out?"

"No. But it should stop you from feeling queasy. Even Admiral Nelson used to get sick at the start of every voyage. And he first went to sea when he was twelve."

"How reassuring."

He chinked the rim of his own glass against hers and downed the contents. "Bottoms up."

With a mental shrug Heloise did the same. Her throat caught fire. Tears sprang to her eyes. When she could catch her breath she croaked out, "Good Lord! That's vile."

Raven grinned and took her empty glass. "Good girl. Now, as you rightly said, I have to 'go captain.' Is there anything else you require?"

"Only your absence," she managed.

He backed out the door with a mocking flourish. "Your humble servant."

Heloise scowled. Ha. There was nothing humble or subservient about him.

As soon as the key turned in the lock she made a thorough search of the cabin. One box was full of charts. The other was a foreign-looking, carved chest that held clothes. The interior smelled like pencil shavings. The desk was unlocked, but contained pens, paper, ink, and nothing remotely interesting. She hadn't really expected to find anything. Raven wouldn't be much of a spy if he left information all over the place for inquisitive people to find.

Perhaps it was the motion of the ship, or the potency of the gin, but she was beginning to feel a little light-headed. Heloise flopped down onto the chair.

"Be careful what you wish for," they said. She grimaced. Her list of "things to do before I die" had included a wish for her mundane life to be more exciting. She'd always been jealous of the closeness the boys shared, that unbreakable bond of friendship, forged in the crucible of war. She'd wished for a chance to travel, too, but it had always been too dangerous; England had been at war with France for so long she'd never had a Paris season or a Grand Tour.

She'd known, on a theoretical level at least, that her code-breaking was important to the war effort, but the comfort of her own home and the genteel luxury of Lord Castlereagh's Whitehall offices had been so far removed from the shadowy world of covert operations inhabited by Raven and her brothers that she'd never truly imagined she could be in danger. Tonight that nebulous threat had become terrifyingly real.

A wave of exhaustion rolled over her. The bed looked extremely inviting. She loosened the laces of her corset, her fingers oddly uncoordinated. That gin must have been extremely strong. She shouldn't have had it on top of the champagne; her head was swimming. She kicked off her cream silk ballet slippers and regarded them dolefully. Ruined. Grass stains never came out.

The boat was definitely moving now; the floor seemed very unreliable. She staggered a little as she crossed the cabin and sank gratefully onto the bed. A key grated in the lock; Raven was back.

Heloise blinked at him owlishly. "Oh, itsh you again, ish it?"

The words came out slurred. She frowned.

Raven affected a scandalized expression. "You're not drunk, are you, Miss Hampden?"

She drew herself up in insulted affront. "Of course not." She tilted her head to one side and gave the matter grave consideration. "I don't think I am." Thinking was hard. "It's possible I'm tipsy," she conceded.

She leaned back against the wall and gave him a slow smile. She was all warm and tingly. "That's one thing I can cross off my list, then."

"Your list?"

She glared at him. He was being particularly dense. "I told you about it. My list of things I want to do before I die."

"Ah. That list. Getting drunk was right next to finding an insatiable lover, I assume."

"Yup. You men all drink with alarming regularity. There must be something to recommend it. Now I see why. It's quite pleasant. Although it does produce the oddest sensation of the floor moving about. That might just be because we're on a ship, of course."

He smiled. "What else?"

She wrinkled her nose. "What else, what?"

"What else is on the list?"

"Oh, all the things I was never allowed to do and wanted to." Her eyelids drooped and she yawned. Raven sat on the edge of the bed. She didn't have the energy to scold him. She listed sideways until her head hit the pillow. Ah. That was better. "I might just take a little nap."

"Not worried I'll ravish you in your sleep?" he teased.

She gave an unladylike snort. "Ha. You don't want me. Never have."

He raised a brow and waited for her to explain.

"In your defense, I do know you didn't turn me down because of my scar. You rejected me a full six months before I got it." She let out a long sigh. "It must have been some other flaw in my personality."

Raven shook his head, his expression unreadable, and Heloise closed her eyes, appalled with herself. Had she really just said that out loud? She needed to stop talking, right this instant.

The mattress dipped as he shifted and she felt him smooth

back her hair from her cheek. His breath sluiced across her forehead, then her cheek, as he bent down.

The touch of his hand disappeared but she sensed he stayed close by. His presence should have been alarming, but instead she found herself oddly comforted.

"Sleep now, Hellcat," he whispered in her ear.

And for possibly the first time in her life, Heloise Hampden did as she was told.

* * *

RAVEN SHOOK his head as he gazed down at the woman in his bed. For someone so intelligent, she was sometimes unbelievably stupid. Thank God.

He tucked the blankets around her and a fierce wave of lust shot through him. He liked the idea of surrounding her in sheets that smelled of him. She nestled further into the pillows, pink lips pouted in sleep.

He forced himself to move away and sit in the chair, enjoying the familiar creak of leather as he propped his booted feet on the desk, and smiled at the memory of her list. He'd done exactly the same thing when he'd been kidnapped, made a mental list of all the things he regretted not doing. Funny how the imminence of death gave one's thoughts a certain awful clarity.

Making love to Heloise Hampden had been high up on his list.

First on the list, if he was honest.

He'd sworn that if he ever got out of that hellhole he was going to go after what he wanted. He'd wanted her, and sod it, he was going to take her, and to hell with the consequences.

Except it hadn't been that simple. He'd wanted to race over and see her the moment he'd escaped, but he'd forced himself to wait, to make himself presentable again. He'd arrived just in time for her damned coming-out ball, spotted her across the room surrounded by a crowd of admirers. There she was, so bloody beautiful, shining like the sun.

The reality of the situation had hit him like a physical blow, more shocking than all the actual blows he'd received during his imprisonment. He couldn't possibly claim her now. He was contaminated, broken. Unworthy.

Raven shifted in his seat, uncomfortable with his thoughts. That had been six years ago and he'd gone even farther down the path of darkness since then. Someone as good as Heloise was forever out of reach.

CHAPTER 11

*H*eloise cracked open one eye and groaned. Her head hurt.

The scuffle of feet overhead and the muted hum of voices confirmed her hazy recollections of the previous night. She was in a cabin. On Raven's boat. A boat that was still moving, judging by the rocking motion and the sound of waves slapping on the hull. The slow side-to-side roll matched the unpleasant pitch of her stomach.

She squinted at the sunlight slanting in through the portholes, which did nothing to help the pounding in her temples. Was it morning? Afternoon? Her throat was scratchy. Was that coffee she could smell?

Someone had partly opened a window, at least; the blessedly fresh breeze gave her the strength to risk moving her head.

She was not alone.

Raven sat in the chair, long legs stretched out in front of him, looking irritatingly refreshed. Heloise moaned and pressed her face back into the pillow. How long had he been there?

"Ah, you're awake." He put down the book he'd been reading,

69

poured a cup of steaming liquid from a silver pot on the desk, and offered it to her.

Heloise held her head with one hand. It felt as if it needed the support. "What time is it?"

"Time to get up. Drink this."

She struggled into a sitting position and shot him a suspicious glare. "It's not alcoholic, is it?"

"Coffee. You'll feel better, I promise." He took a sip. She watched the dip of his throat as he swallowed and cursed the odd feeling in her stomach, which had nothing to do with last night's gin. He handed her the cup. "See? No ill effects."

She deliberately turned the mug so she wouldn't have to drink from the same section his lips had touched. He grinned. She gulped it down. Heavenly. It burned her throat and warmed her stomach, and she felt better immediately.

Raven lifted the satchel he'd brought from the house and tossed it to her. "Look inside."

Heloise opened the top and glanced at him in amazement. It contained her favorite pale blue morning dress, her comb, and a bar of her rose petal soap. "How did you get these?"

"I rode over to your house last night."

"You idiot! You let the servants discover I wasn't in my room?"

"Of course not. I let myself in. Although they'll have noticed you're missing by now, in any case. I left Hodges a note."

Heloise gulped and tried to recall if she'd hidden the embarrassing gothic romance she'd been reading under the volume of Aristotle by her bed. "How did you know which room mine?"

He gave a piratical grin. "I've always known where to find you."

"I imagine you're quite the expert on finding ladies' boudoirs," she sniffed.

The idea of him, prowling round in all his black-wolf potency, touching her things, made her feel faint. A sudden suspicion gripped her and she checked the satchel again. Oh no. There, under the dress, was her favorite teal-colored shift and matching drawers.

Which meant he'd been rifling through her underwear, too, the weasel.

He smiled innocently. "I admit, it was a shock to find your room so feminine."

Heloise bristled. "What did you expect?" Her room was feminine. True, it was pale green, instead of the traditional lavender or pink, with a large desk and several sturdy bookshelves, but it had gilt accents and elegant furniture, too.

"Oh, I don't know. More mummified remains? Jars of pickled newts? The odd sarcophagus or two . . ."

She rolled her eyes. "Ha. You're just intimidated by intelligent women. Someone like me threatens the very core of your masculinity."

"That's not true. I happen to find intelligent women extremely attractive. Especially when they're only partially dressed."

She followed the direction of his gaze. Her dress and loosened corset had slipped down. Heloise gasped, yanked them back up, and scowled at him. Her gaze strayed to the book on the desk, which he'd been reading. She squinted. It looked awfully familiar, like—

"Hey! That's mine!" she shrieked.

Her diary had been hidden in the same drawer as her scandalous undergarments. The battered notebook held mostly mundane scraps of information—notes to herself about new avenues of research, snatches of poetry, quotations she liked—but it also contained her ever-evolving list.

At least she'd had the self-preservation not to commit the myriad erotic fantasies she'd had about him to paper. She'd be spared that particular humiliation, thank God, but still, what she had written was sure to be embarrassing enough.

Heloise made a dive for the book but Raven scooped it up and held it out of reach.

"That is a private notebook! I can't believe—"

"That I'd read it?" he finished with an unapologetic chuckle. "That's the thing about us spies. We're insatiably curious."

She made another lunge. "That is such a betrayal of trust!"

He scanned a page and frowned. "What on earth is a Vigenère cipher? No, never mind, I don't want to know."

"Give that back this minute."

He turned the page. "Too late. I already read your infamous list. It's pathetic."

She bristled. "What do you mean, pathetic?"

"As in dull. Boring. Immature. It needs some serious modification."

Heloise ground her teeth. "And I suppose you have plenty of suggestions?"

"As a matter of fact, I do." He picked up a pen. "Item number one: 'Run in the rain.' " He glanced at her. "What's that supposed to mean?"

"I'd have thought it was obvious. I want to stand outside in the pouring rain and get soaked to the skin, to see if it's as fun as I remember from my childhood."

"I doubt it," he said. "You'll probably catch pneumonia."

"How would you improve it, then?"

He tapped the pen against his lips. Such nice lips. Heloise gave herself a mental smack on the head. She had no business noticing his lips. He didn't need to keep drawing attention to them, either. That was a cheap flirt's trick.

"I'd keep the rain," he mused. "But you should wish to be kissed in it. Then I'd be intrigued."

She rolled her eyes. "This may come as a shock to you, Raven-wood, but I don't spend my spare time dreaming up ways to intrigue you."

"You disappoint me," he said. "In fact, now I think about it, you should wish to be kissed so thoroughly that you cease to even notice that it's raining. If you're striving for decadent abandon, you've a long way to go."

"I'm not striving for decadent abandon."

"That's where you're going wrong. What's next? Ah. Item two: 'Swim in the ocean.' Again, not very exciting."

"Not in England," she clarified. "It's too cold. I meant somewhere warm and exotic. I want hot sand between my toes and warm water lapping at my feet."

She frowned as Raven made an amendment.

"There." He gave a satisfied smile. "Now it says 'swim naked.' " He wrote again. " 'At midnight.' That's far more exciting."

She opened her mouth to protest but he forestalled her by raising his hand. "And while we're on the subject of water, might I suggest another addition?"

"Why not?" she said sarcastically.

"I'm going to include 'Take a bath with someone.' "

Heat curled under her skin and she closed her eyes against an onslaught of incendiary mental images. When she reopened them Raven was squinting at the page.

"Hello. This one's crossed out. Does that mean you've actually achieved it?"

"Maybe," Heloise hedged. "What did it say?"

"I think, 'Acquire a feminine skill.' " He sent her a secret, intimate smile that had her blushing to the roots of her hair. "The mind boggles. Just give me a minute to envisage all the delightful—"

"Not *those* kind of feminine skills," she blurted out. "I meant learn to knit, or sew, or crochet." She almost laughed at his horrified expression.

"God, whatever for? Now, learning skills in the bedroom I can understand—"

"Or maybe make something wearable," she continued valiantly.

"And did you?"

Actually, she'd deleted that one in a fit of frustration after a few complete disasters. "No. I tried to knit a scarf once for Nic, but he said it would be better as a noose."

"All right. We'll leave that one. What's next?" His eyebrows rose. "Smoke a cigar, eh? Now, that I can help you with."

He pulled open the drawer of his desk, extracted a slim wooden box, and drew out a thin cheroot. He lit it and took a few draws that made the end glow red. On the exhale, a cloud of blue smoke curled around his head like a wreath. He held the cigar out to her, his gaze challenging.

Her stomach lurched. Just the smell was making her queasy but she couldn't refuse the challenge. She'd have to brazen it out.

She placed it between her lips and breathed in. Her lungs tingled unpleasantly. The smoke made her eyes water and she exhaled on a cough, waving her hand in front of her face to disband the smoke. "Ugh!"

Raven, the beast, just laughed. He recaptured the cheroot, leaned back in his chair, and took another slow drag. "It's an acquired taste," he said mildly. "I'll cross it off your list." He scraped the pen across the page while Heloise put her hand around her ribs to hold them in place. She was definitely coughing up her own lungs. She was never going to touch a cigar again.

"Now, what else is on here? Ah! I can help you with this next one, too. It says 'Play cards for money.' "

Heloise shook her head. "Not right now, thank you. I want to be in complete possession of my wits before I engage you in card play."

He smirked. "Later, then. What's next? 'Read improving books.' " He glanced around the stark cabin. "Don't keep any books in here. They fall on the floor when there's a storm. I do, however, have several books back in my library at home that might be of interest—"

"I suspect your definition of 'improving' is rather different from mine," she said dryly. "No doubt they're those ridiculous erotic etchings my brothers are so enamored of. They cherish the fond belief that I don't know where they hide them."

He looked impressed. "Sounds like you've read some improving books already, then. What were they? Rowlandson? Gillray?"

"I can't recall."

Heloise willed her blush to subside as her mind brought up with distressing clarity a particularly graphic engraving of the Prince of Wales in bed with his mistress. It depicted the Prince with a ludicrously enlarged male member. At least, she *assumed* it was an exaggeration. She'd never actually seen a man's member—aroused, engorged, or otherwise—but such monstrous proportions were surely ridiculous hyperbole?

She managed an unconcerned shrug. "I don't know why you boys think I'd be so squeamish about it. I'm a scholar. It's a basic human act, depicted on hundreds of historic artifacts. Greek vases are covered in naked men. The Romans put phallic symbols everywhere. They even put wings on them and hung them outside their doors as a good luck charm."

Raven adopted an expression of awe. "You are an extraordinary woman, Heloise Hampden."

She nodded her head in acceptance of the compliment, even though it was somewhat backhanded.

Raven bent to read the next line on the list. " 'Travel.' Well, that's not very specific."

"To Egypt," she clarified. "I want to visit all those exotic places I've only ever seen in drawings in the *Description de l'Égypte*."

Egypt was the place for love affairs, of Anthony and Cleopatra. Where Alexander and the great pharaoh Ramses had built temples that had lasted for thousands of years.

"Egypt, eh? I can do that."

She wrinkled her nose. "You're going to tell the crew to bypass Spain and keep going until we hit Africa?"

He laughed. "No. We're still going to Spain."

"Then how—?"

"It's a trick I learned when I was a hostage."

Her lips formed a soundless O of surprise. Raven had never spoken to her of his imprisonment.

"A man has a lot of time to think when he's alone for hours at a time. For some reason I kept remembering this fragment of a poem: 'Stone Walls do not a Prison make, Nor Iron bars a Cage.' I don't know who wrote it, but it helped me realize that physical imprisonment is not mental imprisonment. You can go anywhere in your mind. I'll show you. Where do you want to be?"

"Sailing down the Nile on a felucca," she said immediately.

"All right. Close your eyes."

Heloise did so reluctantly, half expecting a trick.

"We're not in this cabin. We're in the shade of a palm tree, on the banks of the Nile. I've tied up the boat and sent the servants away. I'm feeding you figs."

Raven shifted his weight and she started to open her eyes.

"No, don't look," he chided softly.

She jumped as he trailed his hand over her forehead and smoothed back her hair. His touch was soothing, magical, and she let herself sink into it, just for a moment.

"There's a cotton blanket beneath us, and warm sand below that. Feel the heat sinking through your bones. The sun is setting, the shadows are turning purple. There's a cool breeze that brushes the palm fronds together so they rustle."

His fingertop stroked across her lips, petal soft. Heloise was just about to part her lips and taste his finger when reality reasserted itself. She reared back, breaking the hypnotic spell he'd cast. "That's quite a trick."

Raven stood with an easy smile. "Isn't it? Come upstairs when you're ready. I'll see you on deck."

Heloise dressed quickly in the pale blue day dress. Raven's effortless ability to affect her was a problem, especially in such close confines. Putting as much distance as possible between them would be prudent, but she was stuck with the man, at least for the time being.

She clearly had two options. She could sulk and complain and generally make his life disagreeable, which did hold a certain vindictive appeal, or she could embrace this adventure as an unexpected opportunity to live. She smiled and made her way up to the deck.

CHAPTER 12

*R*aven tightened his grip on the bundle of clothes he'd gathered and frowned.

Heloise stood on the quarterdeck like a queen holding court. A group of besotted sailors surrounded her and from their enthusiastic gestures he surmised they were pointing out places of interest along the French coast and identifying the various seabirds for 'Her Majesty.'

An accommodating breeze plastered her dress to her body, outlining her curves. No wonder the men were practically salivating. She drew them like bees to honey. It wasn't even deliberate; the infuriating girl had no notion of her own appeal.

Raven stepped up behind her and shot his crew an intimidating look to remind them of their pressing duties. One by one they dropped their heads and sloped back to work.

Heloise turned, puzzled by the loss of her rapt audience. "Oh, it's you, Ravenwood. You startled me, skulking around like that."

He lowered his brows. "This is my own bloody ship. Who else were you expecting? Fat Prince George?"

She ignored that little piece of sarcasm and peered up at the mast. "So. This is your boat."

"It's not a boat. It's a ship."

"There's a difference?"

He ground his teeth. "Yes, there's a difference. A boat is small. For waterways like rivers and staying close to shore. A ship is large. It has a captain and a crew, and sails on the ocean." He tapped the wooden railing with his knuckle.

She gave an unladylike snort. "Ah, so it's a *size* thing. I should have known. You men are obsessed with the relative proportions of everything."

A smile tugged the corner of his mouth and he held his hands up in a gesture of surrender. "I can't. It's just too easy."

"How come ships are always female?"

He slanted her a cynical look from under his brows. "Because men can't resist them, they need constant attention, and they're bloody expensive to keep."

She rolled her eyes. "What's the name of this particular mistress, then?"

"We change the name plates all the time, just to confuse the customs and excise boys. Today she's Hope."

"Very appropriate." Heloise glanced over at him and for a moment he forgot everything, lost in her lavender eyes. Clouds that color meant a storm was on the way.

"You haven't told me where we're going, you know."

Raven shook himself out of his reverie. "Santander, in northern Spain. We'll be there in a couple of hours. Provided you leave my men alone to do their jobs."

Heloise pursed her lips. "I did nothing to encourage them. Besides, what are you going to do? Throw me overboard?"

"I wouldn't want to poison the sharks."

She frowned. "There aren't any sharks in the English Channel."

He pointed to the land mass off to their left and shot her an evil grin. "That's Guernsey. This is the Bay of Biscay." Raven smothered a laugh as she glanced down at the water as if expecting to see ominous gray fins circling the ship.

"Surely this is the Mediterranean?"

He gave a noncommittal shrug and shoved the bundle of clothing at her. "Here, you need to put these on."

"I've only just got dressed." She inspected the shirt and breeches with a dubious expression. "Whose are these?"

"The cabin boy's. Don't worry, they're clean. Mostly."

"I'm not wearing them."

He crossed his arms over his chest. "You know, Hellcat, I don't think you're taking this whole captor-captive thing very seriously. We need to set out a few ground rules. Namely, you have to do everything I say."

"Ha! If I ever consider obeying you, Ravenwood, I'll certainly let you know."

"Try it, if only for the novelty."

She sniffed. "What's wrong with what I'm wearing?"

Raven manfully resisted looking any lower than her neck. "You'll attract less notice as a boy. People will assume you're my servant."

"Another dream come true."

He ignored the sarcasm and pinned her with a challenging glare. "You wouldn't be the first woman to wear male clothes. General Masséna's mistress dressed as one of his staff officers, so she could accompany him on campaign." He went in for the kill. "Come on, Hellcat. You always wanted to be treated like one of the boys. Now's your chance."

"All right," she growled.

She turned and navigated her way unsteadily toward the hatch.

Raven's weathered deckhand, Hardy, who'd accompanied him on countless hair-raising adventures, sidled up and shot him a gap-toothed grin. "Problems wi' the lady, Cap'n?"

Raven watched Heloise's shapely derriere disappear down the

ladder and exhaled loudly through his teeth. "I swear, that woman could make a bishop put his fist through a stained glass window."

Hardy chuckled and gave him a commiserating slap on the back.

Raven scowled. The next few days were going to be absolute hell.

CHAPTER 13

Santander was chaos. The curving harbor teemed with life, so fascinatingly foreign Heloise hardly knew where to look. Fishermen and fishwives decked in straw hats and striped shawls shouted as they hawked their wares on the dockside. Barks of laughter and arguments over baskets of pungent fish clashed with the shouts of men unloading wooden crates onto the jetties and two men cursing as they tried to restrain a rearing horse that objected to disembarking. Colors seemed more intense, the light harsher, and the sun warmer than in England.

She made no demur when Raven steered her down the gangplank and they plunged into the dockside crowds. Her stomach knotted in excitement as she tried to absorb every nuance of this strange, bustling city. She only understood snatches of conversation but gleaned much from the expressions and accompanying gestures. These people were no different from those in any street in England; they gossiped about food prices, naughty children, fashions, errant husbands, prizefights, and livestock.

As Raven had predicted, no one spared her a second glance. She hadn't worn breeches for years, but these seemed indecently tight; they clung to her legs and rubbed between her thighs in a most disconcerting manner. The shirt was a little less revealing, but the leather boots Raven provided were at least a size too small.

Raven purchased a large, floppy straw hat from a street vendor and Heloise scowled as she realized he was having no difficulty communicating. She poked his arm.

"You speak Spanish!"

He gave her a condescending smile. "It's a good thing one of us can. If you're nice to me I might teach you a few useful phrases. Repeat after me. *Me gustaria una aguatinto del puerto.*"

"What does that mean?"

"I'd like an aquatint of the harbor."

She rolled her eyes. "Very useful."

"*He roto mis dentaduras.* I've broken my dentures."

"Idiot."

"Actually, there's only one phrase you'll ever need. *Sí, Cuervo, que siempre tiene la razón.*"

The words spilled from his tongue like love poetry. Heloise suppressed a sigh. Spanish really was a beautiful language. She raised her brows and waited.

"Yes, Raven, you are always right," he translated solemnly.

The boots were good for one thing. She kicked him in the shin.

He sidestepped with a chuckle and slapped the hat on her head. "Can't have those freckles joining up now, can we? A laborer's tan is extremely unfashionable this season. Come on."

He bought two horses from a trader; a handsome Arab for himself and a chestnut mare for her. Neither, she noted, had a sidesaddle. He placed her satchel in one the panniers strapped to the side of his horse and beckoned her to step onto his linked fingers to mount.

"We're not staying in Santander?"

"Afraid not."

He boosted her up and Heloise swung her leg over the saddle. She'd ridden astride as a child, but had endured the more ladylike sidesaddle since she'd turned sixteen.

Raven mounted his own horse with a fluid movement and steered the animal down the street. It wasn't long before they'd ridden out of the city altogether, heading toward a range of distant hills. Heloise glared at the forbidding peaks and her spirits sank. There didn't appear to be much in the way of human habitation up ahead.

"Where are we going?"

Raven squinted at the horizon. "León. It's about fifty miles. We should be there by tomorrow, I expect."

"Tomorrow!"

He smiled at her dismay and Heloise glared at his back as he galloped ahead. He'd donned a rough black waistcoat over his white linen shirt, but it wasn't long enough to conceal the pair of pistols he'd tucked into his waistband or the knife in a leather holster he'd attached to his belt. A tremor of apprehension ran through her. Surely those were just a precaution?

She shook off the worry as she studied her surroundings. There were flowers she didn't recognize, trees she couldn't name. Rabbits scampered out of their path and a few nimble-footed goats scattered into the hills at their approach.

After an hour or so the cultivated land petered out and the path began to climb as they headed into the foothills. Villages became more distant as the sun grew hotter. Heloise prayed they'd stop for a rest. The dust was harsh in the back of her throat and her eyes watered with the sun, despite her ridiculous hat.

At the crest of a hill they discovered a burnt-out village and Heloise frowned at the cluster of weathered, rudimentary crosses that lined the side of the road.

Raven caught her troubled gaze. "This area saw intense fighting at the end of the war. The French used the Ancient tactic of chevauchée, where the retreating army burns the crops behind them. It's effective, but it punishes the locals as much as the enemy. It's no wonder the Spanish fought so fiercely alongside us to expel them."

Heloise shuddered. Peace might have been declared six months ago, but the scars left on the landscape would clearly take far longer to heal. A dark bird flew up from the carcass of a dead animal and she eyed it with distaste. She'd never been able to tell the difference between rooks, ravens, and crows. They all had sharp claws, intelligent eyes, and glossy black plumage. Just like her companion.

"You're well named, you know," she said. "Are you aware of the collective noun for a group of ravens?"

"The collective noun?" He mocked her prim schoolteacher tone.

"The word for a group of them together," she explained patiently. The idiot was feigning ignorance just to amuse himself. "You know, like a parliament of crows. A gaggle of geese. A covey of quails."

Raven shook his head. "I'm sure you're about to enlighten me."

"There are two, actually. An unkindness of ravens and a conspiracy of ravens."

His lips curved upward. "Such flattery."

Heloise fell into a dreamlike reverie as they plodded along. Her body had developed a mass of aches and pains, but she'd be damned if she'd ask to stop. They'd passed a few secluded cottages and a shepherd's hut a while ago, but now there was little more than scrubby brush, lizards, and dry rocks. Heloise slapped her thigh with the palm of her hand and a cloud of red dust billowed out.

Raven reined in so he was alongside her. "You're very quiet. Are you sulking?"

"No."

He leaned over and flicked the brim of her hat.

She swatted him away. "I'm not here for your amusement, Ravenwood. I didn't foist myself upon you. You can't complain if you don't like my company."

"I didn't ask for this either, you know. I'd much rather be back at home."

"My apologies for interrupting your non-stop round of gambling, whoring, and debauchery," she said with razor-edged politeness.

"You're still as annoying as you were when you were ten," he sighed.

She sent him a smug smile. "My brothers call it quietly stubborn."

He muttered something that sounded suspiciously like "pain in the arse." Silence ensued for another mile or so.

It was so hot. Heloise wriggled in the saddle to relieve her aching backside and an unladylike bead of sweat trickled between her breasts. There was nothing for it. She was going to have to beg.

"I need to stop. I can't feel my legs."

Raven glanced back over his shoulder and shot her a cheeky grin. "Want me to feel them for you?"

She narrowed her eyes.

He shrugged. "Stop moaning. Your discomfort's nothing compared to Kit's suffering."

Heloise cursed him to the deepest bowels of hell.

The cheep of crickets was an endless racket. The waves of sound rose to a screeching crescendo then fell again, like a throbbing headache, and a heat haze wavered above the parched landscape, distorting the perspective. There was no discernible trail. They were probably lost and Raven was too proud to admit it. They were going to be eaten by wolves. She hoped they ate him first, so she could watch. At least she'd die happy.

He glanced over at her and chuckled. "Poor little Hellcat."

"I wish you wouldn't call me that."

"What?" he asked, all innocence. "Hell-cat? Hell-oise." He deliberately put the emphasis on the first syllable just to provoke her.

"Yes. And it's the French pronunciation. The H' is silent. I've told you a million times. Ell—Oh—Ease."

* * *

RAVEN WATCHED Heloise's lips form the three distinct syllables of her name and cursed the way his body tightened in response. At the "ell" her tongue peeked out and licked her even white teeth. The soft exhale of the "oh" pursed her lips forward as if she were waiting for a kiss. And the final "ease" stretched her mouth into the same wide, satisfied smile she'd wear after exhausting, mind-altering sex.

Holy hell, it was a provocative name. Everything about the bloody woman sent him into an agony of lust. Hell-oise was apt; he burned for her hotter than the fiery pits of Satan.

What kind of a ridiculous name was it, anyway? It was a houri's name, a courtesan's name. She ought to be in some Persian seraglio, not flitting about the lush English countryside driving people mad. Raven grimaced. Her father might be an English lord, but her mother was quintessentially French. That parental dichotomy surely explained the warring sides of her nature; reserved and composed on the surface, wayward and unruly beneath. It was a lethal combination.

CHAPTER 14

*H*eloise almost cried when Raven stopped and tied the horses—whom she'd secretly named Hades and Persephone—to a scrubby tree. She slid off Persephone and had to clutch the stirrup for support when her knees gave way. Her thighs protested as she walked slowly around the clearing.

"Don't go wandering off," Raven warned. "You have the survival instincts of a day-old kitten."

"I'm perfectly able to fend for myself."

His derisive snort was far from complimentary. "If I left you alone for five minutes, you'd be in trouble faster than you can say 'hieroglyphics.' "

Patronizing ass.

Heloise turned away to study one of the trees at the edge of the clearing. She plucked one of the long, brown withered beans that hung from the branches, snapped it in half, and sniffed. It was rich and fruity, and she smiled in sudden recognition.

Raven marched over and snatched it off her. "Leave that alone."

She snatched it back. "It's a carob. I recognize it from my research on Ancient Egypt. The bean itself," she waved the brown stem at him for emphasis, "is a hieroglyphic symbol, although no one's quite sure what it's supposed to mean." She studied the wizened fruit with a sense of wonder. "I've only ever seen these in illustrations. Did you know that carob seeds were traditionally used by people in the Middle East as a unit of weight? That's where we get the term 'carat' for weighing gold and gemstones."

"You are a fount of useless knowledge."

She ignored his sarcasm and took an experimental nibble. It was sweet and chewy, not entirely unpleasant.

"Don't eat it!" Raven's face was the picture of horrified disbelief. He grabbed her jaw, and squeezed. "What are you doing? Spit it out!"

Heloise swatted his hand away. "It tastes a lot like dates," she mumbled. "Stop being ridiculous."

"What if the hieroglyphic symbol of a carob turns out to denote instant, horrible death? What if you've made a mistake and that's some look-alike relation that's deadly poisonous? Christ, Heloise, there's a big difference between book learning and practical experience. Spit it out."

Heloise shot him a look of pure defiance and swallowed.

He watched her with an expression of fatalistic dread.

She couldn't resist. Adopting a look of surprised horror, she clutched her throat, staggered a little for dramatic effect, and bent over, gasping.

Raven's brows shot together. He stepped forward just as she straightened up and grinned.

He sent her a furious glare. "Hilarious. I'll remember this. Next time you really need my help, don't be surprised if I ignore you completely."

She chuckled. Annoying him was so much fun.

He pointed to a rock. "Sit down and don't move until I come back. And don't touch anything."

She gave him a jaunty, mocking salute and waited exactly

thirty seconds for him to stomp off into the bushes before she went exploring on her own.

This area had clearly once been cultivated. Rows of gnarled trees stood on stepped terraces, now dismally overgrown. Heloise clambered over a broken stone wall and stooped to gather some nuts scattered on the ground. The velvety outer layer was a surprise, but the hard-pitted nut inside she recognized from her mother's Christmas table. Almonds.

A sudden pang of homesickness stole her breath, sharply followed by guilt. The smell of pine resin reminded her of the turpentine Maman used for thinning her oil paints. Had her parents heard about her disappearance yet? Were they worried for her?

Raven glowered at her when she returned to the clearing but said nothing as she shook the almonds from the pouch she'd made in the front of her shirt. He extracted a hunk of bread, some sweaty cheese, and a bottle of wine from his saddlebag and selected a rock next to her.

He'd been foraging, too. A stone nearby held a handful of figs, like dark purple teardrops, and another shiny, red fruit, which looked like an apple with a tiny crown growing on the top.

"A pomegranate," he said, noting the direction of her gaze. "Ever had one?"

She shook her head.

"Another new experience to add to your list, then."

He cut it with his knife and revealed a mass of glistening red seeds. Heloise swallowed as he divided it in two and offered half to her. The gesture seemed oddly symbolic. He looked as tempting and irresistible as the serpent in the Garden of Eden. Would she be entering into some kind of devilish pact if she accepted it?

Raven frowned at her hesitation. "Come on. It's not like you'll be stuck with me for eternity if you eat some."

She glanced up in shock at how closely he'd mirrored her thoughts. "You mean like Persephone?"

"I vaguely remember something about her having to stay with wicked old Hades in the Underworld because she ate a pomegranate."

Heloise took the fruit and adopted her best schoolmistress tone. "Yes. When Hades kidnapped Persephone, Demeter—her mother—demanded her back. They couldn't come to an agreement so they asked Zeus to intervene and he decreed that Persephone would be allowed to leave the Underworld, provided she hadn't eaten any food of the dead. But she'd already eaten six pomegranate seeds, so she had to split her time between the Underworld and the earth above, six months in each."

Raven was uncomfortably close. The front of his shirt hung open in a deep V that revealed the hard line of his collarbone, the cords of his neck. A wave of heat that had nothing to do with the sun burned through her.

Concentrate on the fruit.

She teased a few of the seeds out with her fingernail and brought them to her mouth. Juice, sweet and tart, spurted onto her tongue and she licked her lip as a trickle escaped. She glanced at Raven to see if he'd noticed her unladylike lapse and realized his attention was fixed on her mouth. The intense way he was watching her robbed the air from her lungs.

Oh, goodness.

"You know, some scholars have suggested that the fruit Eve offered to Adam was more likely to be a pomegranate than an apple." Blood rushed to her face. Why on earth had she mentioned that? "Others believe it was a persimmon. Or even a tomato."

A tomato? *A tomato?* She should dash her head against the nearest rock. Why wouldn't her mouth stop working? Why didn't the ground just open up and swallow her whole? She was fluent in five different languages, but in Raven's presence she could barely string a coherent sentence together.

Heloise cleared her throat and busied herself with cracking open the almonds. She selected a large, flat stone and settled it between her legs as an anvil. With a second, smaller rock, she attacked the nuts. She pretended they were his head.

Raven, thankfully, stalked away to check on the horses, offering a fine view of his wide shoulders, slim hips, and tight derriere. Heloise missed the almond, hit her finger, and cursed under her breath.

For years she'd tried to fall in love with someone else, prayed to meet someone who returned her feelings. But the blasted Fates seemed to be determined to ignore her. Raven was the only one who'd do.

He was truly the most obnoxious, irritating man she'd ever met. She was a sensible, educated, enlightened woman. The fact that she still found him attractive, against all logical reasons to the contrary, was extremely vexing.

It was the stress of the situation. Too little sleep and too much excitement was enough to muddle anyone's brain. Even one as ordered as hers.

CHAPTER 15

*H*eloise heard the river before she saw it; a rushing, gurgling sound that increased in volume as they rode toward it. She dismounted, dropped to her haunches to hide the fact that her legs had given way, and pretended she'd meant to test the water all along. It was crystal clear straight off the mountains; she scooped up a handful and drank greedily, gasping as the coolness soothed her parched throat.

She eyed the fast-moving torrent with a leaden sense of dread. "We can't cross here."

Raven dismounted and joined her. "We have to. There aren't any bridges for miles."

"It's too deep."

"Don't be silly," he said with exaggerated patience. "You'll barely get your feet wet."

He cinched the saddlebags higher on Hades's back, stowed his pistols inside, then plucked off her hat and placed that in the saddlebag, too. He caught the reins of both horses in one hand and started forward. "Let's go."

Heloise scuffed the toe of her boot against a stone and sent it skittering into the water.

He leaned closer. "What's that? You're mumbling."

Humiliation engulfed her. She hated having to admit a weakness. "I said, I can't swim."

Raven frowned. "Of course you can. You're the one who saved Tony from that pond, remember?"

"Of course I remember," she snapped. "I still have nightmares about it." She bit her lip. She hadn't meant to reveal that. She hurried on, hoping he hadn't noticed the slip. "But I didn't need to swim to rescue him. The water was frozen. I ran out over the ice. Well, slid, actually. And then I crawled forward on my belly and pulled him out."

She lifted her hand to her forehead automatically, as if to confirm her scar was still there. She'd been helping Tony up the frozen bank, both of them sopping wet, their labored breaths forming icy clouds in front of them. He'd been so heavy. They'd slipped; she recalled the bright, stinging pain as her head hit a snow-covered rock, the festive brightness of her blood against the snow.

Raven's brow creased as he clearly tried to recall a time when he'd witnessed her swimming. He'd fail. She'd always been banned from their naked lake swims and she hadn't dared to try to teach herself. Her injury was a permanent reminder that she'd cheated death of his chosen victim. It would have been tempting fate to go near water again.

He dropped his chin to his chest, closed his eyes, and swore under his breath. "Let me get this straight. You went out on that ice when you *couldn't bloody swim?*"

Hades stepped nervously sideways, reacting to his increasing volume, but Raven controlled the animal with an impatient tug on the reins.

Heloise stood and faced him, her own temper rising at his accusatory tone. "I didn't stop to think about it. Tony was drowning."

He glared at her. "You could have been killed! What if the ice had given way beneath you, too? You'd both have ended up in the water."

She placed her fists on her waist. "What would you have done? Stood on the bank and watched him drown?"

Her anger seemed to diffuse some of his own. He ran a hand through his hair and sighed. "Of course not. I'd have gone after him, too." He glanced down with a frown. "God, I wish I had been there. You wouldn't have been hurt."

The idea that he would have spared her pain, if he could, warmed her and she gentled her tone. "If you'd been there, no doubt you'd have been doing something even more dangerous than ice fishing. I'd have had to rescue both of you."

He bent his head in wry acknowledgment. "You're probably right." He glared at the opposite bank. "There really isn't another way across, you know. I can't just leave you here."

Her knees threatened to buckle. "Can't we ride across?"

"No. I have no idea how the horses will react to the water. I can't risk them throwing you." He stepped closer and gave her a devilish smile. "I won't let you drown, Hellcat. I'm reserving the pleasure of killing you for myself." He held his free hand out toward her. "Come on. Just think of it as another item on your list: 'Cross raging mountain torrent, gain Ravenwood's eternal respect.' "

She couldn't smile at his joke. The idea of going into that water was terrifying, but what choice did she have? She doubted she could find her way back to Santander on her own, even if he'd let her go, and she wasn't ready for her adventure to end. Not yet. And when he looked at her like that, with such utter confidence, she'd follow him to hell itself.

She took his hand.

Heloise started to panic almost as soon as they started. The water was clear and icy-cold. It seeped into her boots with unpleasant speed then crept its way up her legs, getting colder and darker the deeper they waded. By the time it was knee-high, the current was so strong it threatened to pull her legs out from under her and she could barely feel her toes. Her fingers hurt; she was holding Raven's hand so tightly she had to be crushing his knuckles but he didn't seem to mind.

He wasn't having nearly as much difficulty, the swine, being taller and heavier. He simply edged along, sideways to the current, feeling his way across the rocky streambed with his feet.

Her breathing became shallow pants as the water reached her waist. The opposite bank was miles away, and they weren't even at the deepest part. To make matters worse, the horses were splashing and tossing their heads in agitation. Heloise flinched away from the plunging hooves, certain they were going to push her under.

Wonderful. If she didn't drown she'd be trampled to death.

She didn't want to die. She hadn't finished all the items on her list.

She fixed her eyes on the far side. She could do this. She began reciting Shakespeare's Sonnet 18 in her head, the words all running together in her fright. *Shall I compare thee to a summer's day thou art more lovely and more temperate rough winds do shake the darling buds of may and summer's lease hath all too short a date—*

Her foot slipped. She opened her mouth to scream but the current swept her legs out from beneath her and she went under. She lost hold of Raven's hand and inhaled a mouthful of water. Bind panic descended. She thrashed her arms but the flow was so strong it pulled her down and tumbled her over so she didn't even know which way was up. A blurry confusion of light and darkness churned around her and a great rushing filled her ears.

Death must be laughing right now.

Her lungs started to burn and she flailed again, at once desperate and hopeless. A ball of outraged fury welled in her chest. Such a stupid way to die.

And then something caught her shirt and yanked her upward.

She burst through the surface of the water and dragged a great, gasping lungful of air. Nothing had ever felt so good.

Raven's face came back into focus and she struggled to put her feet down on the riverbed. "Don't try. You're out of your depth. Look at me. Only me. Nothing else."

She was too terrified and disoriented to do anything other than obey. He was supporting her in the water, his legs beating a strong stroke beneath her, his hand fisted in the collar of her shirt.

Heloise blinked the water out of her eyes and coughed, clutching his forearm with both hands until her knuckles turned white.

"Breathe with me," he ordered. "Match your breaths to mine. That's it. Slowly."

He became her universe; everything else faded away. She focused on the tiny droplets of water on his eyelashes, the black hair plastered to his forehead, the ridiculous green of his eyes. Her chin dipped beneath the surface and she inhaled another mouthful of water.

"Kick your legs," he said.

She gave a weak kick and was astonished to feel herself propelled forward. She did it again. And again. When her feet finally touched the gravelly bank she uttered a heartfelt prayer of thanks. She started to stagger ashore but Raven swept her up into his arms and carried her the rest of the way. He deposited her a few steps from the bank, letting her slide down his body but keeping his arms around her for support.

Heloise sagged against him, and for a brief moment she allowed herself the forbidden luxury of pressing her face into his chest and absorbing his strength deep into her bones. A shudder racked her body.

She wasn't dead.

Raven rested his chin on the top of her head and simply held her, crooning reassurances into her sopping hair. She clung to him, unable to stop the shaking of her body or the bone-deep chill that gripped her. She had no idea how long they stood there. Time lost all meaning as he rocked her gently, but eventually the tremors abated and she came to slow awareness of their position.

She was clinging to his chest like a barnacle to a ship's hull. Her head rested on his chest; she could hear his heartbeat, a reassuringly solid thump, but she forced herself to release her death grip on the front of his shirt. She uncurled her fists and straightened her fingers, flattened her palms on his chest.

She became intensely conscious of the fact that their wet clothes gave very little protection. Every inch of her body was molded to him, the hard tips of her breasts were squashed flat against his chest. She started to pull back, but Raven had caught her face between his hands. He swept his thumbs over her cheekbones then gently pushed a strand of dripping hair from her temple.

Her pulse missed a beat. There was an ache in her chest that had nothing to do with the water she'd swallowed and everything to do with the tender expression on his face.

"Cats never like water," he said softly. "It's over. Well done."

His gaze flicked to her lips. She tensed, sure he was about to kiss her, but he released her and stepped back instead. She swayed but remained upright through sheer, stubborn pride.

He narrowed his eyes. "You're not going to faint, are you?"

It was just the buck-up she needed. Renewed energy flooded her body and she straightened her spine. "Of course not. I've never fainted in my life."

He gave her a disbelieving look. If he could be so coolly unaffected by a near-death experience then so could she. She gathered her wet hair and wrung it out over her shoulder. "I know, I'm a failure as a woman. I can't summon a half-decent swoon. I've tried, believe me. I can't even cry prettily. My eyes go all red and puffy and my nose runs. It's very unattractive."

"Nerves of steel are far more useful."

She opened her eyes wide in feigned astonishment. "Good God, is that a compliment? I might swoon, after all, from the shock."

Raven smiled. "Ha. You're fine. If you're well enough to argue with me, you're well enough to get back on that horse. Come on."

"The day I lack the strength to argue with you, Ravenwood," she said, "will be the day I leave this world forever."

CHAPTER 16

*R*aven caught the horses, which were grazing contentedly nearby, and Heloise breathed a silent prayer of thanks that they hadn't galloped away. The last thing she needed was to be stranded in the middle of this unforgiving landscape with him.

But Persephone had opted to stay close to the dubious protection of Hades, when she could have made a spirited bid for freedom. Heloise shook her head. Horses were stupid creatures.

Her clothes dried quickly as they rode. The breeches rubbed against her thighs but Heloise refused to utter a word of complaint. She'd asked for an adventure, hadn't she? And this was certainly more exciting than sitting at home. She'd even faced one of her greatest fears and survived, although that was probably more to Raven's credit than hers. Perhaps her wish to swim in the ocean one day wasn't so far-fetched after all.

"Thank you," she said suddenly.

Raven glanced up. "For what?"

"For bringing me with you."

His eyebrows rose. "You're thanking me? I just nearly drowned you."

"I know. But if I'd never come with you, I'd never have felt as alive as I do now. Back in England, it was always like I was half asleep. Like I was just going through the motions of my life, waiting for something to happen. And now it has. So thank you."

He chuckled. "You're welcome."

By the time the warmth leeched out of sky and the sun dipped behind the mountains Heloise had lost all hope of a hot bath, soft pillows, and a down-filled comforter. Her gloomy predictions were confirmed when Raven gestured to a ramshackle building on the crest of a distant hill.

"Here we are."

Heloise groaned as they rode into the deserted yard. The farmhouse itself was a burnt-out shell, nothing but four crumbling walls and some smoke-blackened rafters. Raven strode to inspect a small stone building on one side that, mercifully, still appeared to have an intact roof.

"Welcome to Hotel Ravenwood," he said cheerfully. "I saw a well around the side. I'm going for a wash. Make yourself at home."

Heloise watched in numb disbelief as he disappeared off around the side of the house, whistling softly. Sleeping in a barn was rather biblical, but she didn't feel particularly holy; she felt filthy, sore, and so bone-weary she didn't care if they slept in a ditch. She dismounted and hobbled over to peer through the open door, praying there were no animal inhabitants.

The barn had exposed rafters and a half loft above. Light filtered in through a few holes in the roof and pigeons cooed softly in the eaves. A few scrawny chickens fussed and pecked around, scratching in the dirt. The sweet, pleasant smell of hay filled her nostrils and she wondered what miracle had spared this barn but destroyed the house. A fortuitous wind?

Raven reappeared, his hair damp and his shirt clinging to his chest. Heloise glared at him, envying his cleanliness but too tired to move any farther.

He nodded to the loft. "You can sleep up there."

There was no ladder. Without warning, he simply spanned her waist and hoisted her up. She didn't even have time to gasp. The ease with which he lifted her was astonishing. Flustered, Heloise scrambled up then rolled onto her stomach and peered over the edge at him. "Where are you going to sleep?"

"Down here." He pulled the pistols from his back and placed them to one side, but retained the knife strapped to his belt. He settled back on the pile of straw directly beneath her.

"Tell me you take your dagger off to sleep," she said.

"No. It's always a mistake to disarm completely."

What a telling statement that was. Heloise was certain he was talking about more than physical weaponry. The man wore armor even when he was naked. Still, the idea of him watching over her with a dagger in his hand gave her an odd, primitive thrill. She should not be finding this attractive. It was barbaric. She did not hold with violence except as an absolute last resort. And yet her chest tightened uncomfortably.

"Swear you won't murder me in my sleep?" she teased.

He shot her a dark look that curled her insides. "If I want to kill you I won't bother waiting until you're asleep to do it."

"That's hardly reassuring."

He smiled. "All right. I promise if I ever *do* decide to kill you, I'll give you fair warning. You'll be awake. And armed. And facing me. How's that?"

"That's very generous."

"Sarcasm is not an attractive trait, Miss Hampden," he chided softly.

She rolled over onto her back and settled into the straw. "Good thing I don't aspire to attract you, then, isn't it?" she retorted, then ruined the effect with a yawn. He chuckled and her lips curved upward in an answering smile. He really was fun to tease.

Heloise awoke to daylight and a chicken pecking at her shirt.

She lurched backward with a startled cry as the equally surprised bird darted away with a disapproving squawk. Since there was no hope of going back to sleep she crawled to the edge of the loft and looked down.

Raven was lying on his back on the straw, eyes closed, head propped against his saddlebag, arms folded over his chest and feet crossed at the ankle. A shock of dark hair fell over his forehead. His breeches fitted to his hips like a second skin and his shirt was pulled tight over his arms. His jaw and chin were shadowed with the beginnings of a beard. He looked a perfect rogue, lounging there, and her heart rate quickened. Why did he have to be so damned attractive?

His eyes were closed but she didn't make the mistake of thinking him vulnerable. He was like the guard dog Anubis, no doubt alert to the slightest sound. She wondered if he ever truly allowed himself to relax.

"Admiring my manly physique?" he said without opening his eyes.

Heloise jerked, caught in her shameless ogling. Blood rushed to her cheeks. Revenge was close at hand, however, in the form of a hapless chicken. She nudged it with her elbow. It half fell, half flew downward, squawking in indignation, and landed square on Raven's chest in an explosion of feathers.

Heloise giggled in delight. Raven doubled up with a curse, waving his hands to shoo the creature away while simultaneously trying to avoid the flapping wings, pecking beak, and scratching claws. After a blur of arms and feathers, the outraged fowl finally escaped through the open door and Raven flopped back onto the straw with a final curse. Stray feathers floated down around him and settled on his prone body like snow. Heloise's stomach gave an odd little twist. He looked like a banished angel, just fallen from heaven, and not happy about it one bit.

He glared up at her. "Wretch."

She widened her eyes and feigned innocence. "Me?"

He extended his arms toward her. "Jump down. I'll catch you."

She snorted. "You won't. I'll flatten you."

His mouth quirked at the corners and his eyes took on a mischievous glint. "Oh, believe me, I can handle your weight anytime."

Heloise felt her cheeks warm again. "I can do it myself."

He shrugged and rolled to one side to give her room to land. Without giving herself time to worry about how high up she was, she jumped. The mound of hay cushioned her fall nicely but she couldn't control her forward momentum. She sprawled right on top of Raven.

She tried to push herself off him while simultaneously trying to avoid putting her hands on some utterly inappropriate part of his anatomy, but the unstable straw made the task almost impossible. Raven, the beast, made absolutely no move to help. In fact, he seemed to be thoroughly enjoying her predicament. While she struggled and squirmed, getting more flustered by the minute, he extended his arms out to the side and rested his head back in the straw with an earthy chuckle.

Heloise lost her balance again. Her breasts squashed against his chest and her knee slid between his thighs. She let out a howl of frustration and deliberately dug an elbow into his ribs.

"Oomph!" he groaned, half sitting up. "That's enough!

He made to grab her but she dodged his hands, made a fist, and whacked him on the shoulder. It hurt her hand.

"Hey!" he laughed. "What's that about? You fell on me."

She pummeled him again, aroused, infuriated, and embarrassed all at once. He captured her wrists and secured them above her head with one hand. "Enough," he said again.

Before she could say anything else, he switched their positions and rolled on top of her. Heloise froze. His long body covered hers, pushing her down into the soft give of hay. She held her breath at the full delicious weight of him along her body. Her brain turned to mush.

Slowly, so slowly she could have pulled away, he reached out and captured a tiny feather that had settled on her eyelash. He balanced it on the tip of his finger then blew it gently, watching as it seesawed down to her throat.

A bright spark of longing arced between them, urging her to close the scant distance. Her skin tingled in anticipation as she recalled the exact texture of those lips, the wicked taste of him. Her stomach muscles contracted as she prepared to curl toward him and press her mouth to his. Time stretched to infinity.

"No."

Raven pressed his lips together, shook his head as if to clear it, and rolled off her. He brushed the straw from his breeches with a brisk movement, picked up his pistols, and stalked away.

Heloise dropped her head back into the straw with a groan. This was not disappointment. Or frustration. It was relief. She didn't want to kiss him. He made her reckless and stupid. He made her hot enough to burn.

CHAPTER 17

Bloody woman, Raven thought viciously, spurring his horse. She was a born tease, gnawing away at his self-control. At least he hadn't kissed her again. He should never have bloody kissed her in the first place—because now, instead of just his overactive imagination, he was cursed with the memory of exactly what those lips felt like against his own and exactly how good she tasted. He wanted more. He wanted that soft, smart mouth on his own. If only to shut her up.

He sneaked a glance at her as she turned her face up to the sun, basking like those little lizards on the rocks or a flower unfurling in the heat. Her mobile mouth curled upward in a contented smile. He, of course, found it erotic. He found every-thing she did erotic. She could be eating a piece of burnt toast and he'd find it erotic.

Dressing her as a boy had been a mistake. Yes, it allowed her greater ease of movement and acted as a basic disguise. But those breeches outlined her pert little derriere all too clearly.

"I love this warmth," she said. "It seeps right down into your bones."

Like you, he thought. The damned woman managed to sneak

between the cracks inside his soul. She made him want things he couldn't have. "You'll burn," he warned gruffly. "Keep your face out of the sun."

She ignored his scolding. "So who is this contact we're going to meet?"

"A chap called George Scovell."

Heloise yanked so hard on the reins that her horse stopped dead. "Major Scovell? *The* Major Scovell?"

Raven frowned at her rapturous reaction. She appeared delighted. Enthralled even. "Yes. You know him?"

"I've never met him personally, but of course I know *of* him. He's been our continental counterpart for years. In code-breaking circles the man's a legend." Her eyes gleamed. "Major Scovell's the one who broke the Portuguese cipher back in 1812. Thanks to him, Wellington was able to continue the siege of Badajoz secure in the knowledge that French reinforcements were too far away to threaten Ciudad Rodrigo, the fortress he'd captured a few months earlier."

Raven noted her starry-eyed look with a sharp stab of annoyance and closed his eyes. Oh, wonderful. That's all he needed, a major case of hero worship.

Heloise carried on, blissfully unaware of his darkening mood. "And then, of course, Major Scovell came up with the impregnable system used by our own army."

"No doubt you're going to tell me about that, too?"

If she was aware of his sarcasm she gave no sign. "He gave the same edition of a pocket dictionary to each of the two parties. The code is based on the location of words within these dictionaries, so '134A18' translates to page 134, column A, row 18."

"Thrilling."

She sent him a chiding look for his obvious lack of enthusiasm. "The word 'cryptography' comes from the Greek word meaning hidden writing."

He held up a hand. "No more etymology, you hear me, or I'll throw you in the nearest river myself."

She set her lips into a mutinous line. "Fine."

She looked so chagrined he unbent a little. She was magnificent in a huff, but he preferred listening to her talk. He'd bet she could make even calculus sound fascinating. "How did you get into code-breaking, anyway?"

"About five years ago, just after my accident, Castlereagh came to visit Father. He happened to read a paper I'd written on translating the Rosetta Stone and challenged me to read some basic codes." She smiled in memory. "They only took a couple of minutes—they were simple substitution cyphers—but he was impressed. He gave me more. I cracked every one. He told Father he could use a mind like mine at the Foreign Office and Father agreed, so Castlereagh started sending me messages to decode."

"So how do you go about breaking a code?"

She shot him a suspicious look. "You're really interested?"

"Absolutely," he lied.

Her smile did strange things to his insides. "Well, the simplest type of code is a letter substitution code. That's where you just swap one letter of the alphabet for another by shifting them along a certain number of places. So A is B, B is C and so on. Codes like that have been used for thousands of years. It's called a Caesar shift, after the Roman emperor who often used it."

"I've heard of those. I'm not a complete idiot."

She didn't look convinced. "Codes like that are easy to crack using frequency analysis."

"And that is . . . ?"

"Certain letters are used more often in each language. In English it's E, T, and A. In French, it's E, S, and A. If you find the most common letters in a coded message, the chances are they belong to a high-frequency letter in the original language. You try substituting them and see whether words start to make any sense. After that it's basically a lot of educated guesswork. You use the decoded words to try to deduce the meaning of the coded words from the context."

Raven smothered a yawn. She looked like an erotic nursery rhyme character in that hat. Mary Mary Quite Contrary. Or Little Bo Peep. Except for those damned breeches. They outlined every inch of her long, slim thighs. He imagined them wrapped around his hips and almost groaned.

"Sometimes it's as simple as looking for a repeated phrase. Napoleon's correspondence from his generals, for example, almost always concluded with the phrase 'Vive l'Empereur.' In the same way, you can expect military messages to be concerned with troops, locations, provisions, and so on, so you look for words like 'brigade,' 'division,' 'artillery,' and 'enemy,' to help you guess the rest of the code."

Raven grunted. Would she talk this much when she was making love? He shifted uncomfortably in the saddle as his body urged him to find out.

"French codes of recent years have been much stronger than simple substitutions though," she continued, mercifully unaware of the direction of his depraved thoughts. "Five years ago they started using a new code they called the Great Paris Cipher, which used several different methods of encrypting simultaneously. It was amazingly complicated, but Major Scovell cracked it in less than a year." She sounded as if someone had just presented her with the Crown Jewels.

Raven rolled his eyes. "How did he crack it, if it was so damn complicated?"

Heloise frowned at his irreverence. Clearly the man was a god in her eyes.

"The code wasn't the weakness, it was the French themselves. They were overconfident in the cipher's security. Instead of using it properly, they'd often only encrypt part of a message, mistakenly believing the encoded parts would be strong enough to keep the full meaning a secret. But by leaving some words in common French, they provided Scovell with an invaluable foothold."

Raven tried to pull himself together. She was looking at him expectantly, so clearly some comment was expected of him. He opted for the all-encompassing, "Hmm?"

Heloise inhaled sharply. "Oh, goodness, I just realized something wonderful."

"What?"

"Major Scovell always gets sent copies of the messages we receive in London. And he sends us copies of the ones his men have intercepted. That way we have all our code-breaking resources working on a message at the same time. Sometimes he's been the first to crack a code, other times its been myself or Edward who've managed it."

Her expression clouded at the memory of her murdered colleague, and Raven hastened to regain her attention. "So?"

"Don't you see? I've been feeling guilty for not going back to London to translate those other messages, but now I can do exactly that. Scovell should have copies of them all. I'll be able to show him how to read the code and together we can see if any of them contain any further mention of Kit."

She beamed at him and Raven found himself smiling in response to her palpable excitement. It was highly unlikely that the remaining messages would help their cause, but she seemed so delighted to have a purpose again.

"Have you ever met Major Scovell? I can't wait to meet him."

Raven frowned. "A few times. He's old enough to be your father."

Heloise tilted her head at this apparent non-sequitur and Raven hastened to cover his blunder. "He lost his left arm in some battle or other, so don't let that surprise you." He was saved from having to say more as they emerged from between two peaks and the landscape opened up before them.

Rolling countryside undulated toward the distant city of

León, nestled like a sun-warmed cat among the foothills. The gothic spires of the cathedral rose above a higgledy panorama of terra-cotta roof tiles and sand-colored stone walls.

Raven breathed a sigh of relief.

* * *

It was strange to be among the bustle of a city again, after the solitude of the mountains. Heloise followed Raven through a maze of medieval streets, past scurrying children and vendors hawking wares, until he stopped in front of what appeared to be a monastery, set on one side of a small cobbled square. Arched niches on either side of a huge metal-studded door held weathered stone figures of saints in armor.

Raven seemed unimpressed by the imposing exterior and pounded loudly on the door with his fist. A metal grille slid open to reveal a suspicious eye.

"I'm here to see Scovell. Tell him it's Hades."

The grille slid closed.

Heloise must have made an involuntary sound, because Raven turned to her with an amused expression.

"Your code name's Hades?" she squeaked.

"Didn't I mention that?

She shook her head.

"Rather appropriate, don't you think, considering I've kidnapped you? Does that make you Persephone?"

She was spared having to answer by the creak of the opening door.

The deceptively plain exterior belied an oasis of luxury within, and Heloise gaped in astonishment. The bustle of the street and the cries of the vendors faded away as they rode into a huge central courtyard, framed on all sides by colonnaded cloisters. An elaborate tiered fountain gurgled in the center, flanked by arching palm trees and potted plants.

"This place used to be a Moorish palace. The Spanish comte who owns it fled to England before the war. In gratitude for asylum he allows His Majesty's government to use it while he's in absentia."

"Ravenwood!"

They turned in unison toward the booming voice. An elderly soldier in British army uniform strode out from behind some intricate latticework. His white mustache and bristling sideburn whiskers framed a swarthy, sun-kissed complexion that was the same terra-cotta red as the roof tiles. As Raven had warned, the man's left sleeve was empty, folded across his chest and pinned to his jacket. Heloise felt an instant affinity with the old man whose physical disability was as obvious as her own. His blue eyes were as sharp and intelligent as Raven's.

The soldier noticed the direction of her gaze and bowed. "I might have lost an arm like old Nelson, but at least I've still got both my eyes," he joked.

Heloise smiled as Raven shook the man's outstretched hand. Lord Admiral Nelson had lost not only an arm, but also the use of one eye before he'd died a hero at the Battle of Trafalgar.

"Well, well, Ravenwood. Pleasure to see you again. How's your grandfather? Is he well?"

Raven's jaw hardened. "I assume so. He prefers to stay in London. We seldom visit."

The subtle rebuff was lost on Scovell, who'd already turned an approvingly paternal eye on Heloise. "And who's this charming creature? What brings you to our distant outpost of civilization, my dear? Especially in the company of a hell-born rogue like Ravenwood?"

"Major Scovell, may I present Miss Heloise Hampden."

Scovell raised his eyebrows. "Hampden, you say? Why, you're Castlereagh's girl!" He clasped her hand and shook it eagerly. "I've heard great things about you, my dear. Why, that paper you wrote on the Rosetta Stone's Coptic translation last year was extremely impressive. I—"

"Miss Hampden is extremely fatigued, sir," Raven said. "We've ridden direct from Santander."

The old soldier flushed. "Of course. Where are my manners? Don't get many female guests here, you know. Poor child, you must be exhausted. I'll have one of the men show you to a room and we'll meet up later for tea, eh? How's that?"

Heloise sighed. "That sounds wonderful, thank you."

Scovell turned to Raven. "And you, my boy, can explain why you're here."

CHAPTER 18

A soldier in the green uniform of a rifleman showed Heloise to her room, an enormous chamber off the central courtyard. As the daughter of a viscount she was accustomed to luxury, but she'd never seen anything to rival this.

The furnishings were evocative of another, more elegant age. Every item was of the highest quality, from the exquisite ivory inlaid chest-on-stand, to the giltwood, silk-upholstered chairs and the extraordinary four-post bed that looked fit for royalty. Plumes of ostrich feathers adorned each top corner, dyed to the exact claret color as the shot silk drapes. Colored tiles, too many to count, decorated the floor in dizzying geometric patterns.

Heloise bit back a laugh. Compared to last night's hay barn, anywhere with a feather bed and an intact roof would have seemed like a palace, but here she was, actually *in* a palace. From one extreme to the other.

Her satchel had been placed on the end of the bed, so she stripped and washed herself as best she could using the pitcher and bowl set on a marble-topped cupboard. It was a shame she didn't have time for a bath, but it was still heavenly to be clean again. She combed the tangles from her hair and donned her pale blue dress, glad to be out of those awful breeches. Since she had no other shoes, she put on the accursed leather boots and prayed nobody looked too closely at her feet.

A door opened onto a shared balcony that ran the entire length of the building. Heloise stepped out and gazed over the exquisite gardens that seemed to stretch endlessly into the distance, identifying the purple square petals of a bougainvillea and the tiny star-shaped orange blossom clambering over an arch.

She leaned against the doorjamb and closed her eyes. The scent of jasmine drifted up to her, sultry and exotic, filling her nose and throat. The place reminded her of pictures she'd seen of the great Moorish palace at Granada. She could just imagine the sultan's harem gliding down these corridors, too, see the shimmer of gossamer veils, hear the swish of satin slippers and giggles swiftly hushed.

She stilled as she heard movement in the room adjacent to her own; the sound of feet and a splash of water. And then the door next to hers opened and Raven stepped out onto the balcony.

He wasn't wearing a shirt. She almost groaned. He was like some bad genie, always appearing at the most inconvenient times, making her yearn for wishes he had no intention of granting.

He held a clean shirt bunched in his fist and Heloise couldn't prevent her gaze from sliding over the intriguing ridges of his chest. He was lean and muscular, with broad shoulders that tapered over his ribs to narrow hips and long, long legs. His tawny skin was smooth, except for an intriguing line of hair below his navel that arrowed down and disappeared into the waistband of his breeches.

She swallowed. With great strength of will she dragged her eyes up to his face. His jaw was clean shaven and his hair damp, and his mouth held that annoying half curl at the corners that said he knew exactly what she was thinking. She drew her brows together in a stern, disapproving line. "Put some clothes on, Ravenwood."

He laughed. The muscles on his stomach tensed in relay as he raised the shirt and pulled it over his head, completely unselfconscious. She stifled a private moan of disappointment. He might be a scoundrel, but there was no denying he was pleasing to the eye.

He treated her to a slow head-to-toe sweep that left her body tingling. "What's this? Brushed hair? Clean face? A dress? You look almost female."

She narrowed her eyes and subjected him to the same leisurely inspection. "Why, thank you. You look almost civilized."

He laughed and offered her his bent arm. "Ready? Or do you need more time to sharpen your tongue?"

* * *

"Thank you, Private Canning."

Major Scovell nodded at the young soldier, no older that eighteen or nineteen, who served them tea from a huge silver tray. The china was beautiful, although Heloise couldn't help noticing that every single piece had a hairline crack or a chip to the rim. She smiled, comforted by the familiar ritual that was afternoon tea, the last bastion of Englishness in an exotic land.

"Thank you." She smiled graciously and accepted a cup.

The young soldier flushed beet red at the attention. "Welcome, ma'am."

Raven caught the boy's eye and the private hastily backed away.

"Do try one of these." Scovell offered forward a plate of small, silk-wrapped parcels. "It's a delicacy they bring here from Istanbul. The locals call it locum, from the Arabic for 'morsel' or 'mouthful.' "

"How interesting. The history of words is a particular hobby of mine, you know."

She stole an amused glance at Raven and unwrapped one of the sweets to reveal a pale pink cube covered in a light dusting of white powder. She took an experimental bite and closed her eyes in pleasure at the tooth-aching sweetness that melted on her tongue. It was delicate and exotic, like rosewater mixed with honey.

Unable to resist, she leaned forward and took another. What a sinful, decadent taste. As she licked her fingers to remove the dusting of powdered sugar she became aware of Raven watching her, his eyes fixed on her mouth. Her lips tingled and something seemed to stretch taut between them, like an invisible thread. Her blood warmed. She licked her lip. A muscle ticked in Raven's jaw.

Scovell broke the moment, unaware of their silent byplay. "Legend has it the sultan requested his artisans provide something that would stop the women in his harem from fighting." He chuckled. "This was the answer."

Heloise took a calming sip of tea. "A better solution would have been to stop having a harem," she countered sternly.

"I like this one better," Raven murmured. "Hold still." He leaned forward and caught her chin between his fingers. "You have some on your lip."

Heloise sat paralyzed as he casually traced the contour of her top lip with the pad of his thumb, under the guise of friendly, impartial help. Her heart rate doubled.

"There." He leaned back, licked his thumb clean, and turned to Scovell with a bland, innocent smile. "Delicious."

Scovell, thankfully, was too busy drinking his tea to notice the shocking intimacy of Raven's gesture. Heloise tightened her fingers on the handle of her teacup. The wretch turned her brain to mush. Even worse, he knew it.

"Raven explained the situation to me," Scovell said heartily. "I must say, I think your determination to find your missing colleague is commendable. And I do indeed have several messages written in the same code you've cracked, which we could decipher together." He smiled eagerly. "I'm extremely keen for you to show me how you did it. This code has been annoying me for months."

Heloise nodded, grateful for the distraction. "I'm as eager as you are to read them, Major. We're hoping one of them might contain another mention of Kit Carlisle."

THE LIBRARY of the palace filled Heloise with instant envy. She craned her neck to take in the wall-to-ceiling shelves and the pierced metal rail that ran around the balcony of the second tier. The familiar scent of leather bindings and dust lingered in the air and made her feel instantly at home.

She walked over and touched an astrolabe—a scale model of the solar system with concentric brass rings and tiny metal balls depicting the planets in orbit around the central sun—and set it in motion with a light touch of her hand. The planets started to swing and circle one another like dancers in a graceful celestial waltz. It reminded her of the Ancient Egyptian story of the sun and the moon, chasing each other around the heavens. According to legend, they were doomed lovers who never met except for a few stolen moments at dusk and dawn. The thought was depressing. That was just like her and Raven, always destined to be on opposing paths.

"We have eight messages awaiting translation." Scovell handed her a pile of papers and she glanced down eagerly.

"Can I have a pencil and paper?"

"Of course." Scovell hastened to make room at a handsome bureau plat and pulled out a chair for her. He dragged another over and positioned himself next to her. Raven took up residence in a comfy-looking wing armchair some distance away and sprawled at his ease, watching them.

Heloise began scribbling notes, and Scovell watched closely.

"I am in awe of your skills, my dear," he said.

Heloise blushed. "I've only built upon the methods I learned from your work." She glanced at Raven and saw him roll his eyes at what he no doubt considered a nauseous display of mutual admiration. She bent to the paper once more. "It takes a certain fiendish brilliance to come up with a code as ingenious as this. I have a great deal of respect for whoever it was, even if they are, technically, the enemy."

Raven's jaw clenched. "You admire some cross-eyed French linguistic freak?"

"Speaking as a fellow freak, yes."

"Well, you're never going to meet him, whoever he is." Raven snapped. "Get back to work."

CHAPTER 19

*R*aven sprawled in his chair and watched the unlikely duo at the desk. Scovell, blustery and gray-haired, Heloise, petite and perfect. Both equally brilliant.

They were clearly having a wonderful time debating the pros and cons of something called multiple substitution. They kept muttering words like "polyalphabetic cypher" and "anagramming" and he had absolutely no idea what they were talking about. He wasn't usually the stupidest person in the room, and the feeling of being excluded stung. He drummed his fingers on the arms of his chair.

Heloise's face was animated as she explained her workings and the old man was leaning toward her, enraptured. He had no interest in her except as a fascinating colleague, but Raven still wanted to throw him out the window.

Come to think of it, he hadn't liked the way that young soldier, Canning, had looked at her, either. The randy little sod probably hadn't seen a decent woman in months. Raven frowned at the rush of possessiveness that filled his chest. Heloise needed to be protected. She was under his aegis, his responsibility.

He remembered with awful clarity the way she'd looked when

he'd pulled her from the river; her face pinched and pale, her eyes dazed and far away, still lost in remembered horrors. Something raw and painful had stirred in his chest then, too, as he'd held her. He'd been seized by a sudden urgent tenderness, a need to comfort and protect. To give it all, his strength, his warmth, his life, whatever she needed to make her better. He shook his head. What was she doing to him?

He watched as she bit her lower lip in concentration. Naturally that made him think about kissing her. She'd taste of rosewater, like that pink lokum. He tapped his thigh, impatient with himself. He needed some air.

He stood and strode to the door. "I'll leave you to it."

Neither of them looked up. He suppressed a growl, even though he knew he was being churlish. He'd brought her here to read the codes, as much as to keep her safe. He couldn't complain when she actually did it.

He headed out into the city and spent a couple of hours reacquainting himself with old haunts, making contact with a couple of informants. He was on his way back to the palacio when he saw the bookstore. Buying her a gift was ridiculously impractical. But he'd seen it in the window and known instantly that she'd want it. And that had been reason enough.

In the courtyard he met Scovell, who told him Heloise was still ensconced in the library. She was so absorbed in her work that she didn't hear him push open the door. He leaned on the doorframe and watched her in silence. Dust particles danced in the rays of light that slanted in through the windows. The pink-gold tinge gilded her hair and caressed the curve of her cheek, as if even the sun felt compelled to touch her.

Heloise, of course, was oblivious to the picture she made, head down, studying. He could hear the faint scratch of pen on paper as she made her copious notes. She made a small huff of frustration and crossed something out with a vicious swipe of the pen, then balled the paper in her fist and groaned.

"Time to take a break."

She jumped, then glanced at the windows with a slow blink of wonder.

"Oh. I hadn't realized it was so late. Major Scovell went to talk to his men."

She rubbed the back of her neck and rolled her shoulders. The movement squeezed her breasts up and together above her bodice.

"I found something for you. While I was out. I thought you'd enjoy it," Raven said.

He placed the large book in front of her on the desk with a thump.

She read the embossed gilt letters and glanced up at him in amazement. "*Description de l'Égypte*. For me? Truly?"

"Think of it as a reward for crossing that river."

He hid a smile at her evident delight. She looked like a child on Christmas morning, wide-eyed with disbelief as she stroked the linen cover. "Goodness! Thank you."

He felt her smile like a punch to the gut. She opened the book and he leaned over her shoulder, shamelessly exploiting the opportunity for proximity. Her tantalizing midnight-and-roses scent wrapped around him and sank into his bones.

His elevated position afforded him a lovely view of the smooth curves of her breasts and the shadowed valley in between. With a superhuman effort, he forced his eyes back to the book. The illustration was of a tomb interior. "What's happening here?"

Heloise pointed to a set of giant scales. "Anubis is accompanying the dead to the Hall of Ma'at to have judgment. Their soul is weighed on the scales, see."

Raven murmured something appropriate. At least, he hoped he did. Her nearness was playing havoc with his brain.

"You've heard the phrases 'my heart's as light as a feather' and 'heavy hearted'? They come from the Egyptian." She moved her finger. "The soul is weighed against the feather of Ma'at. If the good deeds outweigh the bad, they're escorted to the afterlife. If not, they're given up to the fearsome Ammit, 'the devourer.' " She pointed to a hideous goddess with a crocodile head, a lion's body, and the rear end of a hippo. "She eats the souls of the unworthy."

"No wonder she's so fat."

Heloise turned the page and pointed to an illustration of a stately cat. "Bastet is the goddess of protection. She's also known as Pasht, which is the root of our word 'passion.' "

A pink flush warmed her cheeks.

"I thought we agreed no more etymology?"

She gave a martyred sigh. "In the Book of the Dead she's mentioned as destroying the bodies of the deceased with the royal flame if they failed the judgment."

Raven raised his brows. "So she's Anubis's partner in crime? Fancy that, a cat and a dog in harmony."

She ignored his teasing and pointed to the figures in another illustration. "Look here. The women are the same size as men, indicating they had equal status. I sometimes think we've gone backward in terms of female emancipation. It's worse now than it was thousands of years ago. A woman today is basically a chattel, but in Ancient Egypt women inherited land and property, made detailed prenuptial agreements, and received fair treatment in cases of divorce."

"No wonder the civilization died out," Raven teased, and watched in fascination as a furious blush made its way up her neck and across her cheeks. He never got tired of baiting her.

"Women's minds are as strong and as cunning as men's!" she fumed.

He injected just the right amount of skeptical scorn into his tone to infuriate her. "You think you're a man's equal?"

"Of course I do! The only reason everyone thinks we're less intelligent is because we're continually denied the right to an equivalent education. If that were remedied I'm convinced there would be equal numbers of females in every single profession."

He leaned in closer. "Mentally, perhaps, you might have a point. But you can't claim to be physical equals."

She rolled her eyes. "Of course not. Women have no need to develop muscles. We have you men to do all the mundane jobs, like lifting heavy objects."

"You don't need to keep proving yourself as capable as your brothers, you know."

She jerked away from him. "I know that."

"It wasn't a criticism," he said. "Don't ever think that what you do is any less important than fighting. Your mind is a weapon that can save lives, not take them."

She shifted in her seat, uncomfortable with his praise. He glanced down at her notes. "So how many codes have you translated so far?"

"Six. But none of them contain anything useful about your friend Kit, I'm afraid."

He shrugged. "I didn't really expect them to. Come on. You've been cooped up here all day. It's time for some brawn instead of brains."

CHAPTER 20

*H*eloise followed Raven out into the gardens. When they were some distance from the house he drew one of the pistols from his back and offered it to her, butt first.

"It's time you learned how to defend yourself. Your mind might be a weapon, but when a man's about to kill you, a pistol is better."

The gun was beautiful, with scrolling tendrils engraved on the silver metal parts and a cross-hatched pattern on the wooden grip. It looked expensive; she was almost afraid to touch it.

"I don't need to learn to shoot."

"You do. I want to know that you can pull the trigger if you have to." His tone brooked no argument and Heloise sighed inwardly. It was pointless trying to change his mind. She'd just have to humor him.

"Fine. Give it here, then."

He stepped behind her and placed the butt of the pistol in her right hand. His arms enclosed her as he molded her left hand over her right, forcing her to grip the gun's handle, then pushed her arms straight out in front of her. The handle was still warm from his body and Heloise was horribly aware of his chest pressed against her back, his cheek so close to hers.

"What am I aiming for?"

He pointed. "There. Shoot that squirrel."

The small rodent was snuffling in blissful ignorance at the base of a nearby tree.

Heloise glared at Raven as if he'd just suggested infanticide. "I'm not shooting a squirrel!"

"Why not? They're just rats with bushy tails."

"They're sweet! I'm not shooting anything sweet."

He gave an exaggerated sigh and glanced upward. "All right. What about a crow?"

"I will not kill an innocent creature."

"You can't just shoot things that deserve it. I'd suggest something repulsive, like a cockroach or an earthworm, but even with a pair of Manton's finest—which is what these are, by the way—you won't manage much smaller than a squirrel. *I* might be able to hit a cockroach, but I'm a damn good shot."

She set her mouth into a stubborn line.

He rolled his eyes. "Fine. Something inanimate, then. Seeing as you're so squeamish." He scanned the garden and pointed at a marble statue positioned on a plinth halfway down one of the walks. "That statue over there. See it?"

Cupid had been depicted in his traditional pose. The chubby cherub balanced improbably on one foot, a quiver of arrows on his back and his bow outstretched, ready to fire at some poor unsuspecting mortal.

"I can't shoot that! It's an antique!"

Raven slid her a smug, patronizing smile. "You won't even hit it, trust me."

Heloise clenched her jaw. Arrogant idiot. She might not be able to swim, but she certainly knew how to shoot. She'd stolen her father's pistols plenty of times and sneaked off to practice in the woods.

Raven's cheek brushed hers and her stomach fluttered. It was hard not to notice the conflicting textures of their skin—his faintly scratchy, like fine sandpaper, hers soft and smooth. He smelled ridiculously good, too, like wood smoke, leather, and man. Ugh.

"Just aim straight down the barrel and pull the trigger."

Heloise closed one eye, aimed, and squeezed her finger. The gun exploded with a loud crack. Her hand kicked back at the recoil and the acrid scent of gunpowder filled her nose as the cloud of blue-gray smoke floated away on the breeze.

Raven strode forward to inspect the statue and she squinted to see if her aim had been true. When she heard him curse she bit back a smile of triumph.

That should give the condescending pig something to think about.

She assumed an innocent expression as he returned. "How did I do?"

"You shot his fig leaf off!"

She opened her eyes wide in feigned surprise. "Really? I was aiming for his head."

He took the pistol from her hand with a sardonic smile. "You can shoot."

She tilted her head. "It would appear so."

"Vixen. You could have told me."

She shot him a jaunty smile, remembering what he'd said when she'd quizzed him about his ability to speak Spanish. "You never asked."

He handed her the second pistol. "Bet you can't do it again."

"Bet you I can." Heloise stepped up close and pressed the barrel of the pistol against his chest, directly over his heart. The air between them thickened at the sudden reversal of power. Heloise found it hard to breathe. He was so close she could feel the heat of him all the way to her bones, feel the strength of his chest against hers. With the pistol between them, death between them, she fought a heady sensation of control.

But instead of backing away, as she'd expected, Raven leaned forward and pressed his chest into the barrel, his eyes glittering in challenge. "You won't shoot me, Hellcat."

The amusement in his voice, the arrogant certainty, was beyond irritating.

"You think not?"

"I know you're tempted, but think of the mess. At such point-blank range, you'll blow a hole in my chest. You'll be covered in my blood."

Bile rose in her throat as she envisioned the warm spatter on her face, her hands. And yet a strange hunger curled low in her belly, too, as if blood and desire were somehow intertwined. She frowned at the contradiction. Raven's gaze flicked down to her lips. Heloise tensed, expecting a kiss, but in a lightning move he grabbed the barrel of the gun and twisted it away to the side, wrenching her wrist. She released the weapon with a cry.

"You're right," she said, glaring at him as she rubbed her hand. "Shooting a statue is one thing, but I could never pull the trigger on a human being, however great the provocation," she added meaningfully. The thought of using the weapon on another person made her nauseous. "I don't believe aggression is the answer to everything."

He glowered at her, as if she were a particularly vexing child. "Grow up, Heloise. You can't fix everything with diplomacy. Sometimes the only thing that works is good, honest violence." His brows lowered. "If the time ever comes when you need to use this in earnest, you will. You win by whatever means you can contrive. In war there are no rules. If you don't win, you die. It's that simple."

Heloise jerked away from him, uncomfortable with the intensity in his eyes. This was one thing they would never agree on. She started walking back to the palace, and decided to steer the conversation to something less incendiary. "Major Scovell told me something interesting earlier. Did you know that we're only three miles from Altamira? I had no idea it was so close."

Raven shook his head. "What's at Altamira?"

"A series of caves, only recently discovered. I read about them last year in the Journal of Anthropology."

His lips twitched. "You'll have to enlighten me. The Journal of Anthropology is not a publication I read with great frequency."

She ignored his gentle teasing. "The walls of the caves are decorated with prehistoric paintings of wild animals. They could be even older than the pyramids." She gave him her best pleading look, all wrinkled forehead and big eyes. "I would love to see it in person."

He lowered his brows. "Absolutely not. I'm not your personal tour guide."

She scowled at his high-handed attitude. "I don't expect you to take me. I can take some of the soldiers as an escort."

"You're not going anywhere. It's not safe. There are groups of bandits roaming the hills, all kinds of unsavory characters lurking around. Have you forgotten the attempt on your life?"

"Of course I haven't. But that was back in England."

"You're no safer here."

She let out a growl of frustration and quickened her pace. "You're worse than my brothers."

"Be sensible. I'm sworn to protect you. I can't do that if I'm not with you."

Righteous fury warmed her chest. "That's all I am, isn't it? An inconvenience. A duty."

"You think I like this situation any better than you do?" He followed her, his steps loud on the gravel path. "This isn't a game, Hellcat. Can't you see I'm only trying to protect you?"

"No, you're trying to make your own life easier, just like when we were young."

Raven caught her by the arm and swung her round to face

him, all his good humor gone. He narrowed his eyes and she shrank back. Good. He wanted her afraid. This was too important to be nice. He needed her to grasp how tenuous her safety really was. "Do you recall my code name?"

She remained stubbornly silent.

"It's Hades. But sometimes I use the code name Anubis. You're the scholar. What do you know of Anubis?"

She tossed her head. "He's the god of the Underworld. The patron of lost souls."

The hope in her eyes was like a kick to his stomach. She was so damned optimistic, looking for goodness in him that just didn't exist. His temper rose. She didn't have him on a pedestal, far from it, but he needed to extinguish the last rays of hope that he was at heart a good man. He was broken and bitter and lost beyond measure. Steeped so deep in the black mire of revenge that there was no way back to the surface.

"What else?"

She licked her lips. "He was the god of the darkness, of death. Of embalming."

He dropped his voice to a menacing whisper. "And what does he do?"

Her throat moved as she swallowed. "He escorts the souls of the dead to the afterlife."

"Precisely." He pressed forward. "What do you think I do, Heloise?"

"You're a smuggler. A spy."

He held her gaze. "And what do you think happened to the man who shot at you in the garden?"

Her eyes widened. "You said he rode away."

He pinned her with his gaze, refusing to let her look away. "He didn't."

She made a choked noise. His chest constricted as first disbelief, then horror filled her expression. "You *killed* him?"

"He tried to kill you. My job is to keep you alive and I will do

whatever is necessary. If I have to kill, then that's what I'll do."
There. He'd said it. The cold, unvarnished truth. He waited for
her inevitable recoil.

"How many?" she whispered.

He didn't pretend to misunderstand her. "I killed my first man
at nineteen—one of the guards holding me hostage. After that I
was recruited by Castlereagh and I've been at war for the past six
years. I've never bothered to count." He narrowed his eyes. "I
don't lose any sleep over the people I've killed. There might not
be dragons anymore, but there are monsters, human monsters,
who prey on the innocent and kill without mercy. Whatever you
might think of me and my methods, it's men like me who deal
with them. It's men like me who keep you safe."

He watched wariness and fear creep into her eyes and cursed
himself for putting it there, but she had to know what she was
dealing with. "You are going to stay here and read those
remaining codes. Do I make myself clear?"

She nodded, her face pale. She pulled free of his hands and
scurried back to the library as if all the devils in hell were after
her. Raven cursed. He hated to frighten her, but he knew he was
right. Her safety was paramount.

CHAPTER 21

Georges Lavalle stood in the rain overlooking Raven's empty dock and swore with impressive Gallic fluency.

"Fils de putain!"

Not only was his colleague dead, but the bungling amateur had failed to kill the English code-breaking bitch. Now he, Georges, had been sent to the far ends of this miserable, rain-sodden country to track down some scarred nitwit of a girl. Except she'd managed to escape, and it was no coincidence that it had happened at the property of her neighbor, Lord Ravenwood, the English spy known as Hades.

Georges knew Raven. They'd crossed paths on a handful of occasions in Europe over the past decade, never close enough to engage, but close enough to recognize each other by sight. The world of spying was relatively small. All the major European players had a reputation in the field, and Raven was no exception. His code name was appropriate. He was rumored to be a devil in a fight, unforgiving and merciless. Much like Georges himself.

He almost admired the bastard.

It had felt good cutting the throat of that London scholar, Edward Lamb. Georges smiled. Such a stupid name; he'd truly been like a lamb to the slaughter—he'd barely even put up a fight. The little lamb hadn't bleated, though. He'd stubbornly refused to reveal the location of their senior code-breaker in Spain.

Georges detested such pointless heroism. These stupid English, with their mad, German king and their corpulent prince. They should have risen up and lopped off their ruler's head years ago, as his brothers in France had done.

Georges sighed and huddled deeper into his greatcoat. Defeat left a bitter taste in his mouth and there wasn't even a decent bottle of wine to be had in this piece-of-shit country to drown it out. It would be a pleasure to return to France, even if he'd have to tell Savary about his failure to find the Hampden bitch.

* * *

IT TOOK HELOISE another few hours to translate the remaining coded messages, but they were no more helpful than the others, and she returned to her room and sank onto the bed, battling an overwhelming sensation of anticlimax. She plucked at the fringed cover of the bedspread. If only she could have done more, discovered where Kit was being held. But life was never that convenient, or that kind.

According to Scovell, Raven had gone to try to locate a contact who might have heard of the man called Alvarez. She had little hope that talking to his informants would yield any results. Alvarez was surely an extremely common Spanish name.

He hadn't needed to be so bossy, either. Her irritation grew as she thought of his high-handed order to stay. As if she were a good little dog. Now that there were no more codes to read, she'd outlived her usefulness. No doubt Raven was wishing he could send her packing, on the next ship home. But of course he wouldn't do that, because of his own perverse, self-appointed role as her protector.

A whisper of defiance unfurled in her chest. Raven had no

right to order her around. She'd done everything he'd asked of her. Come with him to this godforsaken place. Translated his codes. Faced her worst fears in order to cross that dratted river.

The rest of her staid, conservative life stretched ahead of her like a prison sentence, an eternity of dutiful acquiescence and good, proper behavior. The faces of Lord Collingham and Lord Wilton floated in her mind and her defiance coalesced into resolve. She was not under arrest. She'd come here of her own free will. Sort of.

This was her last chance for an adventure.

She found Scovell in his study, deep in a weighty tome on linguistics. He glanced up with an absentminded frown.

"Well then, my dear, what can I do for you?"

"I've been thinking I might visit the caves at Altamira. With your permission, I'd like to borrow some men to escort me."

"Would Lord Ravenwood mind, do you think?"

Heloise tossed her head. "Lord Ravenwood has no interest in seeing the caves." That, at least, was perfectly true. "Since there are no more messages to translate, I'll be returning to England shortly, and I would like to see the caves before I go. I want to see whether there are any visual similarities between these pictograms and Egyptian hieroglyphs."

Scovell gave a genial shrug. "What an interesting idea. Well, I suppose they aren't too far. Only a few miles. If you leave now you'll be back before sundown." He gave her a twinkling, paternal smile. "And I'm sure the men would be more than happy to oblige you. Squiring a pretty lady around the place is bound to be far more popular than guard duty," he chuckled.

Heloise's escort turned out to be the skinny youth who'd served them tea, whose name was Private Canning, and his superior officer, an enormous Irishman with twinkling eyes and a nose that was permanently squashed to the side, called Sergeant Mullaney.

She smiled in delight as they rode out of the city gates,

reveling in the open air, and quashed a twinge of guilt at disobeying Raven's orders. He'd been exaggerating the danger to frighten her into obedience, and besides, she had two strong, armed men with her.

She turned to her escorts, curious to learn more about people so far removed from her own usual social circle. "So, Private Canning? How long have you been in the army?"

The young man jumped in surprise at being directly addressed and she watched in amusement as a tide of red crept up his neck and over his cheeks. His voice cracked a little as he spoke.

"'Bout a year, miss. Joined up right after Waterloo, I did."

His accent, she noted, was pure East London. "And what did you do before you were in the army?"

His Adam's apple bobbed as he swallowed. "I were a palmer, miss."

Heloise frowned, mystified. "What's that?"

Canning looked down sheepishly. "A pickpocket," he mumbled.

Heloise laughed in delight. "Oh! Were you really? How fascinating! I've never met a pickpocket before." She really should have included something like this on her list. *Make disreputable acquaintances whenever possible.*

Canning had clearly anticipated disapproval because he looked a little surprised at her enthusiasm. "I never stole from anyone who'd earned their money," he defended quickly. "Only rich bucks too stupid to hide their cash. Flaunting it, come to town to blow their allowance. They could afford it. All they lost out on was a new cravat or an extra bottle of claret. I needed the blunt for the doctor, 'cause me mum was sick."

Heloise bit back a smile. He was just like Raven, with his warped sense of morality. Both had dubious notions of right and wrong, but an oddly pure code of ethics. It was an intriguing contradiction. Besides, who was she to disapprove of someone trying to care for their sick family? She'd probably have done the same thing.

"I weren't one of 'em sneeze lurkers, neither." Canning wrinkled his nose in distain. "That's them wot throws snuff in a mark's face. I had skills, me." He held up one thin hand and wiggled his fingers. "Lightest touch in St. Giles."

His cockney accent became more pronounced as he reminisced.

"What did you steal?"

"'Ankerchiefs mostly. They're not attached to belcher chains, like watches, see. Easy to sell, too. Unless they got letters on."

"Letters? Oh, you mean an embroidered monogram," Heloise said. "How exactly do you go about it?"

"First you got to pick the right place. Somewhere there's lots of jostlin', like a fair or a market. Public executions were always good. Then you make one big contact with your mark—bump into 'im hard on the shoulder, say, or trip and fall up against 'im. He'll be so busy concentratin' on that, he won't notice your 'and in 'is pocket. It's misdirection, see?"

"I see," Heloise said, enthralled.

"I got a good face for it, too. I look much younger than I am. All innocent, like." Canning shot her a cheeky grin. "No one never suspected me. If they grabbed me, I'd just furrow my brows and act like I was scared, or about to cry, and suddenly I was the victim. Most of the marks ended up apologizing for bumping into me!" He chuckled, utterly unrepentant.

"So why did you stop?"

He shrugged his thin shoulders. "A few of me mates got nabbed and sent to the Clink. I realized it was only a matter of time before I ended up there, too. After Waterloo the army was cryin' out for new recruits—they'd lost so many men, you see, and they was offerin' regular pay and decent meals, so I signed up." He sniffed eloquently. "It's not so bad, really."

Sergeant Mullaney's hearty laugh interrupted him. "Young Canning thinks it's deadly dull here."

Canning scowled. "I didn't join the army to sit around doin' nothin'. I still 'aint never seen no action. Never even fired my gun, 'cept in practice." He glumly patted the long- barreled rifle slung over his shoulder.

Mullaney shrugged. "Better peace than war. Give me dull over exciting any day."

"'S all right for you. You've been in hundreds of battles."

Mullaney leaned across and gave Canning's hair an affectionate ruffle then he turned to Heloise. "A slight exaggeration. But I've seen some action, right enough."

"Mullaney was in the division." Canning whispered the words with reverence, his face worshipful.

Heloise frowned. "And, ah, what's that?"

"The light division," Canning explained with a touch of asperity.

Mullaney nodded. "Seven years in the 52nd Light Infantry, I was. Under Colonel Colborne."

"Goodness. You must have seen a lot of fighting."

"Yes, ma'am. Corunna was my first taste of it, back in '09. Got nicked on my arm at Ciudad Rodrigo in 1812." He rolled up his sleeve to show a long, jagged scar. "But I was good for Tolouse and Bayonne, and then of course Waterloo, this time last year."

Heloise regarded him with new respect. "What was it like? Waterloo?"

Canning nodded, his face eager. "It must have felt pretty fine to give Boney 'is last good thrashing."

Mullaney's eyes took on a faraway look, as if he'd turned his gaze inward. Heloise recognized that expression. Raven had it sometimes, when he spoke about his imprisonment.

"I was at the farm at Quatre bras." Grim lines bracketed Mullaney's mouth. "That first French cannonade lasted for two hours. Then came the cavalry. Lads were dropping like flies. The ground was churned up, all trampled crops and corpses of men and horses."

He shook his head. "Three days we were at it. Back and forth, advance and retreat. The French had double the guns we had, but they got stuck in the mud. Old Boney would try with the cavalry and we'd push 'em back. We lost over half our men." Mullaney's face held the haunted look of a man recalling countless horrors. "Just when we thought it was all over, that we were done for, the Prussians under Blücher came round the right of the enemy's line. That was when we knew we had 'em."

Heloise found herself leaning forward in the saddle, straining to hear the story.

"The Imperial Guard came at us and we went in with our bayonets. It was a mud bath. You could hardly see for the smoke, hardly hear for the screams and the crack of the shot. A Frenchie came at me and made a thrust at my groin with his bayonet. I parried, and cut him down through the head with my sabre. Then a lancer had a go. I threw off the lance to my right and cut him up through the chin." He demonstrated the move with an imaginary sword, so lost in his memories he seemed unaware of how unsuitable such gruesome detail was for a lady's ears.

"When the Imperial Guard broke ranks the whole French army turned tail and ran." Mullaney looked a little dazed. "There was such an odd silence when the firing suddenly stopped."

He shook himself out of his reverie and turned to Heloise. "Didn't realize I'd been wounded till it was all over." He lifted his shirt to reveal a hideous slash to his side. The puckered skin ran in an angry welt from his hip to his ribs and Heloise winced in sympathy. It made her own scar look like the tiniest of scratches. She shuddered and glanced over at Private Canning. His eyes were wide in his pale face. He looked like he was about to vomit.

Mullaney turned to him. "They say it was a great victory." He snorted. "But Wellington understood; he said there's nothing worse than a victory, saving a defeat." He patted Canning's shoulder. "Don't go wishing yourself into battle, son. There's no glory in bloodshed."

Heloise decided it was time to lighten the mood. "And what did you do before you joined the army, Sergeant Mullaney?"

"Me? I'm an emperor of the pugilistic arts. A lad of the fancy."

"A boxer," Canning translated. "A prizefighter."

Ah. That explained the broken nose.

"I went nine rounds against Gentleman Jackson, once, at Tom Belcher's place in Holborn." Mullaney's chest puffed out proudly. "He gave me a right blinker that time, but I still beat him." He chuckled at the memory. "That's how I ended up in the army. Jackson became a recruiting sergeant. The sneaky blighter convinced me to sign up one evening after I'd had a few too many pints."

They came to a fork in the road and Mullaney turned his horse to the right. "Nearly there, miss. The caves are just along here."

Heloise let out a relieved sigh. If she could see the caves and get back before Raven, he'd be none the wiser. And if he happened to get back first, well, there was still nothing he could do about it, was there? What was the worst he could do? Send her home? He was going to do that, anyway.

CHAPTER 22

*R*aven returned to the palacio in a foul mood.

He'd ventured into parts of the city few civilized people dared to go, to find someone to deliver a message to his Romany ally, Alejandro.

He'd worked with the guerilla band many times during the war, haranguing the French supply routes across the Pyrenees, and using their incredible knowledge of the terrain to ambush scouts and intercept messages. The Rom comprised a vast network of horse traders, blacksmiths, gunsmiths, innkeepers, fences, all bound by ties of blood or marriage. Alejandro himself was married to the niece of the parish priest. If anyone could help track down Kit, it was the gypsies, and Raven was seething with a restless irritation. All this inactivity was wearing on his nerves. He needed action, something to slake the rising need to punish whoever had his friend. He could feel the need for violence within him, like a dark cloud, knew he was reaching the limits of his control.

Whenever he felt like this at home he took his aggression out on one of his colleagues—usually Heloise's brothers, if they were around. They'd spar or fence or box until his anger was tamped down to a dull roar. If they weren't available, he did the next best thing and went to a high-class brothel and bedded some enthusiastic harlot until he was too exhausted to stand.

Unfortunately, neither of those diverting outlets was available to him right now. So his frustration and his lust were just simmering away, feeding off each other. Heloise distracted him, aroused him, and infuriated him by turns, and he needed his wits about him if he was going to find Kit. But sending her home wasn't an option; she wouldn't be safe until the threat to her was dealt with.

He dismounted in the stables and sought out Scovell in his study.

"Where's Miss Hampden?"

Scovell glanced up, absently chewing the end of his pencil. "Hmm? Oh. She's out."

A cold prickle of premonition trickled down his spine. "What do you mean, out? Where is she?" His heart began thudding in dread. "Don't say she's left the palacio."

"Well, yes. She expressed a desire to visit the caves at Altamira. She's with Canning and Mullaney. Expect she'll be back soon."

Raven took a deep breath and counted to ten.

He was going to wring her neck.

Someone should have spanked her backside for disobedience a long time ago. Unfortunately, imagining that scenario gave him an instant erection, which infuriated him even more.

The stable boy seemed quite surprised when Raven stormed back into the stables, swung up onto his horse, and kicked the stallion's sides.

If anything happened to her . . . He couldn't finish the thought. Heloise Hampden might be the most irritating woman alive, and certainly not the woman for him, but the idea of a world without her in it, somewhere, making his life a misery, was inconceivable.

He should have told her the truth, but he hadn't wanted to scare her any more than he already had. The French agent in his garden had talked before he'd died. The little bastard had wriggled like a worm on a hook.

"Who killed George Lamb?" Raven had hissed.

"Let me go, m'sieur. It wasn't me! I swear. It was the Butcher. Lavalle."

Raven stilled at hearing that name and the worm smiled, showing a mouthful of rotten teeth. "You know of him. And you know this: If I fail, they will simply send him, in my place." He gave a grotesque, triumphant smile. "They will keep sending men until she's dead."

Raven grasped his head and broke his neck.

The relief that engulfed him when he caught sight of Canning and Mullaney sitting on a rock at the cave entrance, playing dice, only fueled his fury.

The two soldiers leaped to attention and saluted.

"Where is she?" he growled, dismounting and tying his horse to a tree.

"Inside the cave, sir. Been in there a good hour already. She has a lantern, sir."

Raven nodded. "Wait here. I'll get her."

The first few meters of the cave were sunlit, but after that it tapered into darkness. Names had been scratched into the stone: Aberdeen 1803 and H. P. Pope 1799. Raven understood the need to make a mark for future generations to see. Something permanent, indelible, that would echo through the ages long after you were gone. The Ancient Greeks believed you never truly died if people still remembered you and spoke your name. If that was right, then Hector and Achilles had surely gained their longed-for immortality.

As he ventured deeper, the sunless chill wrapped around him

and his chest tightened with a pervasive sense of dread. The dark, dank cave reminded him of the bone-deep cold of his cell and he closed his eyes, unwillingly transported back to his own imprisonment. His palms went clammy and his heart started to thump against his ribs.

There had been writing on his cell walls, too; short parallel lines he'd initially mistaken for the claw marks of an animal, until he noticed they were in orderly batches of five. A previous inmate had been counting the days he'd been held. So many lines. The walls had been covered in them. Had the poor bastard been trying to impose some sort of order on the madness? Or maybe he'd been praying for madness to take him.

Raven had sometimes wished he could go mad. That would be a freedom of sorts, wouldn't it?

At least his mind had been free to wander, to go wherever he willed. It had gone to her, Heloise. His candle in the darkness, a symbol of everything that was worth fighting for. If he was the shadow, then she was the light.

He'd pried a nail free from his water bucket and used it to scratch her name into the stone. Heloise Caroline Hampden. As if doing so could somehow summon her presence. It seemed to work. He hadn't felt so alone.

Raven clenched his fists as the memories kept coming, unbidden. He hadn't just written her name. He'd written the name he wanted her to have: Heloise de l'Isle. Lady Ravenwood. Like some damned giddy, lovesick sixteen-year-old girl practicing her signature.

He'd drawn the Hampden coat of arms and the Ravenwood crest, too, side by side, and then he'd combined them into a new imaginary crest, an amalgamation of their sigils.

Raven shook himself out of his reverie. He'd killed his guard with the same nail he'd used to write her name. Stabbed him in the neck with it to escape.

He'd been nineteen, so young to be a killer, but he hardened his heart. He felt no guilt. It had been kill or be killed. Except he had no excuse for all the killings that had come after that one. It had been the start of a downward spiral. His thirst for revenge was never slaked, because every death diminished him, stained his soul a little blacker, instead of bringing him peace. And he'd embraced it, sinking deeper every day.

He could see no sign of her light up ahead. Bloody woman.

He edged forward carefully, hands out in front to shield his face, feet feeling their way along the uneven dirt floor. Then his eyes got used to the dark and he became aware of a faint glow around a bend in the tunnel. He followed it through a series of small chambers until he finally found her, lantern propped on a rock, inspecting the walls.

He experienced a queer light-headedness at seeing her alive and well. In the flickering light of the lantern she looked like a Renaissance goddess, some Old Testament heroine picked out in chiaroscuro by a master. The glow caressed the straight line of her nose and laved her cheeks, lush lips, and stubborn chin.

She traced her fingers over the curves of rock and he imagined her shaping his body in the same reverent way.

Anger rose up again. As usual the fool woman was completely heedless of potential danger. What if there had been a wild animal hiding in here? Or a rock fall? She didn't even have a weapon. Had she learned nothing?

"For a woman who speaks five languages, you seem to have a remarkably difficult time understanding basic commands. I thought I made myself perfectly clear."

She jumped at the sound of his voice and spun round with a gasp, but recovered her composure quickly enough. "Someone once told me it's easier to ask for forgiveness than permission."

He ground his teeth until his jaw hurt. Impertinent little baggage, quoting his own words back at him.

"And as you can see, I've come to no harm," she said.

He forced himself to stay across the cave from her, when what he really wanted to do was go over there and shake some sense into her. "This is all one big adventure to you, isn't it? But there's danger everywhere, Heloise. We might as well still be at war, for all the safety there is in this country right now."

She gave an infuriating, dismissive shrug. "I feel perfectly safe now that the invincible Lord Ravenwood is here."

He clenched his fists and released them. "You shouldn't have come. No one is invincible. Not even me."

"Goodness, are you admitting to limitations?" she mocked. "I think I need to sit down."

Infernal woman. Raven scowled at her but she'd already turned away to study the walls again. She placed her hand over a painted handprint and matched up her fingers and thumb over the top. Whoever had made it had small hands, almost same size as hers. He wondered if *they'd* ever been tempted to strangle somebody for disobedience.

She glanced at him over her shoulder. "Just think, someone did exactly this, possibly thousands of years ago. They put their hand here and blew pigment over it to leave a negative image." She craned her head back and studied the ceiling. "Isn't this incredible? I've never seen anything like it."

Raven looked upward. A huge herd of bull-like animals stampeded across the curved expanse, each drawn in earth tones of black charcoal, iron red mud, and yellow ochre. The side walls, too, teemed with animals; horses and goats, a large doe, and something that looked like a wild boar.

The natural contours of the cave walls had been used to give the animals a three-dimensional effect, enhanced by the flickering light of the lantern. The unsteady light made them look as if they were moving.

"This is a sort of code, too," Heloise said. "A story without words." She pointed. "The artists had a lot of respect for these animals. Look, they're all different. Each has its own personality."

Raven settled back on a rock and folded his arms across his

145

chest. "They drew what was important to them. What they loved."

Heloise beamed at him. "Yes! Exactly."

"That's what I did," Raven admitted.

CHAPTER 23

*H*eloise stilled at his unexpected admission. "What do you mean?"

"When I was kidnapped. I drew on the walls, too."

Her face immediately clouded with guilt and compassion. "Oh God, I'm so sorry. I didn't think. Does being in here remind you of being imprisoned? Do you want to leave?"

He shook his head, inwardly amazed that he'd even brought the subject up. "No. It's all right."

"Were you kept in darkness like this?"

"For eight weeks."

He heard her swift intake of breath. "How did you survive?"

"I embraced death," he said simply. "I remembered something I must have read at school, by a Spartan poet called Tyrtaeus. He said 'learn to love death's ink-black shadow as much as you love the light of dawn.' "He tilted his head back and stared out into the darkness. "He meant don't fear death, embrace it." His lips curled in self-mockery. "But that's easier said than done. The will to survive persists, no matter how hopeless the situation."

Heloise made no sound, so he continued. "Death was always there, a specter looming every second of the day. One day I saw my captors making nooses out of rope. I thought they were going to hang me."

She gave a choked gasp but he didn't look at her.

"I was terrified until I realized it was just halters to tie up their horses." He bent, picked up a stone, and began tossing it from one hand to the other. "They held a mock execution once. No last requests or anything like that. They just said time was up. They tied my hands and blindfolded me and led me outside. They made me kneel. They put a pistol to my head—I heard the click as the hammer was drawn back. I honestly thought I was about to die."

He glanced over at Heloise. Her eyes were wide, her fingers covering her mouth as if to protect herself from his words.

"I braced myself. Swore that if I died I'd come back and haunt those murderous bastards. But then the hammer was uncocked and they all started to laugh. 'Later,' one of them said. And then they left. I just sagged there, on my knees in the dirt, and retched, although there was nothing in my stomach to throw up. After God knows how long, one of them came and pulled me up and returned me to my cell."

"Oh God," she whispered.

He kept his voice matter-of-fact, his tone even. "I considered killing myself as a way to escape. But that would have been the coward's way out."

He stopped, surprised to hear those words tumbling from his lips. He'd never told anyone that, not even her brothers. He didn't want her pity, her sympathy. But he owed her something for the way he'd made her face her own demons back at the river. The least he could do was offer his own most shaming experience in exchange.

"I never told you what happened when I was kidnapped." He leaned one shoulder against the wall and crossed his arms, staying at the very edge of the glow of light, half in shadow. "I was nineteen, just down from University, staying in our London town-house. One evening I got blind drunk and decided to stagger home." His voice was rich with cynicism. "Being young and stupid, I was supremely confident that my elevated position in society meant nothing and nobody could harm me. I was an easy mark."

He gave an empty laugh. "A London underworld kingpin thought the same thing. He figured my doting grandfather would pay handsomely for the return of his sole heir."

A bitter smile twisted his mouth. "Ah, but there was the irony: He clearly hadn't done his research on my skinflint grandfather." He kept his tone dry and amused, as if he were recounting an entertaining anecdote at a card party instead of the story of his youthful suffering and humiliation.

"You see, kidnapping only works if the threatened party actually values the person taken hostage. If not, they sign the prisoner's death warrant, because their life is literally worthless to the kidnappers. They become an expense they don't need. It's a simple monetary transaction."

His expression darkened. "They miscalculated badly with my grandfather. His pride was offended by their audacity. He flatly refused to be blackmailed. He pretended to negotiate to stall for time while he hired Bow Street Runners and private investigators to find me. But he took too long.

"I should thank him, really. It taught me a valuable life lesson. No one was going to rescue me. If I wanted to get out of there, I had to do it myself." His eyes bored into hers. "I vowed then that I would never again be at the mercy of another human being. When I got back I confronted my grandfather in his study. We argued. The old bastard collapsed of an apoplexy as a result. He went back to his London townhouse and I've barely spoken to him since."

"I heard he's dying," Heloise said quietly.

He curled his lip. "The bastard's been threatening to die for the past six years. I don't care. He can keep his money and his poxy titles." He scowled at her disapproving expression.

"Your father's titles are yours by right. I don't understand why you refuse to accept them."

"I don't need them, or the money. I've made my own fortune, without any help from him."

"But you could be the duke one day."

"The title will die with my grandfather. He wants forgiveness, but absolution is something I will never give him."

"You can't mean that. Whatever he's done, he's still your grandfather, still family."

Raven sighed at her endless, unquenchable optimism. "We share blood, but he's not my family. Your brothers are my family, and my brothers in arms. Tony and Nic, Richard and Kit."

She shook her head. "You should still forgive him. He'd lost his son and daughter-in-law. He could have had you, but instead he alienated you. You should pity him that money was more important to him than family."

"Christ. You're so much kinder than me, Hellcat. I can't do it."

She sighed and he steeled himself against her look of reproach.

"What did you think about?" she asked, clearly realizing he would not be drawn on the subject. "When you were alone in that cell?"

He considered lying to her. Considered telling her he'd quoted Shakespeare and dreamed of desert islands. But the truth streamed out of him and he was helpless to stop it.

"The same thing I thought of when that gun was at my head," he said quietly. "I thought of you."

CHAPTER 24

*H*eloise stilled.

"Me?" she whispered.

The air between them thickened. The look in his eyes stirred something primitive within her, like the warmth of flames or the need for food and shelter. He threw aside his stone, crossed to her in two strides, and gripped her shoulders so tightly she could almost feel the bruises forming on her skin. Heloise lifted her face, anticipating his kiss, craving it.

A cry of alarm and gunfire echoed from outside. Raven released her with a curse and sprinted toward the cave mouth. Heloise grabbed the lantern and followed him, stumbling in her haste. Two more shots rang out, their sound a monstrous echo that filled the cave, as Raven fired his own pistols.

She ran straight into a nightmare.

There was no sign of Mullaney, but Canning lay facedown in the dirt next to the bodies of two men she didn't recognize. Raven must have shot them. Three more strangers, each armed with a knife, surrounded Raven, who threw down his spent pistols and drew his own blade as he advanced.

"Stay back," he shouted to her.

One of the men lunged. Raven leaped back as the man slashed, then parried the knife and caught his attacker around the neck. He kicked out a leg and knocked over the second man. While he fell backward onto the ground, Raven put his hands around his captive's head and gave a quick twist. There was a sickening crack. The man's shoulders and torso contorted, and his limbs fell limp.

Raven dropped the body to the ground just as the third man leaped forward. The man swung and Raven hissed as the knife caught him across the ribs. He grabbed his assailant's arm, pushed the blade aside, and punched him twice in the face, breaking his nose. Blood sprayed onto the dusty floor and the man howled in pain, but he didn't go down. He swung wildly and managed to catch Raven on the jaw.

Heloise pressed herself against the uneven rock at the mouth of the cave, her breathing harsh and uneven. Bile rose in her throat.

The man who'd been kicked to the ground heaved himself up with a groan. Ignoring the fight between Raven and his friend, he advanced on Heloise, an ugly look of determination on his face. She shrank back against the wall, then realized she still held the lantern. As the man came closer, she swung her arm with all her might and caught him across the shoulder.

He batted her arm aside with a roar and grabbed her hair, twirling her around to imprison her from behind. His scrawny forearm tightened across her neck and Heloise froze in terror as she felt the cold sting of a blade at her throat. His other arm caught her around the waist and he started to drag her backward into the cave.

Heloise clawed his arm, but desperation had lent him a demonic strength. She cringed away from the overpowering stench of him, rank with sweat and dust. His hand cupped over her breast and he squeezed, hard. He panted something in her ear, and while she didn't understand the words, his meaning was terrifyingly clear. He inhaled deeply, drawing her scent into his lungs, then sniffed her hair.

Heloise cried out in disgust and renewed her struggles. She threw a desperate glance at Raven and saw him deliver a brutal punch that sent his opponent sagging to the ground, unconscious. Chest heaving, he turned and advanced with the predatory grace of a stalking panther.

"Don't come any closer or I'll kill her," her captor shouted.

Raven's eyes flashed.

The man holding her must have read their murderous intent. "I mean it. Stay back."

He pressed his knife harder into her neck. Heloise whimpered as it pricked a sharp slice into her skin and a hot trickle of blood slid down the side of her throat.

Raven tilted his head, as if pondering the many ways to end the man's life. His relaxed smile was chilling. "Let her go and I'll kill you quickly."

His voice was low and mesmerizing, a total contrast to the other man's panicked squeak. Her captor backed away, dragging Heloise with him, using her as a human shield. "I don't think you're in any position to make demands. Put down your weapon."

"All right." Raven made a show of straightening his fingers away from the knife hilt. He bent and placed it slowly on the floor. "Now what do you suggest?"

"Kick it away. That's better. Now, I'm—"

Raven's arm moved so quickly it was a blur. Heloise saw him move at the same instant the arms restraining her went limp and the man's body dropped away. A thud and a hideous gargling noise sounded behind her. Confused, she started to turn, even as Raven shouted, "Don't—!"

She glanced down. Her captor was on the ground, a knife protruding from the front of his throat. He clutched at it feebly, his eyes wide with shock. His heels dug tracks in the stony gravel as he writhed and then stilled.

Horror crawled like maggots under her skin. That was Raven's knife. He'd thrown it right past her head. She backed away. A wave of nausea threatened and she pressed her hand to her mouth. A buzzing sounded in her ears.

A muffled whimper her made her turn. The soldier Raven had punched had regained consciousness and was trying to crawl away back to the horses, dragging his injured body over the rocky ground. Heloise turned her head and found Raven watching her with an expression that was impossible to define; dark and helpless and furious all in one.

"I told you not to look," he said.

There was no inflexion in his voice. He shot her a last hard look, as if to satisfy himself she wasn't going to faint, picked up his discarded knife, and strode over to the retreating survivor.

Heloise murmured a protest as he grabbed the man's shirt and threw him over onto his back. The man cried out and raised his hands to protect his face but Raven dodged them easily and slapped him across the face with an open palm.

Heloise let out a moan at his brutality. "Don't—"

He ignored her, bent down to place his face in the whimpering man's line of vision. "Why are you here. Who sent you?"

The very quietness of his voice acted as a warning. Raven rarely raised his voice; a whisper was far more effective than a shout. The man was trying to scuttle backward like a crab, but Raven kept hold of his shirt.

"No one! We were just going to steal the horses, that's all. I swear."

Another slap. "I don't believe you. Who sent you?" Raven raised his hand again but did not strike.

It was threat enough. Blabbering now, the man spat blood and wiped his mouth with a shaking hand. "I don't—Nobody sent me." He glanced in horror at his two dead comrades and started to sob. "Let me go. I just want to go home. Please. Just let me go home."

Raven nodded, as if the information were confirmation of what he already knew. He transferred the knife to his right hand.

"No!" Heloise cried.

He looked over at her and his eyes were cold. He bent over the man, ready to kill.

"No!" she repeated. She kept her eyes on him, knew they must be wide with horror and fear. "Don't kill him."

"Why not?" The cool, inhuman look on his face was terrifying and Heloise took a step back from the casual savagery she read there. He seemed a stranger, suddenly remote, with infinity between them; a distance so vast it could never be breached.

"Let him go." She heard the quaver of panic in her own voice but didn't dare look away.

Raven's knuckles whitened on the man's shirt. He shook his head. "He would have killed you. Raped you."

"He's a victim, too." She took a tentative step toward him, maintaining eye contact, certain that if she broke the connection, the man would die. "Desperate men do desperate things. You of all people should understand that." She kept her voice low, reasonable. "Let him go. You don't need another murder on your conscience. Have mercy."

Raven shot the man a disgusted, uncomprehending glance, like a wolf being ordered to spare the lamb. "He would have killed you," he repeated. "How can you have any compassion for such a piece of human filth?" He made clemency sound like the worst kind of insult. A defect. A weakness.

"Please," she whispered. "For me."

He stilled. And then all the tension leeched out of him. He gave the man a disgusted shake and dropped him back into the dirt. The man moaned in wordless relief, then shrank back as Raven leaned in close.

"You will not touch her. Not so long as I draw breath. If I see you again, I will kill you."

The man whimpered in agreement.

Heloise almost sagged in relief as Raven sheathed his dagger and stepped back, but then his fist whipped round and he punched the man clean across the jaw, causing him to slump senseless onto the ground. She shot Raven a look of reproach, of condemnation.

He returned it with his own, mocking, insolent. "Stop looking at me like that. He's not dead, is he?"

Her breath caught on a shuddery sob as she pressed shaking fingers to her lips. "You were going to kill him."

"Yes." He looked at her as if she were an idiot. "He hurt you. And if I have to choose between you or him, it's simple. I choose you."

The words hung in the air between them like a dark promise, a vow. He sent her an immeasurable look; both savage and beautiful at once. Heloise's stomach lurched. He was a terrifying sight, his fists red with blood, his lip split, his hair dirty and disheveled. Her heart gave an uncomfortable jolt as he strode toward her, stopping a foot away.

His eyes narrowed. "For God's sake, cover yourself."

She glanced down and realized that the front of her bodice had been torn. Her left breast was almost completely exposed to his view. She clutched the sagging cloth to her chest as a hot wave of shame and outrage scorched her skin.

He raised his hand and she flinched. A bitter smile twisted his lips at her unguarded reaction. He reached out again, slower this time, his expression silently challenging her to stay still. He steadied her jaw and brushed the pad of his thumb over her lips, the silent gentleness at odds with the fierce expression on his face.

Her lower lip tingled as he rolled it down and brushed the slick inner lining. The tension that had started inside the cave sprang to life again. Total prickling awareness. It arced and fizzled in the air, so tangible she half expected to see it.

Her breath caught in her throat. A bright red smear of blood streaked his thumb. She watched, spellbound, as he brought it up and licked it clean, exactly as he had done with the rose-flavored sweet. She stilled, both repulsed and inexplicably aroused by such a primitive gesture. Her blood in his mouth. She felt faint.

"Are you afraid now, Hellcat?" He leaned in, and his huge shoulders blocked out the sun. "Because you should be."

She swallowed painfully and nodded.

"Good."

CHAPTER 25

The moment was broken by a rustle from the bushes. Heloise braced for another attack, but Sergeant Mullaney staggered into the clearing, almost bent double.

"Bastards jumped me from behind," he groaned, sinking down on a rock and trying to staunch a wound at the back of his head. He pulled his hand away and scowled at the red smear.

A pitiful groan diverted their attention.

"Sergeant Canning!" Heloise rushed to the boy's side and turned him gently onto his back. His right eye was a mess, swollen shut and turning black, but he was alive. Heloise breathed a silent prayer of thanks.

He struggled to speak. "I'm so sorry, my lady. I—"

Heloise stroked his forehead. "Shh, it's all right. Don't try to talk."

He tried to sit up, the stubborn child. She rubbed his back as he linked his arms around his bent knees and dropped his head onto them in an attitude of pain and exhaustion.

Raven strode off into the scrub and returned leading Hades. He stopped in front of Canning.

"Let's get you back to camp. You'll ride with me."

Canning cried out as Raven helped him to his feet, but made no complaint when Raven swung up behind him on the horse. His face was as pale as a ghost. Heloise winced in sympathy. From the odd angle of his left arm it was clear he'd broken a bone.

She helped Mullaney bind the gash on his head with his sash, untied Persephone, and followed behind without a word. Canning passed out before they even made it halfway down the hill, which was probably a mercy. Raven was ominously silent.

The setting sun pained the landscape with a glorious palette of colors, as if mocking her dark thoughts with its beauty. A wave of guilt washed over her. Canning's injury was all her fault. He could have been killed. If she hadn't insisted on ignoring Raven's advice . . .

The silence began to wear on her nerves. Her teeth began to chatter and she wished Raven would just shout and rail at her for her stupidity. She deserved it. But no, this was worse, this silent, brooding disapproval.

Their arrival at the palace elicited cries of alarm, but Raven brushed them all aside. Directed by a visibly shaken Scovell he carried Canning to his barracks room, sent someone for a doctor, then strode off without a glance at Heloise. He remounted Hades and started toward the doorway.

"Where are you going?" she called out after him, hating the catch of panic in her voice.

"Wherever I damn well please," he growled.

* * *

RAVEN HEADED out of the city. Bloody woman. She probably thought he was going back to finish off that last attacker. He wasn't. Not that he wasn't aching to kill the bastard, slowly and painfully. The whoreson had threatened her. He'd make it last a full week. The ones he'd killed straightaway had been let off too lightly. Swift deaths had been far too merciful. But no, he'd told her he wouldn't, hadn't he?

When he reached a stream he stripped off his clothes and waded in. He washed the blood from his swollen knuckles, then ducked under the water and washed his hair.

The frigid water was a relief. It cooled some of his anger and cleared his head. He closed his eyes as the appalling truth crystallized. He'd killed four men. Right in front of her.

He kept seeing her face, white with fear, eyes wide, lips bloodless, that murderous knife at her throat. She'd been bleeding—her lip from where she'd bitten it in her struggles, her neck from where the bastard had nicked her with his knife. His stomach rolled. That knife had been right over her artery. All that spirit, gone in the blink of an eye.

A black tide of despair engulfed him. He'd tried to warn her. He'd told her he was a killer. But she hadn't comprehended the horrifying, visceral reality of it. Not until today. Despair gnawed away at his insides.

He groaned and sank under the water again. She'd seen him at his most violent. His most feral. And yet she'd cut through his black rage. The little idiot had begged for mercy for her attacker. And, miracle upon miracle, he'd listened.

He should have known she wouldn't sit meekly and wait for him back at the palacio. If he hadn't been so intent on finding Kit he'd have remembered she wasn't the kind of girl to take no for an answer. She was disobedient, stubborn, headstrong, infuriating. He hated the turmoil she aroused in him. Hated himself for wanting her so fiercely.

Raven scrubbed a hand over his face and winced at a bruise forming on his jaw. He should have comforted her at the cave, should have gathered her into his arms and just stroked her back or something. But how could she welcome his touch when she'd seen him kill with those same hands?

She was going to be terrified of him now, and rightly so. Part of him wanted it, but most of him rebelled at the idea. She had to know that he'd never hurt her. He'd rather kill himself than harm a single hair on her head.

He dropped his chin to his chest. At least now she'd keep her distance, exactly as she'd done after that god-awful night six years ago.

He'd made her hate him then, too.

Her brothers had always taken advantage of her inability to turn down a challenge, no matter how outlandish, and that day they'd told her to go and hide, knowing she was such a stubborn little devil she'd refuse to come out unless she was actually "found." They'd enjoyed a good hour of uninterrupted fishing, and when the time came to go and find her, Raven had drawn the short straw.

He'd had a fairly good idea of where she was hiding: the grotto, a shell-encrusted monstrosity created by one of his ancestors, right on the border between their two adjoining properties. The folly had been built to resemble artless ruins, with a series of seashell-covered caves built into the natural tunnels that led through the cliffs to caves at the coast.

He'd ducked under the low doorframe and dodged the moss and ferns growing from the walls.

"Hellcat? Come out, I've found you."

"I can't." A whimper, barely heard. Then a sniffle, barely concealed.

Immediate guilt flooded him. Oh, shit, they'd left her down here for well over an hour. Alone.

Dread clenched his gut. "Are you hurt?"

"Of course I'm hurt, you idiot! Do you think I'm still down here because it's fun?"

Oddly, he felt a measure of relief at her aggrieved wail. She couldn't be too badly injured if she was still sniping at him. He made his way down to her. It was pitch black and he cursed the fact that he had no flame. "What did you do?"

"I slipped on this stupid moss and then the stupid step crumbled under me. I've twisted my ankle."

He edged his way closer to her, using his ears more than his eyes. He could hear her breathing. He reached out with his hand and encountered something soft and squashy. He frowned and tested it with his fingers. It fitted perfectly in his palm. Shit! It was her breast. He reared back at the same time she did.

"That is not my ankle," she said in a small, choked voice.

"Sorry."

He didn't feel sorry. In fact, he felt instantly aroused, the blood pooling in his groin making his cock stand to attention. He ground his molars and forcefully reminded himself of his mantra. Best friend's sister. Out of bounds. *Not. For. You.*

He became intensely aware that it was just the two of them inside the small, dark building. The mossy ferns gave off a fecund scent, earthy and moist, like sex.

"Raven?"

"What?"

"I'm glad you found me."

Heloise leaned forward, slid her arms around his neck, and unerringly found his lips in the dark.

Raven froze. God, her small breasts pressed against his chest and her sweet, soft lips molded themselves over his. The scent of her filled his nose and for one dark moment he'd been utterly unable to resist.

He opened his mouth and gave her his tongue, slanting his head and kissing her fully, slowly, deeply. She released a breathy little moan and accepted him into her mouth, mimicking his actions with an artless enthusiasm that made his blood boil. It was awkward, rough, unpolished. It was the hottest thing he'd ever experienced in his life.

And then he bashed his elbow against the wall and in a horrifying flash realized where it would lead—to a marriage proposal, not a pleasant screw in the dark. Heloise was a woman of worth.

Innocents were a bad idea. He'd find himself shackled and betrothed before he'd even had time to live.

For one crazy moment he actually considered making an offer for her. Would that be so bad? God, yes. He was eighteen. The grandson of a Duke. Too young to be tied down. Not by her, not by any woman.

"Raven?" she whispered, trying to pull his face back down to hers.

He panicked. Faced with her shining, girlish adoration, when there was nothing childish about his lustful feelings for her, he'd done the only thing he could think of. He pushed her off and plastered a fierce scowl on his face even though he knew she couldn't see him in the dark. "What are you doing?"

"I thought, well, we're friends . . . aren't we?"

"Friends?" He gave an incredulous laugh. "No. We're not 'friends.' Your brothers are my friends. You're their annoying little sister."

She gasped at the cruelty of his words, as he'd predicted. He made his tone even more scathing. "You're a child, Heloise. Now go home and leave me be."

She pulled away. Sniffed.

To make it worse, he'd laughed.

She slapped him.

She'd tried to run then, but her ankle had denied her a dignified exit. She'd been forced to suffer the ignominy of him carrying her back to the house. She hadn't looked at him once, but he'd felt the shaking of her body she hadn't been able to hide, the wetness of her tears against the front of his shirt. He'd felt like someone had slipped a knife between his ribs.

She'd ignored him for months afterward. And then, while he'd been immersing himself in all the ruinous debauchery London had to offer, she'd been scarred. He'd rushed back to see her immediately, their stupid rift forgotten. It had broken his heart, to see her face like that, still red and obviously painful. Not because it made her ugly in his eyes, but because it reminded him that horrible things happened to good people. It reminded him that she'd already had enough bad things befall her without ever getting involved with him.

Sometimes he wished he'd never set eyes on her. Most of the time he wished he'd just pulled her down onto the cold stone floor of the grotto and simply taken her. It would have been so easy. She'd wanted him with a passion that was both desperate and astonishing. A passion that was completely underserved.

Of course, his restraint had backfired. He'd been haunted by her taste, the feel of her, that sound of choked amazement she'd made when he'd cupped her breast. He'd never forget it, even if he sailed a thousand leagues away from her. He'd become an expert at ignoring the inner voice that insisted she was the woman for him.

It had taken his own kidnapping and the better part of six years for them to get back onto any kind of normal footing. And now he'd ruined it again.

What was she doing now? Would she shrink from him? She was probably in her room sobbing. Wishing herself as far away as possible. Raven sank under the water again, wishing he never had to resurface.

CHAPTER 26

*H*eloise was not crying.

Two of Scovell's men brought a hip bath full of hot water up to her room and she sank into it gratefully, washing herself with the rose-scented soap from her satchel. She scrubbed at her skin until not a single trace of the caves remained, then used the water to wash her dress as best she could. There was nothing she could do about the ripped front, but she draped it over the windowsill to dry and lay on the bed and closed her eyes.

She couldn't relax. Her mind churned and her body felt restless and agitated. She had the niggling sense that something remained unfinished. She had to clear the air between them.

He'd saved her. From rape and possibly murder. She'd needed protection and he'd been there for her. Yes, he scared her, but who better to protect her than the most frightening man she'd ever met? Who better to keep her safe than the angel of death himself?

He wanted her, she was sure of it. It was there in the way he watched her when he thought she wasn't looking. There in the way he simultaneously pulled her close and kept his distance.

She knew his ways. He had some stupid chivalric idea that he wasn't good enough for her. Every time he started to relax and open up he deliberately introduced some painful topic to give her a disgust of him, as if to remind them both how unsuitable he was for her. So wrongheaded. She was the only one for him.

Today he'd proved himself a killer, and yet she trusted him instinctively. She wanted to reach him. To show him he was more than he gave himself credit for.

Heloise let out a sigh and opened her eyes. He was *her* killer. She needed him. Wanted him, despite everything he'd done. She thought back to his admission in the cave, before they'd been interrupted. He'd thought of her while in prison. He cared for her. However much he wanted to deny it.

She stared at the damask canopy above her head. He was her protection, her strength and shield. She'd ride with him into whatever hell he chose to take her.

She could have died today. Without ever taking what she wanted. Without ever admitting how she felt about him. *Carpe Diem,* Horace said. Seize the day, and put no faith in tomorrow.

It was time to stop being a coward.

She heard him return half an hour later, the echo of his boots in the room next door. Her dress was still soaking, so she simply slipped her shirt over her head. It was so big it reached almost to her knees. She didn't bother with the breeches. The tiles were warm on her bare feet as she slipped out onto the balcony and opened the door to his room.

He was lying on the bed, dark hair in disarray, but sat up at her unexpected entry and glared at her. She watched him warily, unsure of his mood. Of her welcome.

He wasn't wearing a shirt, and for a moment she paused to take in the naked beauty of his chest, the flex of his forearms, the bulge of his biceps. She clasped her hands in front of her to stop herself reaching for all that luscious skin. He lowered his lashes and she stared at the bruises already forming on the side of his jaw, a dark red bruise starting to darken his ribs. A nasty slice, where a knife had caught him, marred his side. Her stomach lurched in guilt. He'd been hurt because of her stupidity.

He opened his mouth to speak but she forestalled his objection. "I'm sorry I went to the cave. I didn't take your warnings seriously. I should have listened to you."

"Yes, you should have," he said sullenly.

"It was stupid."

"Yes."

"Thank you for rescuing me." She risked a glance up at him.

"You're welcome," he growled. His jaw set tight and he lowered his brows moodily. "Now go back to bed."

Heloise didn't move, sure there was more to be said. Raven slid a slow glance along her body and she felt heat rise under her skin at his knowing look.

* * *

RAVEN SWALLOWED. Bloody woman. He watched her take inventory of his injuries: the bruise that reddened his jaw; the cut over his ribs—not bad enough for stitches, but it caused a catch in his breath when he moved. It hurt like the devil.

She stood there in that damned oversize shirt, flesh rosy from her bath, little curls framing her face, and apologized to him? A wave of disbelief and remorse rolled over him. He wasn't worthy to wipe her feet.

He had to make her leave. He knew just how to do it, just how to find a person's weakness, a dubious talent he'd honed while questioning enemy operatives. He could frighten her, prey on her insecurities, say all the things perfectly calculated to wound her and drive her away.

"'I'm not going to apologize, if that's what you've come for," he said. "I'm not sorry for killing those men. I'm only sorry you had to see it. I hate that the violence has touched you."

She just looked at him, unwavering. "I'm glad you did it. You saved my life."

God, the way she was looking at him. Like he was some sort of savior. What was wrong with her? He'd warned her about the darkness in his soul. She'd seen firsthand proof of it this afternoon. Why did she still insist on seeing him in a positive light?

His lips twisted bitterly. "Grow up, Heloise. I'm not some knight in shining armor."

She regarded him solemnly. "I know."

"You've seen what I am. Killing's all I can do."

"No it's not," she whispered. "You're loyal, and brave and fearless. You haven't stopped searching for Kit for almost two years. You protect the people you love. You've kept me safe."

He stared at her, his eyes burning. "I bring death, Heloise. And I enjoy it. You hear me? I like delivering justice, seeking vengeance. I like the fact that the last face they see in this world is mine."

She moistened her lips with the tip of her tongue. His eyes followed the movement and the air in the room thickened with sudden awareness. "Stop looking at me like that," he snarled.

She blinked. "Like what?"

"Like you want me inside you."

She gasped at his crudity and he suddenly knew exactly how to get her to leave. He'd call her bluff. She might be foolish enough to imagine she still wanted him, but when it came right down to it she'd run. All he had to do was shock her sufficiently.

"You think I don't know why you're here?" His mouth twisted. "I've seen it a thousand times before. You're restless and edgy and you don't know why. Soldiers feel the same way after a battle. Let me explain it to you. You want sex. You want the confirmation of life to erase the smell of violent death still in your nose."

Her eyes widened. "That's not why I came!"

His kept his expression cynical, faintly mocking. "It's *exactly* why you came."

He was off the bed and in front of her in three long strides, backing her up until she hit the bookshelf behind her. He placed his palms on either side of her head and stepped in, crowding her with his body. "I know, because I feel the same way."

Her gaze flashed down to his crotch and her eyes widened as she took in the bulge of his arousal. Her eyes flew back to his, her lips parted in shock, and it was all he could do not to kiss the look off her face.

With a stifled curse, he caught her wrist and dragged her hand down between their bodies, forced her to feel the rigid length of him through the fabric of his breeches. She sucked in a breath as he curled her fingers around his shaft. He found it hard to breathe.

He leaned forward so his lips brushed her ear. "It's lust. That's all it is," he managed hoarsely. "Nothing personal, just healthy bodies needing a release. The good news is, it's easy to remedy. I can make it go away, Hellcat. You know I can. I can give you pleasure without taking your virginity. You know my reputation. Apart from killing, this is what I do best."

There. That ought to do it. He'd reminded her of his other women, of his shocking character, and impressed upon her that this was pent-up tension, nothing more. She'd be disgusted.

His heart hammered against his chest as he waited for her to pull away. Or slap him. "All you have to do is say yes," he taunted, just for good measure.

She tilted her head back and looked him straight in the eye. Her fingers tightened around his shaft.

"Yes," she breathed.

* * *

RAVEN'S HEAD REELED. *Yes?* Was she insane? He pulled back,

169

dislodging her hand, and stared at her in disbelief. "What?" he choked.

Her thunderstorm eyes didn't waver from his. "I said, yes."

He let out a shaky exhalation. "You don't mean that, Hellcat."

Her eyes narrowed dangerously. She lifted her chin. "Don't tell me what I mean, Ravenwood."

Oh God. He would have laughed if he hadn't been so turned on. Had he really hoped to call her bluff? Heloise had never once done what he expected.

She put her hand on his chest and he realized he was breathing hard, as if he'd run a race. Her midnight-and-roses fragrance sneaked into his lungs and knotted his stomach, making it hard to think. The ferocious depth of his desire for her roared in his ears. She moistened her lip with the tip of her tongue and his cock throbbed in response.

He couldn't take her. That would be a monumental mistake, a line he'd sworn never to cross. But the vital distance he needed to maintain had been swept away by the violence at the caves and his stupid confession. Hell, he might as well have told her he loved her.

He growled low in his throat, breath hissing out between his teeth, his entire body taut with exquisite tension.

Why *couldn't* he give her what she wanted? He could pleasure her and preserve her virginity, though the effort might actually kill him.

This was all he had to give. She had his heart, but he could never offer her marriage, permanence. Still, he could give her his body, his expertise; sweet, perfect satisfaction. And he could steal this one, brief selfish moment for himself.

"You trust me?" he asked hoarsely.

She nodded.

He closed his eyes in defeat. They'd been coming to this moment for years. And while it was all new to her, he had a wealth of experience. His every sexual encounter had been in preparation for this, every other woman a poor substitute for the one in his arms. He smiled in fierce satisfaction. Oh, yes. This was what he was good at. What he loved. He'd make it so good she'd forget her own name.

* * *

Heloise couldn't believe what Raven had just offered. Or that she'd actually accepted.

Oh God. When she'd teased him at the ball about taking him as her lover, she'd never imagined he'd actually propose it in truth. Her heart hammered, even as a thrilling rush of physical desire mingled with the panic. Would he really go through with it? Would she? She'd never wanted anything more in her life.

His bare chest was mere inches from hers, his skin heated under her palm. The steady thud of his heart pounded beneath her fingertips. She brought her other hand up and circled his bicep; her fingers barely curled halfway around it. Her body tingled.

The look he gave her was so direct, so predatory, she felt it in the pit of her stomach and the tips of her breasts. She stared up at him, trembling. He leaned forward and his beard-stubbled cheek rasped against her skin like fine sandpaper.

His voice was a low, hoarse whisper in her ear. "I'm going to use my mouth on you, Hellcat. And my hands. Until you scream with pleasure."

She gasped as he bit her earlobe, then pressed his lips against the small cut on her throat where the assailant's knife had been; he soothed the sting with a flick of his tongue. He moved lower and she thought he would go to her breasts next, but instead he dropped to his knees in front of her. His hands caught her hips and he rested his forehead against the curve of her stomach, almost as if he were saying penance.

Heloise froze in astonishment. The warmth of his breath

through the thin fabric of her shirt sent shivers of excitement racing through her. Her hands went automatically to his head and she tangled her fingers in his hair.

He turned his head and pressed an openmouthed kiss against her stomach, then another, lower down. A throbbing ache started between her legs. His hands moved from her hips and cupped her bottom, then slid down the back of her thighs and up again, underneath the shirt. The feel of him on her naked skin was astonishing.

The muscles in his shoulders rippled as he lowered his head and pressed a gentle kiss to the inside of her leg, just above her knee. Her legs turned to water. His lips trailed upward, to the soft skin of her inner thigh, and Heloise squirmed in embarrassment as she realized his destination. Slick heat bloomed between her legs but she clutched at his shoulders, trying to push him off.

"You can't!" she gasped.

She felt his deep sigh, the rasp of his faint stubble against her thigh as he glanced up at her, his expression both exasperated and wicked.

"You seem to be forgetting which one of us is the expert."

His voice was teasing, but there was a roughness there, too, as if he was having difficulty holding himself in check. A flush stretched over his high cheekbones.

"Now, if I want advice on code-breaking, or things of a linguistic nature," he kissed her thigh again and she sucked in a breath, "I'll ask you, the expert." He swirled his tongue and edged higher. "But when it comes to *this*, and what we should or shouldn't be doing, I'm afraid, Miss Hampden, you have no opinion whatsoever."

She shuddered. Her heart was beating so hard in her throat she thought she might pass out.

"Open your legs for me, Hellcat."

Shaking with desire, Heloise widened her stance, even as her

cheeks flamed in mortification. Cool air touched her most feminine place. She was completely bare to his gaze.

For a long moment he simply looked at her and she tensed,
anticipating some taunt.

His hands caught her hips. "Oh God, you're beautiful." His
voice was hoarse, reverent.

He leaned forward and put his mouth between her legs.

Heloise jerked in astonishment and bit back a cry. *He was
kissing her, there!* All she could feel was his wicked tongue, the
erotic scrape of his chin and mouth as he lapped her. He found
the slick petals at the entrance to her body and parted them,
sliding in the betraying wetness. *Good God!*

It was like nothing she'd ever imagined. Heloise tightened her
fingers in his hair and arched into his touch, urging him on,
unable to help herself, past shame. For whatever reason she'd
broken through his self-imposed ban on touching her, and she
wanted this, wanted him, in any way she could have him. She'd
take whatever he chose to give.

"You taste so good." His growl of satisfaction held a fierce
note of triumph.

Heloise could barely think. She let go of his head and gripped
the edge of the bookshelves for balance as he teased her sensitive
flesh with his lips. She gasped as she felt his finger, just the very
tip, push inside her. He withdrew and pressed again, easier this
time, and she cried out at the unbelievable sensation.

She couldn't draw enough air into her lungs. She arched
against him but he held her tight, only his hand moving, teasing.
He flicked her with his tongue and Heloise almost sobbed in
frustration. She was striving to get somewhere, some unnamed
peak just out of reach. She held her breath.

A shimmer of pleasure danced along her skin. Her body was
on fire, her heart racing, and she bucked her hips, trying to get
closer to the maddening friction. His tongue invaded her, mimic-

king the action of his hand, and the brief penetration was almost more than she could bear.

Perhaps he was right? Maybe this *was* only lust. Maybe she'd feel this way for any man. She doubted it, but it was hard to think when his fingers worked their magic, made her burn and melt and writhe.

"Let it go, Heloise. Come for me. Now."

She had no idea what he was talking about, but she was almost there, almost there, and the combination of his voice and those wicked fingers sent her flying over the edge. Blinding pleasure radiated from her core as she splintered apart. Her whole body convulsed, clenching and releasing around his fingers as she gasped for air, blinded, falling, dying.

She sagged, boneless, against the wall and would have sunk to the floor if not for Raven's support. He stood and wrapped his arms around her, enclosing her in his embrace. Dazed, Heloise rested her head back on the shelf. Her heart was hammering against her ribs, her skin was flushed. For a few seconds all she could hear was labored panting—Raven's as loud as her own.

She started to pull away but he tightened his arms and buried his face in her hair. She tensed as she realized he was still fiercely aroused. His shaft pressed hard and unyielding against her stomach.

"Wait," he panted. He let out a half laugh that sounded ragged, almost desperate. "Don't move just yet, all right? Just . . . give me a minute."

She stilled, let herself soften and relax in his embrace. Her mind was still reeling from what they had done. After a few moments Raven moved back from her. The shirt fell demurely back into place against her legs with a whisper of cool air.

She was burning up with embarrassment, but pride demanded that she lift her chin and meet his eyes. She wanted to say something flippant, witty, but she was too shattered, too raw. Words, her fail-safe friends, deserted her.

Raven let out a long sigh. He studied her face for a long moment, opened his mouth to say something, then closed it again. She didn't struggle when he gathered her up in his arms and carried her back to her own room. He lay her down on her mattress and left her without a word.

CHAPTER 27

Raven fell facedown onto the bed, his entire body burning with unsatisfied lust.

He punched a pillow, his stomach roiling in a complex muddle of fury, frustration, and desire. He was as hard as a rock but he wasn't going to do anything about it. He deserved the discomfort, this aching, throbbing need.

Christ, what a mistake. This was going to complicate everything. Heloise wasn't one of his panting, easy conquests who'd take what he'd given and walk away with a contented smile. She wasn't a sophisticated flirt he could pay off with a diamond choker and the empty promise of a rematch.

He rubbed his palm over his face and caught her scent; sweet and spicy and so bloody delicious that he wanted to howl. He was shaking with the need to go back into her room and finish what they'd started. God, he'd been so close to losing control. The sight of her, the taste. Better than he'd ever imagined.

He exhaled slowly. At least he hadn't taken his own pleasure. She was still, technically, a virgin. And he hadn't kissed her this time. Not on the mouth, at any rate.

He bit back a groan and pressed his face into the pillow as he

176

recalled the feel of her body around his fingers; warm, tight, slick. She made him mad. That was the only explanation. Heloise Hampden had been merrily rearranging his wits for years, oblivious to the trail of havoc and destruction she left in her wake.

He couldn't risk touching her again. His vaunted control was hanging by a thread. From now on he was going to stay as far away from her as humanly possible.

* * *

HELOISE LAY on her bed and stared sightlessly up at the canopy.

Embarrassment at the liberties she'd allowed Raven mingled with amazement at the pleasure he'd given her.

No wonder the Ancient Romans made constant references to the sexual act. If the last ten minutes were anything to go by, it was a miracle they'd done anything else at all. Who on earth wanted to build an aqueduct or construct a coliseum when they could be doing *that* all day? Her entire body felt awakened, tingling, but her skin heated as she remembered her own lusty response to Raven's skillful manipulation.

He'd let her get close, but no closer, as if he'd drawn some invisible emotional barrier in his mind that could not be crossed. Heloise bit her lip. Part of her resented how easily he'd controlled her. He'd wanted her to understand that it was just bodies—physical pleasure without any emotion other than raw lust.

She took a deep breath. Her mother, ever the Frenchwoman, had taken great pains when Heloise had turned sixteen to explain to her the intricacies of physical love, so she knew Raven had restrained himself from completing the act. He must have known she wouldn't have resisted if he'd wanted to take her fully. He could have taken advantage, but had not. In his own, warped, typically convoluted way, he'd been honorable.

And he hadn't been entirely unaffected himself, no matter how cool he'd tried to be. She'd felt his physical response, that rigid length of him against her stomach. There had been a certain equality in that. At least she affected him as much as he affected her.

Heloise closed her eyes, suddenly exhausted. How on earth was she going to face him tomorrow?

CHAPTER 28

*R*aven watched Heloise closely as she stepped into the library the next morning, interested to see how she was going to react. She lingered uncertainly by the door, obviously eager to escape. Her cheeks were flushed—embarrassment for last night, or fury at his behavior? Either way, it didn't matter. The messages he'd received at breakfast had changed everything.

He held up the first of them. "From Castlereagh. The French have officially proposed the prisoner swap they discussed in that first message you read in England."

Heloise's face lit up in a smile, her nervousness forgotten. "That's wonderful!"

He lifted his hand to forestall her celebrations. "It would be, except for one minor problem. Their agent, the Baker, is dead."

"Dead? How?"

"He managed to get himself killed during an escape attempt a few days ago. He clearly hadn't heard his release was imminent. It's damned inconvenient."

"The death of another human being isn't *inconvenient*," she admonished sternly. "It's tragic."

Raven rolled his eyes. "There you go, feeling sorry for the

enemy again. The man was a sadistic bastard. He got what was coming to him."

She scowled and he felt his heart lighten. It was nice to be back on their old footing.

"As soon as the French discover he's dead they'll kill Kit in retaliation. For all we know, there could be a message on its way to Savary right now telling him the news. They have their spies in London, as we have ours in Paris."

Heloise's brow wrinkled. "So what will you do?"

"Castlereagh's replied to the French, agreeing to the swap."

Her nose wrinkled. "Even though the prisoner they want is dead?"

"How many people know what the Baker looks like? Savary does, and so do a few of the other French agents, but none of them will be present at the handover. Do you think the guards making the exchange will be able to identify him? Because that's one of the good things about us spies. Very few people know our faces."

"So what are you going to do?"

"Kit's going to be at that church in the foothills of the Pyrenees in three days. I'll go to the rendezvous point and pretend to be the Baker, under British escort. When we get close enough, we'll ambush the guards and rescue Kit."

Heloise frowned. "Who are you going to use to help you? Scovell's men?"

"No. A group of gypsies who know the land better than anyone. I've worked with them before. They're good fighters."

She nodded.

"You need to pack your things."

Her face fell. "Are you sending me back to England?"

Was that disappointment he heard in her tone? Or eagerness? He shook his head. "You're not going anywhere. You're staying where I can keep an eye on you. I had another letter this morning, from your brother Richard. Edward Lamb's murder apparently had all the hallmarks of a kill by a French agent named Georges Lavalle. From the intelligence he's received, Richard thinks Lavalle's already left London with orders to come after you."

Richard's note had merely confirmed what Raven had already gleaned from the agent he'd killed in his garden, but seeing the threat in writing had hardened his resolve.

Heloise opened her mouth to argue, of course. "But—"

"I've had run-ins with Lavalle before. His code name's the Barber." Raven watched her throat work nervously.

"Why the Barber?"

"Because he's good with a knife." He paused to let that sink in. Heloise shivered. Good, she was scared. He needed her to be on alert. Maybe now she'd take the threat to her life seriously, instead of gallivanting off on sightseeing trips.

"You're lucky Lavalle was sent after Edward first and not you. He wouldn't have missed that shot through the window, not at such close range."

He couldn't tell what she was thinking from her expression. Was she disappointed to not be going home? Angry at his order? Or was she glad that her adventure was continuing?

"The good news is, I doubt Lavalle will be able to work out where you've gone. Even if he suspects you're with me, he won't be able to discover our destination."

Her face brightened. "Well, that's good, isn't it? I mean, if this Lavalle doesn't know where I am, he can't be a threat, can he?"

"He's not a threat while you remain here in Spain, no. But I can guarantee he'll be able to get to you as soon as you set foot back in England. That scar of yours makes for an extremely recognizable face, sweetheart."

He saw her flinch at his jibe, but it was nothing more than the truth. "So you'll be safe as long as you stay here with me." He glanced down, dismissing her. "Now go and pack."

He heard her inhale as if she was about to speak, then she

clearly thought better of it, released her breath in a huff, and left. Raven breathed a sigh of relief.

It was a measure of the depth of their friendship, he supposed, that Richard hadn't even questioned his decision to bring Heloise with him to Spain. He'd merely offered whatever assistance he could provide. There weren't many men you could write to and say; *I'm taking your sister abroad, and by the way, there's a corpse in my garden that needs disposing of discreetly. Thanks. R.*

Richard's own brief signoff, *Keep her safe*, was sufficient to convey a whole host of meanings, including the unspoken threat: *Hurt my little sister and I'll castrate you, Ravenwood,* and the absolute confidence that Raven would lay down his life for hers. It was good to have such a friend.

Castlereagh's note, in contrast, had specifically ordered Raven to send Heloise home. He was furious that his best code breaker had been taken out of action, even for a few weeks. He wanted her back in England and working on new codes immediately.

Raven ought to comply. The next stage of the rescue would be even more dangerous, but the simple truth was he didn't trust anyone else, especially if Richard was right and Lavalle truly was after her. The idea that the Frenchman could be out there even now, waiting for his moment to strike, made Raven's blood run cold. Lavalle wasn't a bungling amateur; he'd need to be dealt with before Heloise could return to England. Hopefully, that was something Richard could accomplish soon.

This wouldn't be the first time Raven had ignored a direct order, and it probably wouldn't be the last. Castlereagh might punish his disobedience by pulling him from future missions, but Raven didn't care. This way she'd stay safe.

To his surprise she was ready and waiting in the courtyard, dressed in her shirt and breeches, when he emerged from his room half an hour later. She thanked Scovell for his hospitality, asked him to take care of her copy of *Description de l'Égypte* until she returned, and mounted her horse.

Scovell came to his stallion's head and frowned up at him, mustache bristling. "Are you sure Miss Hampden can't stay here, Ravenwood? Seems a plaguey dangerous thing, to have her go with you." Seeing his closed expression, Scovell harrumphed in defeat. "Well, you look after that young lady, you hear me? I want to work with her again. Mind like a razor, that one."

Raven bit back a sarcastic retort about it being her tongue, not her mind, that was razor-sharp, and nodded instead. "I'll protect her with my life, sir."

Whatever Scovell saw in his face apparently satisfied him, because he nodded and patted his horse's neck in farewell. "Off you go, then. And good luck."

CHAPTER 29

They met up with Raven's friends a few miles north of León.

Apparently he and the ruffians were old acquaintances—the leader hailed him like a long-lost brother. Both men leaped off their mounts, clapped palms, and then came together in a masculine hug that included much enthusiastic backslapping and ruffling of hair.

The leader's outfit consisted of flowing black pants tucked into black leather boots, a billowing white shirt, a red embroidered waistcoat, and a matching red sash tied around his waist. His hat bore some sort of military medal that appeared to have been stolen from a French general.

Raven beckoned Heloise forward. "Miss Heloise Hampden, meet Alejandro Amaya, self-proclaimed King of Santander," Raven said dryly.

The gypsy laughed, his wide smile revealing one solid gold tooth. A silver charm of St. Nicolas flashed around his neck as he swept her an extravagant bow.

"Senorita 'Ampden," he said, with the native Spaniard's

trouble pronouncing the hard H in her name. "Welcome. Is good to meet Raven's woman at last."

Heloise felt her cheeks heat. "His—? Oh, I don't—I mean, I'm not."

The gypsy laughed again and made a comical face at Raven, who merely shrugged.

One by one Heloise was introduced to the rest of the disreputable group, which consisted of Carlos; Alejandro's cousin and his two brothers, Luis and Antonio; the two Perno brothers, Federico and Pedro; and their cousin Sebastiano, apparently a famed horse tamer. All the men nodded to her or touched their forehead in a sign of respect. Introductions finished, they remounted and set off.

"Their camp is located higher up in the mountains," Raven confided, nudging his horse closer to hers on the narrow trail. "We'll reach it later today."

Heloise took the opportunity to study her companions. Their clothes were an odd assortment of styles; flamboyant waistcoats, bright sashes, and items of uniform that had clearly been looted. One of the Perno brothers wore a navy French jacket incongruously paired with a white British uniform sash. Sebastiano wore the dark green jacket of a British rifleman, complete with Baker rifle over his shoulder.

All seven of them had the same arrogant swagger and athletic ease in the saddle as Raven. No wonder they were friends.

Having run out of subjects to ponder, Heloise finally turned her attention to Raven. She narrowed her eyes. He had no right to look so attractive in such scruffy clothes. He wore the same white shirt and waistcoat as before, but he'd exchanged his dark breeches for a pale buff military pair—scrounged, no doubt, from one of Scovell's recruits. Despite being borrowed, the damn things fitted him like a second skin. They were practically indecent. Heloise found it impossible to tear her eyes away from tight curve of his behind and the way the material molded itself to his long, muscular thighs.

Raven was strong but sinewy, lethal and elegant. He looked like a gypsy himself, with his dark hair slightly overlong, curling over the collar of his shirt. The hollows of his cheeks appeared more prominent with the darkened stubble on his cheeks, and the tan he'd developed over the past few days made his green eyes even more striking.

She felt a traitorous flutter in her stomach as she recalled the hot slide of his skin against hers, the response he'd drawn from her so skillfully. She wanted to feel it again, that sweet ache and hectic race toward pleasure. Wanted his arms around her, his panting breath against her neck, the sudden desperation and arching bliss. She fanned herself with her hand.

He was a beast.

Her brother Nic had once told her that guerilla fighters like these were called "*chacales*." Jackals. Of course.

Raven whistled as they rode, something tuneless, as if he hadn't a care in the world. He was content here, she realized suddenly, with nothing but the clothes he stood up in and his own wits, as relaxed as if he was in a formal London ballroom.

Heloise sighed. She'd spent years trying to shed light on obscure codes and illuminate dark corners. Raven had spent the same time learning the art of concealment.

Undulating foothills gave way to fertile valleys and steep-sided trails as they rode, the snow-capped peaks of the Pyrenees appearing on the horizon. The bleating of animals and the tinkle of bells heralded their approach to the gypsy encampment. Two men carrying a pole with the carcass of a goat tied onto it hailed Alejandro from the trail.

The gypsy led the way to a wooded clearing, where an odd assortment of brightly colored canvas tents and caravans had been drawn up around a central fire. Children chased one another about the trees and several men and women sat on the steps of their caravans.

Heloise peered around in fascination. The caravans were all garishly decorated, their spoked wheels picked out in yellow or cornflower blue, while every inch of their exteriors had been painted with an assortment of flowers, birds, and other fanciful embellishments.

Several women ran over and greeted their men. One woman practically dragged Antonio from his horse by tugging on his waistcoat and planted a huge kiss on his mouth. Federico's lady exclaimed over a tear in his breeches. Raven was greeted with joyous shouts and exclamations—handshakes and friendly punches from the men and extremely familiar kisses and hugs from the women.

And then they noticed the newcomer and Heloise blushed as she became the center of attention. The gypsy women crowded round, apparently fascinated by her pale skin and freckles and the fact that she was wearing boys' clothes. One girl touched her hair reverently and said something. They all nodded and laughed.

Heloise turned to Raven for translation. "What did she say?"

"She called you '*Luz*.' It means light."

"Oh."

"The gypsies refer to themselves as *cales*. '*Calo*' means black." He touched his own dark hair. "You and I are both *payllos*, which is a word they use to describe anyone not of the gypsy race."

He spoke with one of the women in rapid Spanish and then nodded. "Go with Maria. They'll show you to a caravan to sleep in."

"That's very kind." Heloise smiled warmly at the woman, trying to make herself understood despite the language barrier. "Thank you very much."

The women led her to a caravan set among the trees, a little way from the fire. The exterior was a gaudy apple green with yellow trim. Almost every inch of the surface was decorated with painted roses and flowers, castles, curling scrolls, pierced fretwork, and arched frills. It looked like something out of a fairy tale. Heloise mounted the steps set between the lowered shanks and peered inside.

The arched ceiling had been painted to depict the night sky, a deep midnight blue flecked with golden stars. A raised bed took up the entire far end, piled high with jewel-toned cushions. A padded bench sat below a window on the right wall, and a tiny iron wood-burning stove and more cupboards lined the left one. Various utensils, frying pans, mugs, and bunches of dried flowers hung from hooks on the walls and the ceiling beams.

One of the women brought Heloise's satchel and filled a bowl with water. The ladies showed no inclination of leaving her alone, so Heloise washed her hands and face. With her blue dress still unmended, she withdrew her only other option, the sadly creased—but clean—white evening dress, the one she'd last worn to Raven's ball.

A little embarrassed at having an audience, she stripped off her shirt and breeches to reveal her silk drawers and matching lace-edged shift, which drew a ripple of appreciative gasps. Heloise realized they were as intrigued by the foreignness of her clothing as she was by theirs. Language was irrelevant—the exclamations of women admiring one another's outfits crossed barriers of race and fortune.

With reverent fingers the girls touched the straps of thin ribbon tied in bows on each shoulder and the embroidered hem of her chemise, exclaiming over the quality of the lace, the fineness of the silk. They admired her figure, too, using shaping actions with their hands to remark on the narrowness of her waist and the pertness of her breasts. From that, they proceeded to tease her about her freckles. Their own skin was brown and smooth, their straight, long hair the black-blue sheen of a raven's wing.

Heloise blushed furiously, but cherished the sense of feminine solidarity. Having grown up with three brothers, it was rather nice to have some purely female interaction.

She reached for the white dress but it was snatched from her with much shaking of heads and miming of potential disasters, which she eventually understood to mean that she shouldn't wear such a fine thing outside by the fire, where it might get ruined.

One of the younger women went out and reappeared with a bundle of clothes. Heloise's protests were brushed aside, so she gave in with good grace and allowed them to dress her in the long skirt, ruched peasant top, and loose embroidered corset—worn, oddly, over, not under, the shirt.

Twilight had fallen by the time they emerged from the caravan and Heloise glanced around, looking for Raven. She found him deep in conversation with Alejandro on the other side of the camp, so she allowed the women to drag her to the fire and accepted a bowl of soup with a smile of thanks.

RAVEN KNEW the exact moment Heloise came out of the caravan.

He took one look at her, dressed in her gypsy clothes, and scowled. They weren't much of an improvement on the breeches. Her breasts spilled from the top of the blouse, peachy and pale, pushed up by some fiendishly effective external corset. His body, naturally, hardened to the point of discomfort. The damn woman could wear a flour sack and he'd still want her.

She'd left her hair loose, too. The firelight caught the long strands, highlighting copper streaks and flashes of burnished gold around her head, like sparks. The glow licked over her, caressing all the parts he wanted to touch, while leaving other bits mysteriously shadowed in a sublime juxtaposition of darkness and light.

He wanted to be the one turning her cheeks pink.

The sun had brought out even more of her freckles; he imagined tracing them with his tongue, dragging her into some dark corner and putting his hands on her skin.

One of the men picked up a guitar and began to strum. Another joined in, a cheering song about bandits and robbers picking off members of a party on their travels. Raven sighed. Nice tales of murder. Heloise looked delighted, probably because she had no idea about the gruesome subject matter. The next song was no better, about a woman crossed in love and dying for passion. Raven rolled his eyes at the melodrama.

Maria demanded a dance and the musicians began a rhythmic hand clap. Alejandro began a crooning chant to accompany the strum of the guitar, while Maria clicked her fingers and twirled in the firelight, swishing her skirts and twisting her body in a sinuous flamenco. The fringed shawl around her hips flared out as she spun, arms raised, heels stamping in the dust, black hair way past her hips.

The music throbbed through his chest, sweet and heartrending one minute, proud and defiant the next. How different this was to the stately quadrille, even the scandalous waltz. Flamenco was dramatic and aggressive, graceful and playful. And unashamedly sensual.

Raven had seen it before, of course, but he glanced across the fire to watch Heloise's reaction. She sat forward on her seat, lips parted in rapt attention. Some of the women tried to pull her to her feet to dance, but she refused, laughing, and joined in by clapping her hands instead.

They'd chosen the perfect name for her. Luz. Light. She beckoned him like the warmth of the fire. He sighed. If she was the sun, then he was the moon, something with no light of its own. Just a cold gray lump of rock that needed the sun to glow.

A profound yearning tightened his chest as he watched her across the clearing. So much more than physical space separated them. He was trapped in a cage of his own making, drawn to her like an alcoholic drawn to a tumbler of whisky, like a gambler to the snap and whirr of the cards. Helplessly, angrily, against his will.

Her innocence made him want to weep. He'd seen the very worst of life and she saw the best in everything. He wouldn't touch her again. No matter how much he wanted to. One drop of poison was all it took to contaminate a pure glass of water. Once it was in, there was no getting it out. He would corrupt her, taint her. Inch by inch.

She rose and came toward him, still clapping in time to the dance, and flopped down next to him, laughing.

"What's so funny?"

"You. The heir to a dukedom, sitting here quite at home with a bunch of lawless gypsies."

He scowled.

She tilted her head toward the group by the fire. "Do they know about your exalted position back home, *Lord Ravenwood?*"

"No. They only know me as Raven. Smuggler, gunrunner, spy. But they wouldn't care if they *did* know. The Rom aren't impressed by wealth. They have a saying: Why have two horses when you only have one arse?"

She chuckled. "I suppose that makes a lot of sense. But better not bring up such heresy at a *ton* party. You'll incite a riot."

She yawned and he frowned. "You're exhausted. Time for bed. You know which caravan's yours?"

She nodded. "That pretty green one. Where are you going to sleep?"

"Out here."

"What? On the ground? That's stupid. You can sleep in the caravan with me."

He thoroughly enjoyed her instant blush as she realized her innocent offer of shelter could be twisted into an invitation to sin.

"I mean that you can sleep on the floor, if you want. There's plenty of room."

He put her out of her misery. "It's a tempting offer, but I think I'll pass. After you've been incarcerated, it's a pleasure to sleep free under the stars. Go to bed."

CHAPTER 30

*G*eorges Lavalle took another look through his telescope
and gave a cracked laugh of disbelief.

Fils de putain!

He didn't believe in coincidences; everything was preor-
dained, and here, at last, was proof that God was smiling on his
efforts once again.

His idol, Napoleon, had been raised to the rank of emperor
over those inbred Bourbons by divine right. His overthrow and
subsequent imprisonment on Elba had been a minor setback, but
the Lord had helped him escape and march on Paris again.

The defeat in Belgium last year had been unfortunate,
certainly—a combination of a freak rainstorm and the devil-
aided luck of the Prussians arriving just when the English were
on the cusp of annihilation. The emperor had been imprisoned
again, this time on St. Helena, but Georges had no doubt that he
would escape that prison, too. And when he did he would reward
his faithful followers appropriately.

Had he not paid the Austrian spy Schulmeister enough to buy
his own chateau for his help in capturing the Duc D'Enghien? He

would offer a similar reward to Georges Lavalle for killing these English spies.

Savary had not been pleased when Georges had returned to Paris with news that he'd failed to kill the Englishwoman, but he'd entrusted him with another mission almost immediately. He was to travel just over the border with Spain and make sure that those perfidious British didn't renege on their promise to exchange his colleague Marc 'the Baker' Breton with one of their own.

Since there was only one route up to the agreed rendezvous point, Lavalle had set up his observation post here, in a high-sided ravine, where there was plenty of cover from rocks, several avenues of escape, and a nice elevated position.

He'd thought to kill the British bastards before they even made it to the exchange site and free his friend, but this band of travelers was larger than he'd anticipated. There was no sign of Marc, either, although he was no doubt secured in one of those covered gypsy wagons.

But now he'd been handed the sweetest of opportunities. The agent sent to deal with the Spaniard Alvarez was none other than that British bastard Ravenwood! And, even more amusing, George's initial target—that scarred code-breaking bitch—was with him. Truly, the fates were smiling on him today.

Georges mopped his brow and stifled another giggle of delight. The only difficulty, of course, was which to eliminate first?

It would have to be Ravenwood. He was the more dangerous of the two. With him dead, the woman would be easy to pick off, even with an armed guard.

Georges rolled onto his stomach, steadied his rifle, took aim, and squeezed the trigger. He had divine support. He couldn't miss.

* * *

CRACK.

A small clod of earth exploded on the bank of grass to Heloise's left. She looked up, confused, and saw a puff of smoke floating above a nearby stony ridge. Her horse reared, but before she could control it Raven practically pulled her off the plunging mount and pushed her roughly down behind the bank of earth that bordered the trail.

He already had his own pistol raised. She covered her ears as he fired toward the smoke, then craned her neck to tried to see what he'd been aiming at, but he reached over and shoved her cheek back down into the dusty grass.

"Do you want to get shot?" he growled.

There was a *ping* as another bullet ricocheted off a nearby rock; it spat a hail of sharp chips.

"Sniper. Stay down. And don't move until I come back."

He didn't even sound shaken, just his usual cool, slightly irritated self. Did nothing rattle him? He started to move away from her.

"Where are you going?" she hissed.

"After him. Why? You worried about me, Hellcat?" He shot her a daredevil grin, totally self-assured. "I'll be back, I promise."

"You can't promise not to get killed, you idiot."

He had a dimple, just on the one side when he smiled. With his tanned skin, that hint of stubble, and his utterly boyish charm, he was almost irresistible. There was a vitality about him, a sort of gleeful madness in the face of danger; he looked lithe and virile and extremely capable.

He crawled forward. She followed him.

"Where do you think *you're* going?"

"With you," she said.

"No, you're not."

She pushed his restraining hand away.

He gave a skeptical lift of his brows. "What are you going to do? Argue the man to death?"

She opened her mouth, but he wasn't finished.

"Good with a knife, are you? Handy with a garrote? No? I didn't think so."

"I might be useful."

"Only as a target. Now stay here."

"Do you even have a plan?"

He grinned. "I never make plans. Plans are for people with no imagination. Like lists." The look he gave her was both arrogant and amused. "Now stay."

With a signal to Alejandro and Carlos to follow his lead, he took off into the rocks, certain his high-handed command would be obeyed. Heloise clenched her jaw. Stay! As if she was some sort of barely-trained house pet. *Insufferable man!*

She was still seething half an hour later when he returned. He strode in with Alejandro and Carlos, all dusty swagger.

"Did you catch him?"

"No. But I hit the bastard. We found a spatter of blood up there where he was hiding. I just don't know how badly he's hurt."

"Who do you think it was? A robber?"

Raven shrugged.

"Think he'll try again?"

"If he's not dead, he might, but it's unlikely."

She frowned and crossed her arms. "I wish you wouldn't just go running off like that."

"Did you miss me, angel?"

"Hardly. My concern's purely self-interest. If you go and die falling down a ravine or get yourself shot, who's going to protect me?"

He snorted. "Credit me with a little coordination, please. Besides, I thought you didn't need protection?"

"I'm not so foolish as to deny myself the services of a perfectly competent bodyguard if one happens to be around."

He clapped a palm to his chest and staggered as if he'd

received a fatal blow. "Did you just call me perfectly competent? Good God."

She ignored his foolery. "It's clear in this area you have skills that surpass my own."

The corner of his mouth curved up in a wicked smile. "Oh, I think you'll find my skills surpass yours in several areas." The look in his eye had her flushing to the roots of her hair. "This is the second time I've saved you from a bullet, you know."

She raised her chin. "And?"

"Most people I rescue are grateful."

"I'm grateful."

One dark eyebrow rose in disbelief.

"I am, damn you!"

Raven mirrored her defensive stance, folding his arms over his chest. "Prove it."

"What do you mean?"

He tapped his cheek with his finger. "Come over here and kiss me."

"Do you make everyone you rescue do that?"

His eyes glowed with a wolfish, predatory gleam. "So far they've all been men." He stepped up close, toe to toe, and tilted his head. "What's wrong with one, innocent little kiss, hmm?"

Heloise strove to recover her composure even though her heart was racing. "Nothing to do with you is ever innocent, Ravenwood."

His chuckle rumbled in his chest. "One kiss."

He thought she'd forfeit. Heloise sighed loudly. "Oh, *fine*. Never let it be said that I don't honor my debts." She pursed her lips and leaned up on tiptoe, but even then she couldn't reach his cheek. She braced herself on his arm to keep her balance.

His eyes crinkled at the corners. "I'm waiting."

"Come down here, then," she said crossly.

He bent until they were an inch apart. She closed the distance just as he turned his head; she made contact with his lips instead of his cheek.

She gasped in protest and started to draw back, but he followed her. She felt him smile against her lips. "You know, you're much more attractive when you're not talking, Hellcat."

"That is so—"

He kissed her, hard, cupping the back of her skull in his hands, his mouth clinging and shaping the contours of her own, coaxing a response.

She punched him.

"You're utterly depraved," she panted, when he finally released her.

"Thank you."

"It wasn't a compliment."

He grinned and kissed her again, slower this time. His tongue stroked hers in a maddening swirl and retreat that left her dizzy and aching, and Heloise surrendered with a moan of defeat. *Why was she fighting something that felt so good?*

This was stupid and reckless and would only lead to disaster, but she threaded her fingers through his hair and kissed him back. He dragged her down into a whole new world. Not a place of sunshine and flowers, but somewhere darker, deeper, more complex. Somewhere infinitely more alluring. His hands framed her waist, then skimmed over the curve of her buttocks, and a low hum of arousal rumbled from his chest into hers. Her brain shut down. The world narrowed to all the places they touched.

Heloise closed her eyes and let her head fall back as he pressed feverish kisses across her nose, her cheek, the sensitive skin just below her ear. Her legs turned to water. He widened his stance and pulled her between his thighs; his hard maleness pressed against her stomach and she felt a thrill of feminine satisfaction at his unmistakable reaction. She wanted her skirts gone, no barriers at all, only this wonderful hot rush of need.

A loud whistle and a peal of masculine laughter jolted them apart.

Heloise fell back, shaken and panting. A tide of heat rose to her cheeks as she realized she'd just made a public spectacle of herself like some ill-bred harlot. She dropped her gaze, totally unable to look at him. *Idiot.* She'd meant to kiss him once and step back. She should have known better than to try. She had no control when it came to him.

He flicked one finger carelessly across her cheek. "I'll have to rescue you again, Hellcat, if this is the thanks I get."

She took only slight gratification from the fact that his voice wasn't entirely steady. "I have never met a man as infuriating as you."

His smile was cocky. "You've never met any real men at all, sweeting. All you know is soft boys in silk waistcoats and pasty-faced fops." He tilted his head. "You know, the gypsies believe that if you save a life it becomes yours."

She snorted. "So I belong to you now, is that it? That's ridiculous."

His intense look made her stomach quake. She turned and stalked away.

"Maybe I'll keep you," he called out after her.

"Maybe I'll stab you in your sleep," she shouted back.

His laugh was genuine. "You can *try*."

"I might get lucky."

"Sweetheart, if someone as talentless as you gets anywhere near me with a knife, I *deserve* to die."

CHAPTER 31

They made camp that evening in a lush valley nestled between the foothills.

Heloise retrieved her journal and sat herself down on a rock near her caravan. She wanted to record as many ideas and impressions as possible for when she was back in dull, rainy England.

A rustle behind her made her turn. A boy, no older than eight or nine, was hiding in the shadows, watching her with huge liquid eyes. He lingered at the very edge of the circle of light, and when she glanced at him he froze like a frightened animal. When she smiled and beckoned he sidled closer but kept his distance, staying well out of arm's reach.

The child was thin, a cadaverous Anubis puppy with dark hair and golden skin and black, haunted eyes that looked as if they'd seen far too much.

Heloise bent back over her writing and pretended to ignore him. He sneaked closer. She tapped the pen against her lips as if struggling to think of a phrase. He edged forward and slid onto the rock next to her. He peered over her arm at her book, intrigued. She repressed a smile.

"What is your name?" She kept her voice low, soothing, so as not to scare him off.

He didn't answer.

She glanced over at him and tapped her chest. "Heloise." She pointed at him and raised her brows. Nothing. Just big eyes as he stared at her, uncomprehending. "No?" she tilted her head. "Can you read?"

No answer.

"Can you understand me? Speak English?" Heloise sighed. "No, probably not," she muttered to herself. "And I don't speak much Spanish. Bother."

She couldn't even remember how to ask for an aquatint of the harbor or tell him her dentures were broken. At least those phrases might have coaxed a bemused smile.

The boy shook his head, which sent his inky black curls tumbling around his little face. Maybe he was a mute? Heloise turned to a clean page in her journal and wrote out her name, then pointed to it. "Heloise. That's me. See?"

She gestured at his chest again. "You?"

Nothing. She sighed. How to entertain him? He looked so serious, watching her as if she were some kind of oddity, like an exotic animal in a zoo. She'd received similar uncomprehending looks when talking about etymology to her suitors. "All right. How about this, then?"

She tried to recall the parlor games she'd played with her brothers and remembered the silhouette shows they'd performed for their parents. Turning to the side, she used her hands to make the shadow outline of a bird's head upon the side of the caravan, lit by the distant fire.

She made a dove, waggling her fingers to make it flap its wings. The boy's eyes widened with delight. She smiled at him.

"You like that, do you? How about a swan?" She elongated one arm to make the neck and made bobbing motions with her hand for the head.

He smiled wider.

"What else? Um, I can make a stag." She did so, splaying the fingers of one hand for the antlers. "Oh, and a wolf. AUOOOO!" She howled softly.

To her delight the boy nodded enthusiastically.

She racked her brains, determined to keep up the entertainment, some instinct telling her that this boy hadn't smiled in a long time.

"How about a rabbit?" Two upraised fingers created the animal's ears. She made it hop.

When the boy laughed, the ancient look fell from his face and she smiled at him, perfectly in charity. To her surprise he reached out toward her with his hand, then pulled back partway, watching her apprehensively as if he expected her to scold him. He tilted his head to one side in silent question and when she didn't refuse, he reached out and traced his finger over her scar. He had the gentlest touch, and Heloise swallowed a lump in her throat at the look of sympathy and understanding on his face.

He dropped his hand to his skinny chest and tapped it, moistened his lips, and whispered. "Rafa. Rafael."

His voice was a low croak. She smiled. "That's your name? Rafael?"

He nodded shyly. "*Sí.*"

"Like the angel," she said, gesturing vaguely at the sky.

He shook his head earnestly, clearly having understood the word. He took a strand of her hair between his fingers. "No. *Usted es el ángel.*"

His little face was so solemn, his voice so low and rough that she had to dip her head to hear it. She nodded but glanced up when she heard a sharp intake of breath.

The woman made the sign of the cross on her chest and stared in astonishment at the child as if she'd seen a ghost. "*Qué dice?*" she gasped.

Heloise realized she was asking what the boy had said. She

frowned and glanced behind her, but the boy had already slunk back into the shadows.

The woman's urgency was alarming and Heloise's stomach dropped at the thought that she might have inadvertently done something to offend. Had she crossed some invisible social boundary by talking to the boy?

"Ah, something about angels, I think. And his name. That's all."

The woman caught her arm. "*Madre de Dios!* He speak? *Verdad?*"

"Well, yes," Heloise said, confused.

"God be praised, signora!"

The woman dragged her forward to the fire and erupted into a stream of Spanish too fast for her to follow.

"I'm not sure I've done anything, really . . ." Heloise stammered. "I just—"

Raven stepped up to translate the sudden babble that had arisen. "The boy is a distant cousin of Alejandro. He hasn't said a word since he witnessed the massacre of his parents and entire village two years ago."

Heloise gasped, her eyes wide.

"He survived by playing dead while the French soldiers looted and raped."

"Oh, my God," she whispered.

"They think what you've done is a miracle."

Heloise flushed. "Oh, well. I'm just glad I could help."

An elderly woman pushed her way to the front of the crowd now surrounding them and pinched Raven's arm. She studied Heloise critically for a few seconds, then said something to Raven and beckoned Heloise forward with a welcoming gesture. "Come. You come."

Heloise frowned.

"Elvira's offered to tell your *baji*, your fortune," Raven said. "It's a great honor. You're an outsider."

Heloise glanced at the old crone uncertainly but she looked so expectant it was impossible to refuse. "Oh, well then. Thank you."

She followed the woman to a red-painted caravan and sat down on the front step as directed. The elder settled herself opposite her and drew a pack of worn pictorial cards from a pocket in her skirts. She handed them to Heloise and indicated that she should shuffle them, then held up four fingers. Heloise dutifully lay out four cards, facedown on the step.

"Past, present, future, outcome," Elvira said in accented English.

Heloise started, surprised to hear her own language coming out of the woman's mouth, but Elvira merely gave an enigmatic smile and tapped the back of each card, her gnarled knuckles like the twisted limbs of an olive tree.

Heloise nodded. She'd seen a tarot reader perform once before, at Lady Vane's. The woman had been so vague in her pronouncements that the guests had interpreted them to mean whatever they wanted to believe. There was no magic in it, merely the power of suggestion, but Heloise had been intrigued. The tarot was, in effect, another code—one from which the reader could tease practically any desired translation.

She turned over the first card.

CHAPTER 32

"Six of swords."

The card showed a boat carrying six upright swords and a woman and a child being ferried from rough water to smooth.

Elvira nodded. "This means a passage away from difficulties, recovery after trials."

She'd recovered from the trial of her scar, Heloise thought. And accepting Tony's death had been extremely difficult. Or maybe the card was more literal? She'd taken a trip across water in Raven's boat. Ship. Whatever. But she'd passed from the still waters of home into treacherous seas, not the other way around.

"There is sadness for those you leave behind, but this trip will do you good." Elvira tapped the second card. "The present."

Heloise turned it over.

Elvira nodded again, as if the card confirmed what she'd been expecting. "*La luna.*"

The image was a wolf, howling at the moon.

"The wolf is the wild, untamed aspect of our nature."

Heloise swallowed. Raven had certainly brought that out in

her. He seemed to spend his entire time encouraging her to set it free, the subversive devil.

"The moon appears when you do not know your destination, or even the path you are traveling, but you travel nonetheless."

Well, that was certainly true. Heloise had no idea where they were headed, except that it was north.

"The moon is the card of our dreams. You have lost your way, and walk in the dark, guided only by your inner light."

Heloise frowned. She wasn't sure what that meant, exactly, but it sounded rather frightening. She turned over the third card. Future.

Elvira smiled, showing several gold teeth. "The Magician."

Heloise glanced up in alarm. The dark-haired figure on the card bore an uncanny resemblance to Raven.

The old woman gave her a knowing wink. "We see what we want to in the cards."

Heloise shifted on the wooden step. Was she imagining Raven in her future? That was ridiculous. She concentrated on the card. The figure's right hand held a staff raised toward the sky, while his left hand pointed to the earth. Above his head was a sideways figure eight, the symbol of eternity, and around his waist a snake biting its own tail, another symbol of eternity.

"One of my favorite cards," Elvira murmured. "The Magician is skill, logic, and intellect. He represents the ability to transform the world and have power over it."

That sounded like Raven, all right. The man turned her world upside down.

"He is the bridge between the world of the spirit and the world of humanity."

Like Anubis, Heloise thought. And Hades. One foot on earth, the other in the Underworld.

The gypsy's finger pointed to the card. "His robe is white, for innocence, but his cloak is red, for worldly experience and knowledge."

Heloise almost snorted. There was nothing pure about Raven. The swine had provided her with "worldly experience" aplenty. The worst of it was, she had an awful suspicion that he'd ruined her for anyone else. Not physically, but emotionally. He'd opened her eyes to a whole new world, tied her to him in ways she couldn't explain. He'd shown her adventure, friendship, and breath-stealing passion. She couldn't imagine wanting any other man. The thought was profoundly depressing.

"Is this supposed to represent my future?"

Elvira nodded. "You will soon be offered a situation that contains all the elements needed to bring your desires to life. Those desires may be spiritual, physical, emotional," she reached over and put her palm on Heloise's breastbone, "or mental." She tapped Heloise's temple with her finger, directly over her scar. "Only you have the ability to make it happen."

She indicated for Heloise to turn over the last card. "Outcome."

The old woman raised her brows in surprise, then chuckled. "Strength. Of course."

The card showed a woman patting a lion, gazing down at it with a peaceful smile. The sky held both a sun and a moon, and above her head hovered the same infinity symbol as in the Magician card. She stood unprotected in an open green field, wearing a white pleated dress suspiciously like the one Heloise had worn to the ball, and a crown of flowers. She looked exactly like the Persephone painted on Raven's ceiling.

Heloise shook her head. It was pure coincidence. She was reading far too much into things, seeing connections that didn't exist.

"The fact that Strength is a woman shows this card is not focused on pure physical strength. Do you see how the lion is sticking out his tongue? Animals that are preparing to bite do not stick out their tongues. This lion is happy to submit and surrender to the woman." Elvira's gaze was shrewd. "The woman offers love and patience to the ferocious lion to tame him. She uses compassion and her wits."

Without thinking, Heloise glanced over at Raven, sitting across the fire. The handsome, elegant lines of his face were outlined in fire glow and shadow and Heloise felt a painful fullness in her throat, a constriction in her chest. Every sense seemed heightened around him; the stars were brighter, the night darker, the scents sharper, the crickets louder.

"He's so beautiful," she was astonished to hear herself say.

The gypsy shook her head, her eyes dark in her walnut-wrinkled face. "No, cara. He's as scarred as you. But his scars are all on the inside. It takes a strong woman to love a man like that."

Her inference was clear. Heloise could be the lion tamer. If only she had the courage to go after what she wanted. Was she that woman? Heloise shook her head. It was stupid to wish it. Raven had no desire to be tamed. She might as well try to tame a jackal.

Elvira tapped the strength card with a long fingernail. "Time does not heal scars. Only love can do that." She glanced up at the sky and frowned. "Storm coming."

Heloise had no idea how she knew that. It was cloudless and clear. Perhaps she meant an emotional storm? That didn't bode well either.

A woman in a head scarf and red apron approached them and murmured something to Elvira.

"This is Rafael's aunt," Elvira said. "She wishes to present this shawl to you."

The woman nodded and pressed a folded piece of pale yellow fabric into Heloise's hands. It was fringed, and embroidered with flowers so intricate Heloise squinted in awe at the delicacy of the work.

"Oh no, I can't accept this!" she stammered. "It must have taken hours to sew."

The old woman smiled. "Child, what you have given Rafa's

family is greater than any gift. You have brought their nephew back from the dark place he inhabited."

"Honestly, there's no need, I didn't—"

"You will insult them if you do not take what is offered." The soft tone held a hint of reprimand and Heloise was suddenly reminded of old Doctor Gilbert at home, scolding her for hurting herself as a child.

"Oh, well, of course. Thank you." She nodded and smiled.

The woman backed away, still bowing and murmuring blessings.

"You go to your *minchorró* now," Elvira said.

"I'm sorry, I don't know that word."

The fortune teller grinned and nodded across the fire at Raven. "Ask him." She gathered up her cards and made a shooing gesture with her hands. "Now you go. This old woman needs her sleep."

"Thank you."

Elvira waved her away and hobbled up the steps to her caravan.

Heloise walked over to the fire and accepted a cup of warmed wine from Sebastiano with a smile.

CHAPTER 33

*R*aven frowned into the flames. Who the hell had been firing at them today?

His first suspicion had been Lavalle, but it just was too unlikely. The odds that he could have tracked them from England were simply too remote.

A random attack was similarly unlikely. Why would a single gunman take on a much larger force? If robbery had been his aim, he must have known he would fail.

If the French had discovered the Baker was dead, and decided to ambush them on the way to the prisoner exchange, surely they would have sent more than just one man to ensure the job got done? Raven shook his head. It didn't make any sense. The most likely explanation was that the French had sent someone to scare away any random travelers so there wouldn't be any accidental witnesses to the prisoner exchange.

Raven rested his elbows on his knees and hung his head. He hated uncertainty, especially when it endangered Heloise. He looked up to check on her, and found her smiling at Fernando.

Alejandro sidled up and whacked him playfully on the shoulder. "Stop scowling at Fernando. He's not interested in her. Nor she him."

Raven took another sip of wine. "I don't know what you mean."

"Oh? Then there must be some other reason you look like you're measuring him for a shallow grave."

Raven grunted. Alejandro had a point. He was a hypocrite, wanting other men to keep their eyes off her when he couldn't control the same impulse in himself. God, the woman was a menace.

"A blind man could see what you feel for her, my friend."

Raven scowled. "Most of the time I want to kill her."

Alejandro snorted. "Ha. You lie to yourself. It's only a little death you want to give her, eh?" He nudged Raven in the ribs with a ribald laugh.

"I need her like the devil needs holy water."

"Would you not kill for her?"

"Already done that."

"Die for her?"

Raven shot him a disgusted look. "What do you think?"

Alejandro gave a fatalistic shrug of his huge shoulders. "Then it's love, my friend. Nothing so simple, or so complicated."

Shit, Raven thought, as Alejandro ambled back to the fire. Was he really that obvious?

Heloise detached herself from Fernando and came toward him and Raven schooled his features into a semblance of polite interest. He dragged his eyes from her entrancing face and nodded at the fabric in her hands. "What's that?"

She showed him.

"You made quite the impression."

"I didn't do much to deserve it. I only spoke to him a little."

"You don't give yourself enough credit, Hellcat."

Her scar had given her an affinity with broken things. And unlike him, she hadn't let the darkness that touched her make her bitter. Instead, she used the glow of her personality to heal others.

She flushed, uncomfortable with his praise. "What does *minchorró* mean?"

"It means someone's 'fancy,' their lover." He shot her a questioning glance. "Why?"

Her blush intensified. "Oh, no reason. I just heard one of the women using it, that's all."

He smiled. "Did Elvira read your fortune?"

"Yes."

"Was it all dragons and knights?"

She bit her lip. "Not exactly. More like lions and boats."

He raised his brows. "Stands to reason. You're hardly the distressed damsel type. I doubt you'd want a dragon-slaying knight doing all the dirty work for you."

She laughed. "You're right. Knights are always galloping off on ridiculous quests. I'd much rather have the dragon. Big. Strong. Fiery breath to keep me warm on cold winter nights . . ." She ticked the list off on her fingers.

"I thought all young ladies spent their days dreaming of happily ever after?"

"Heavens, no," she said, genuinely appalled. "Just think about that phrase. Happily. Ever. After. Even if it were possible, it's not at all desirable."

"It's not?"

"Who'd want to be *perpetually* happy? And how would you even know you were happy if you had nothing with which to compare it?"

He frowned. "You think you need to experience unhappiness just so you can feel happiness?"

"Yes, of course. Every shadow needs a source of light. Heaven can't exist without hell."

Raven didn't even want to consider that argument. It was far too close to the way his own thoughts had been leading him recently. She might be as necessary to his existence as oxygen, but she was still Not. For. Him.

He stood and started to walk her back toward her caravan. It was set a little way from the others, near a stand of tall pines. A shard of broken pottery crunched under his boot. He bent and picked it up, turned it over in his fingers, filled with a sudden need to make her realize how extraordinary her own achievements were. She was such a positive force. She charmed and helped almost everyone she came into contact with.

"My mother used to collect porcelain," he said. "She had cabinets of the stuff. Vases and plates and teapots and bowls. Beautiful things, all delicate, exquisite, expensive."

Heloise froze, and he knew it was in surprise; he rarely spoke about his family. He didn't know why he was doing so now, except he needed to somehow apologize to her for the way he'd treated her at the palace.

He cleared his throat. "Father used to buy them for her as presents. One day, when I was maybe nine or ten, about a year before she died, she asked me which piece was my favorite. I told her—the two fat sumo wrestlers."

Heloise smiled.

"She asked me to guess which *she* liked best. I thought it would be one of the plates, or maybe the fancy tulip vase, but she reached in and brought out this little tea bowl, like a cup without a handle, so small it fitted in her palm.

"I thought she was teasing me. The thing had been dropped at some point, broken into four or five pieces then put back together. It had metal in the joins, like golden veins. Mother smiled at my confusion. 'Don't you see, Will?' she said. 'It isn't the prettiest because it was broken, it's prettiest because it was mended.'"

Raven's heart thumped against his ribs. He wasn't talking about porcelain.

Heloise cleared her throat. "Oh?"

"It's taken me years to understand what she meant." He glanced at her, but her expression was unreadable. "Someone loved it enough to repair it. It's called Kintsugi, the art of fixing things with gold. In Japan, they believe the piece is even more beautiful for having been damaged and restored."

God, he wanted to cry. He felt the constriction in his throat, hot and tight. His eyes were stinging. Only she could do this to him, make him strip his soul bare. Unable to help himself he reached out and stroked her cheek, her chin, a lingering caress. She didn't move. "Those suitors of yours who withdrew their offers? They're all fools."

She closed her eyes.

"You want to pretend this scar isn't there, but it's what makes you you." He stroked one finger over the slight ridge and felt a shiver course through her. "Don't be ashamed of it. It's a badge of pride. You should wear it like a bloody medal. It's proof that you're stronger than the thing that tried to hurt you. It's proof that you're a survivor." He cupped her nape, drew her forward, and grazed the scar with his lips. She stood utterly still, but he heard her swift intake of breath.

"You're like the moon. It has craters and scars and shadows. But only an idiot would deny that it's beautiful."

Heloise swayed toward him and he forced himself to step back, gesturing to the caravan steps. "Up you go."

Her brows lowered in confusion. "Aren't you coming in? Elvira says there's going to be a storm."

He glanced up at the sky then back at her. Going inside would be a very bad idea. "No."

A rumble of thunder echoed in the distance. "It's going to rain," she said. "You'll get soaked if you stay out here."

"I'll be fine. Go to bed."

A crack of thunder sounded right above them. It rumbled around the mountains and Raven felt the splash of the first fat raindrops with a certain inevitability. Slow at first, then faster, a persistent hiss as they hit the leaves and grass around him. The camp emptied, people scrambling for cover.

Her silhouette shadowed his face. "Come in here. Don't be a stubborn ass. You'll be no good to Kit if you catch a fever and die."

Raven ground his teeth and mounted the first two steps. The rain was coming down in earnest now, soaking his hair, his shoulders. It drummed on the wood of the caravan, an insistent beat that mirrored the pulse in his temples. Heloise just stood there. She was trying to drive him mad.

She half turned, thinking he was about to follow, but he reached out and grabbed her wrist. Her eyes widened, her lips parted in surprise, and he cursed himself for a fool.

To hell with it.

With a single tug, he pulled her out into the downpour. She gave a startled yelp but he caught her in his arms and spun her down to the ground. "Here's one more to cross off that list of yours," he growled. "A kiss in the rain."

He caught her chin, tilted her head, and kissed her full on the mouth, drowning in anger and frustration, passion and despair. He kissed her just long enough to get light-headed, just long enough for the heat and the desperation to build. And then he shoved her up the steps. "Now bloody well go to sleep."

This time, thank God, she got the message.

The door slammed shut in his face.

CHAPTER 34

aven settled himself beneath the trees and tried to get more comfortable.

The walls of her caravan were too damn thin. Despite the patter of the rain he was sure he could hear her undressing. His mind, of course, provided an image for every rustle and thump. The minutes passed. He heard the splash of water, the sound of bare feet on wood, the whisper of sheets across her body. Not even the bloody French had devised such torture.

He waited a good hour, until he was certain she was asleep, before he slipped into the caravan. The doorway was so low he had to duck his head, and once inside he could barely straighten up, but at least it was dry.

He sat down on the edge of the bed, careful not to wake her. She wore that damnable teal chemise again, little more than scraps of silk and lace, designed to entice rather than conceal. One thing you could say about the French, no matter how wrong-headed their politics, as a nation they were masters of producing undergarments that could drive a man to the brink of insanity.

He watched the rhythmic rise and fall of her chest, listened to her breathing, and lost all track of time. He could stay like this forever, watching her, guarding her. It was a total invasion of her privacy, just as reading her journal had been, but he didn't care. He'd steal whatever moments he could to nourish his dark soul.

His eyes traced the delicate lines of shoulder and collarbone. Awake, she was so feisty, so fierce, like a tiny force of nature. He kept forgetting how fragile she was. Each time he lifted her he was shocked at how little she weighed.

And yet she constantly surprised him with her resilience. He'd mocked her ability to survive, but she was as adept at self-preservation as he. She'd endured the barbs of the London ballrooms after her accident, avoided marriage as successfully as he'd avoided sniper's bullets. She'd faced the challenges of traveling as an adventure rather than an ordeal.

His chest constricted. That bullet today had been too close for comfort. He'd hit the shooter, but there was no way of knowing whether it had been enough to put the bastard out of action.

Heloise stirred restlessly. Her forehead puckered as she turned her head and she muttered something incomprehensible.

He ought to leave. He had no business spying on her.

She flailed and kicked a leg out from underneath the blankets. The chemise pulled taut, baring the upper curve of one breast, and Raven swallowed. She needed rest, and all he could think about was putting his mouth on her skin.

Her eyelids flickered. And then she screamed.

"Tony!"

* * *

THE ICE CRACKED beneath her feet, hideous gray lines radiating out with every step she took. Heloise raced forward, her panicked breaths white puffs in the freezing air.

"I'm coming, Tony! Hold on!"

She was almost there, so close. And then the ice gave way and she was falling, down, into the frigid black water. She flung out her arms and kicked her legs. Surfaced with a gasp. Somewhere, nearby, Tony was shouting her name, frantic, desperate, but she couldn't see him, couldn't reach him. The weight of her skirts dragged her down, wrapping round her legs in an icy embrace as she thrashed. "Wait! I'm coming! Wait!"

She clawed and grasped nothing. Tony's voice was fading, slipping away, and a scream tore from her throat, of rage and frustration and grief. This wasn't what had happened. Tony couldn't leave her!

Heloise sat bolt upright, her heart hammering, her throat tight and raw. Strong arms enveloped her and she didn't even question their presence. She let out a choked sob and buried her head in the comforting warmth and strength. Raven. Of course.

A shudder ran through her. "I dreamed of Tony. On the ice."

Soothing hands rubbed her back. "Shh. It's all right."

She could barely breathe past the weight of loss crushing her chest. "Oh God. Why did he have to die?"

"I don't know."

She suppressed another shuddering sob. "It's so bloody stupid. What was the point in me saving him from drowning, when he went and got himself killed a few years later in the war?" Tears threatened behind her eyelids but she refused to let them fall. She buried her face against Raven's shirt instead. "I couldn't save him. He died."

Raven stroked her hair, smoothed the damp tendrils back from her face and simply held her, offering wordless comfort. Heloise lifted her head and stared at him in the shadows. "I miss him so much. It still hurts. Every day, you know?"

Oh, yes, Raven thought helplessly, he knew. That gnawing sense of loss. The impotence and hollowness and rage. He'd never wish it on his worst enemy.

She made a soft sound, a little sigh, and burrowed her face into his chest again. He stiffened but didn't move.

"I was afraid for you this afternoon," she sniffed, her words muffled against his shirt. "What if you'd been shot? I've already lost Tony. I couldn't bear to lose you, too."

Raven stilled at her admission, then forced his muscles to relax. "You won't get rid of me that easily. I'll stay on this earth just to haunt you." He smiled when she chuckled, and felt an instant gratification that he'd eased a little of her pain. "I thought you hated me, Hellcat?" It came out gruffer than he would have liked, but she didn't notice, thankfully.

She gave a watery laugh. "I might want to kill you, Ravenwood, but I'd never want you dead."

That was paradoxical, but he knew what she meant. He felt the same way about her. She lifted her eyes, and he felt himself weakening. That pleading look was killing him, as sure as a knife through the heart. He stood abruptly and stepped to the door. He had to get out of there.

"Stay," she said softly.

CHAPTER 35

*H*eloise couldn't believe she'd just said that out loud. But she didn't want to take it back. She tensed, waiting for his reaction.

Raven paused, one hand on the doorknob.

"I need you. Stay with me tonight."

"You don't have the first clue what you're saying."

Heloise swallowed. This wasn't her real life. This was just a temporary interlude. No one would know what happened here. She could take what she wanted and damn the consequences. She wanted him. His body, if not his heart. "I know this isn't forever. I don't care. I want you to be my first lover."

His lip curled in a snarl. "You don't need anyone. Least of all me."

"I do." Her heart was hammering in her throat but she attempted an insouciant shrug. "If anyone finds out I've been with you this past week, I'll be ruined."

"No one's going to find out," he growled. "Your family will tell everyone you've been ill."

She ignored that piece of logic. "Someone might. And if I'm

going to be labeled a fallen woman, I might as well find out what all the fuss is about."

He ran his left hand through his hair in a distracted motion. The movement flexed his bicep, bunched it up tight beneath his shirt. "No. Someone has to have a care for your reputation."

Anger warmed her chest. "Why? It's not as if I'm ever going to marry. And I'll be damned if I go to my grave without knowing what it's like to be with a man."

He narrowed his eyes at her, his knuckles white as he clutched the doorknob. "I'm not going to overpower you so you can tell yourself afterward that I forced you into it."

"I know that."

His eyes burned into hers. "You'd better be sure, Hellcat. Because if we start this, I won't stop. Not this time."

The rain beat down on the roof and the caravan suddenly seemed far too small. She could barely breathe. "I won't want you to stop."

His hand dropped from the door. Raven tilted his chin at her chemise, a faint, challenging lilt in his tone. "Then take that off."

Her heart almost stopped. Oh, good God in heaven. He'd agreed!

She came up onto her knees on the bed. Her hands shook as she grasped the hem of her shift and drew it upward, slowly. The cool silk flowed over her thighs like water, and her stomach fluttered in the cold air. The scandalous garment slid over her breasts as she lifted her arms. Her hair caught up and then dropped down her back as she drew it over her head.

She couldn't believe she was doing this. She wanted to hide behind the fall of silk forever, but she forced herself to bring her arms down and look him in the eye.

Raven was staring at her naked body. Heloise couldn't move. His gaze was like a physical touch as it swept her shoulders, her neck, her breasts. To her horror she felt her nipples rise, as if begging for his hands. Her stomach muscles tightened when he looked lower, down to the pale curls at the juncture of her thighs. She squeezed her knees together. A wicked pulse throbbed as she thought of his hands there, as they had been before. Heat scalded her skin.

Her initial bravery faded as the silence stretched. She felt drawn tight as a bowstring. Was this just another of his cruel jokes? Was he going to take one look at her and dismiss her again as unworthy?

Why didn't he *say* something?

* * *

RAVEN WAS DYING.

He needed to do what he always did, make some cruel, flippant taunt that would have her diving under the covers and safely hating his guts.

He couldn't do it. He was tired of fighting. Tired of playing it safe. Either one of them could have been killed by that sniper today. Anything could happen at the prisoner exchange. If he was going to die—which was a distinct possibility—did he really want to go without a single taste of the thing he craved most in this life?

God, no.

Why the hell should he save her virginity for some undeserving bastard like Wilton?

Life was sex and death and pain and pleasure. You had to grab it all while you could. His pulse hammered in his throat. Of all the places he'd imagined making love to Heloise Hampden—and they'd been legion—he'd never once imagined a gypsy caravan in the rain. It was oddly fitting, though, a place out of time, something magical, a fantasy.

He let out a breath, half sigh, half groan. "A million times I've dreamed of you like this."

He stepped forward until he stood directly in front of her.

The height of the bed and her kneeling position meant the top of her head was level with his chin. He extended his hand.

She jumped when he shaped the curve of her waist, then inhaled sharply as his forefinger traced the underside of her breast.

"That's because you're depraved," she managed shakily.

"Yes," he breathed, half to himself. He flattened his hand over her stomach then made his way up the valley of her breasts to describe a lazy crescent over the top swell. A tremor passed through her.

God, she was perfect. Small and sweet and soft. His skin was dark upon hers and he watched with something akin to amazement as he let his finger spiral down, around and around, in ever-decreasing circles until his thumb brushed her nipple and she gasped.

He replaced his thumb with his whole palm, cupping her, squeezing gently, and she gave a wordless moan and leaned into the sensation. So responsive. So trusting.

He looked down at her, a bitter twist to his lips. "You want to know the truth? I'm *glad* you're scarred. Glad you've fallen from your pedestal into the realm of mere mortals like myself." He flicked his thumb again and watched her lips part in wonder. "It makes you real. Makes you touchable."

He matched the words, trailing his hand up the side of her neck until he cupped her jaw. He stroked her lip with his thumb and felt his body tighten in response as she closed her eyes. The blood was rushing in his ears and he couldn't recall a single time when he'd desired a woman more.

He stroked her scar. "Everyone who looks at your face sees this scar. I want to know the marks no one else knows about. The secret ones only a lover would know."

She opened her eyes, raised her hand to the center of his chest, and he was caught in the swirling lavender-gray of her stare.

"Yes," she whispered.

He kissed her then, hungrily, deeply. Oh Christ, he should be going slowly. But he couldn't seem to catch his breath, couldn't stop his hands. He was feverish, shaking, so utterly lacking in his usual finesse. The scent of her filled his senses, a warm perfume of arousal that rolled off her skin and sent him reeling.

He forced himself to pull back. He nibbled on her mouth until she began to mimic the movement, her lips reaching for his, clinging. And then her tongue stroked his, a warm slick slide. The taste of her was delicious, addictive, and he wanted more, this glorious rush of pleasure through his veins.

He pressed her with his body, allowed her to feel the full strength of him, both a warning and a promise. The disparity between them amazed him, made him want to weep. She was small and fragile and yet at the same time so brave and strong.

He dipped his head and buried his face between her breasts, cupped them with his hands, and heard her moan. He turned his head, his cheek grazing her soft skin, and tugged a nipple into his mouth. It beaded against his tongue like a tiny, perfect pearl and she arched her back with a gasp of delight and fisted his hair, holding his head in place.

"Oh!"

This was undoubtedly stupid, but it was too late to stop now. He'd rather cut off his own arm. Heloise was the only important thing in his universe. He wanted to raze cities to the ground for her, to burn her up with the heat of his passion. He couldn't tell her that he loved her, but he could show her in a thousand different ways. He could worship her with his body, love her with his lips, his tongue.

She didn't protest when he lowered her to the mattress and stretched out on top of her. No, she tugged at his shirt, yanked it over his head, and threw it away. His heart sang at her impatience. This was the real Heloise Hampden, this fearsome, intoxicating, untamed creature. And just for tonight, she was his.

CHAPTER 36

*H*eloise's skin was on fire.

Each of Raven's kisses was like a tiny flame, their cumulative effect increasing her desperation, each touch curling through her blood and heating it to a slow boil.

He kissed his way down her body and she let out a shocked gasp as he ran his tongue around her navel then went lower. She put her hands down to cover herself, then squirmed in embarrassment as he bent her knees up and moved down so his shoulders were between her thighs. For a few seconds he just stared at her, his breath teasing her sensitized flesh. And then he turned his head and kissed the inside of her knee.

Heloise fell back and drew her hands into fists on the bedcovers. He moved higher, between her legs. And kissed her there.

"Oh, good Lord!" she gasped.

It became a battle of wills. She tried to fight his mastery, but it was no use. He was a magician, teasing with his lips, his tongue. She arched her hips to encourage him to increase the pressure, but he just drew back and blew softly on her. Her skin pebbled and she wanted to scream at him to keep going, to stop playing and have mercy. She didn't, of course. She had her pride. She could endure. And then he started all over again and she dug her heels into the bed, staring blindly at the infinite stars painted on the ceiling above.

He slipped his tongue inside her, then his fingers, and she clenched her muscles around him, trying to keep him inside. Close, so close, so—

He withdrew again and his knowing laugh made her want to hit him. "Not yet. Not without me."

He rose up, wiping his mouth on his palm, and kissed her. She tasted herself on his tongue, musky and strange, and her stomach clenched in anticipation. Raven rolled over onto his back, shucked out of his breeches, and returned.

It was too dark to see much of him and Heloise bit back a moan of disappointment. And then he settled between her legs, a luscious, heavy weight that spread her thighs and pressed her into the sheets. His bare chest rubbed hers and the head of his shaft pressed against her, hot marble-smoothness where his mouth had been. She shifted, restless, urging him on. He slid over her slickness and groaned deep in his chest.

"I need to be inside you."

"Please. Yes, please."

"Don't beg," he said roughly. "You don't *ever* have to beg." He dropped his forehead to hers and exhaled in a despairing sigh. "God, Hellcat. I don't deserve to be your first. Are you sure this is what you want?" He swallowed with an effort, his arms shaking as he held himself above her. "It's not too late, we can still stop, I—"

Heloise curved upward and answered him with her mouth, stopping his ridiculous words. Idiot man. Of course it was too late. It had been too late for years and years.

She kissed him with every fiber of her being, with a force beyond decency and civilization, with a need to claim, and mark, and possess. She wrapped her arms around him, marveling at the contrast of soft skin and solid muscle on his back, embracing him with a kind of loving despair. This man stole her heart and soul, and she waved them both away, helpless to resist. She pressed her face into the curve of his shoulder and inhaled, taking him deep into her lungs.

He reached down and positioned himself at the entrance to her body. "You want me?" His voice was taut with urgency.

"Yes."

"Inside you?"

"Yes."

He changed the angle of his hips, and suddenly he wasn't sliding against her, but into her, a sensation of heat and a brief unaccustomed stretch; not pain, exactly, but not quite pleasant, either.

He drew back and she gripped his sides in panic, thinking he was leaving her. He supported himself on his elbows, forearms cradling her head, and brushed her hair back from her flushed face. He pressed forward again, entering her a little more. "Good?"

She nodded.

"Liar," he chuckled. "But it will be."

The look he gave her was so full of wicked promise that it made her pulse rocket even more. She could detect a certain arrogance alongside the concern, as if he knew some brilliant joke and hadn't yet told her the punch line.

She was finding it hard to think, let alone converse. He was over her, around her, inside her. As close as two people could be. She bit her lip and watched in satisfaction as his eyes followed the movement. She licked it, just to tease him, and raised her brows.

"Is that it?" She tried to sound unimpressed, but her voice held a betraying quiver. "I have to say, I'd expected something . . . different."

He raised his own brows. "Different how?"

"Well, something . . ." words failed her ". . . more."

His lips curled upward. "More, as in, like this?"

He rocked his hips and slid inside her fully. Heloise gasped as her chin tipped up. "Umm . . . well, yes . . . " she managed. "That's . . . ah—"

He withdrew and did it again, a slow, voluptuous slide that pulled him back and then eased back in. Each time was easier than the last. A ripple of delight shimmered through her as the fire he'd built with his mouth returned. Heloise closed her eyes. Oh, the beast, he knew full well the torture he was inflicting. But it was hard to complain when it was so insanely pleasurable.

He pressed again and she arched instinctively as he increased the pace.

"Oh God." He bent his head and kissed her, openmouthed, his tongue mimicking the movement of his body in hers in a wicked, insidious rhythm. They were both gasping when he pulled back. "I don't want to hurt you," he panted.

"I don't want you to hold back," she countered fiercely. "No half measures, Ravenwood. I want everything."

Whatever restraint he'd still had vanished with her words. With a groan he pressed feverish kisses onto her face and then dropped his forehead to her neck and abandoned all pretense of control. His hand gripped her hip as he pulled her up to meet him, the other threaded through her hair to cradle the back of her head.

Heloise gloried in his tender violence. His body was twice the size of hers; he pushed her down into the mattress with breath-stealing force, but she felt only a thrill at his possession, his dominance. All this strength was hers. She defeated him, owned him. Loved him. She'd wanted this forever, wanted him to be a part of her. Even if he left her eventually, she'd have this—this thing they could never undo. Never take back.

He filled her whole world. All she could see was the outline of his shoulder, the strong curve of his neck. His breathy encouragement rasped in her ear, praise and beseeching and nonsense.

Heloise almost laughed aloud. Before, at the *palacio*, it had only been about her pleasure, with him firmly in control, but now he lost himself, too. His big body trembled as he took her, thrusting with urgency instead of control. He drove her upward until she was clutching at his shoulders, sobbing for breath. Closer and closer, as if she were running, but couldn't run fast enough, as in dreams.

And then he put his hand between them, teasing her with his fingers too, and Heloise forgot to breathe.

"Now, Heloise."

Blinding sweetness pierced her; beat after beat of pleasure, of blackness and falling and total annihilation. Raven threw his head back as shudders racked his body and Heloise pressed her face into his shoulder, tasting the salt on his skin, feeling the frantic pounding of his heart beneath her lips.

He relaxed heavily on top of her and she held him, loving the weight of him as the world swam back into focus. Every nerve ending in her body tingled with repletion.

Raven pulled back, still within her, and met her eyes. He looked as shaken, as shattered, as she felt. A lock of his hair had fallen over his forehead and she reached up and stroked it back lovingly. He closed his eyes and rolled off her and she felt a twinge of discomfort as he withdrew.

Well, she was no longer a virgin. Now what? She had no idea what sophisticated women did in circumstances like this. What was the etiquette? Was he going to leave? Should they talk? Have a drink? Go to sleep?

She held her breath as Raven turned on his side and wrapped his arms around her. She opened her mouth to speak but he let out an exhausted chuckle and pulled the blankets over them both.

"Don't you dare say anything," he murmured into her nape. "You'll only ruin it. Just be quiet and go to sleep."

Heloise scowled at his high-handed attitude but she was too exhausted to take him to task. She struggled to muster up even an

ounce of regret, and failed. According to the strict rules of the
ton, she was ruined, but she could find nothing but joy in it.

Her scattered thoughts went back to what he'd said outside.
When he'd kissed her scar it had been the most amazing, heart-
stopping moment, a healing and a benediction all in one. Not
even her mother had ever done that. Heloise had always seen her
injury as a failure, a flaw, but *he* saw her as unbowed. Not a
ruined beauty, but a survivor. No wonder she was in love
with him.

He was delusional, of course. Someone like him was bound to
have warped ideas of beauty. But she wanted to believe him with
every fiber of her being.

Heloise closed her eyes and snuggled deeper into his embrace,
amazed at how natural it felt to be held against his naked body.
Her limbs were suffused with a wonderful languor, a feeling of
peace and contentment unlike any she'd ever known.

* * *

WHEN SHE AWOKE it was daylight, and she was alone. She hadn't
expected otherwise.

As tempting as it was to hide in the cocoon of the caravan
forever, she wasn't a coward. She could be mature about this.
Sophisticated. There was no need to make Raven feel uncomfortable. She'd asked him to stay. And then practically begged him to
make love to her.

She refused to wonder how she compared to all his other
women. It crushed her to think of him doing with other women
what he had just done with her. She was nothing like the voluptuous Lady Brooke.

She'd worried that he'd find her inexperience boring and
gauche, but he'd seemed to enjoy himself well enough. Heloise
flushed, recalling the unaccustomed stickiness between her legs
when she'd washed. Her mother, ever practical, had told her what

to expect. There had been no blood that she could see. She had nothing, in fact, to show for her experience except a few aches in rarely used muscles and a wistful pang in her heart.

Raven wasn't in the camp when she went to the fire, and from a series of mimes and gestures she discovered he and Alejandro had gone ahead to scout out the trail. She helped the women and children pack up, and before long they all set out on a lumbering procession, guarded on all sides by the Alejandro's men, their rifles slung over their shoulders.

They traveled all day, through winding passes and verdant valleys. She caught sight of Raven a few times, up ahead, but he didn't approach her. When he didn't reappear that evening, she ate some rice-filled soup, tried to teach Rafael how to write his own name, and excused herself as soon as it got dark.

So, the bloody man had decided to ignore her, had he? Fine. Two could play at that game.

CHAPTER 37

*R*aven knelt by the stream and splashed cold water on his face. He'd slept beneath Heloise's caravan but left long before she woke. He'd avoided her all day yesterday, hadn't trusted himself to go near her. It had been almost impossible to pretend a distance he didn't want, to feign an indifference he didn't feel. But he was a master at camouflaging his emotions.

He ought to be regretting what they'd done, but it had felt so right it was scary, like suddenly putting his shoes on the right feet after six years of wearing them wrong. He ran a hand over the back of his neck. He'd known it would be good, despite her inexperience, but he'd been shaken by exactly *how* good. What she'd lacked in knowledge she'd made up for in enthusiasm.

Every time he looked at her his mind flooded with erotic images. He kept seeing the tiny perfection of her body under his, her lips parted in an artless gasp of pleasure as he sank into her. Her cheeks flushed with passion, her lips swollen and rosy from his too-hard kisses. His fingers twitched, recalling the satiny feel of her pale skin; the closest thing to heaven a sinner like him would ever experience.

He'd stayed awake for hours after she'd fallen into an

exhausted asleep, assaulted by a whole host of unfamiliar emotions. The feel of her warm, naked body curled around his filled him with such a sense of perfect belonging that it was terrifying. He'd never once spent the night with a woman. Never wanted to, after the sex was done. But with Heloise he'd savored the rightness of holding her in his arms. He'd gazed up at the painted stars and wished that time would stop. That he could deny the inevitability of the coming dawn and simply stay in that moment, perfectly at peace. But every heartbeat, every breath, was one closer to the moment he'd have to leave her.

A profound and hopeless yearning had twisted his gut as he'd tried to imprint the image of her lying next to him into his mind forever. He'd reached out and pushed a stray tendril of hair from her cheek and discovered, to his amusement, that his hand was still trembling. She'd wrinkled her nose and sighed in her sleep and he'd smiled in bittersweet longing.

He'd wanted to wake her and take her again. Wanted to kiss her, long and deep, to stoke the hunger that burned in her until it was a conflagration that matched his own desire.

He'd had sex with women far more skilled, but not once had he so lost himself that he'd forgotten to use a sheath or withdraw. With Heloise he'd done neither. It was as if his body was trying to sabotage his brain. The odds of her becoming pregnant from just the one encounter were slim but his stomach still knotted at the idea of his child in her belly. Every primitive instinct howled at the rightness of it.

If she was pregnant there'd be hell to pay. He'd have to marry her. For one, brief moment he allowed himself a vision of the unthinkable, of himself married to Heloise, allowed to touch her without guilt. Anytime. Anywhere. Every day of his life. All the blood left his head.

Raven shook it. She deserved better that. Better than him. She deserved a man with a whole, unsullied heart, not one who'd inevitably hurt her, frighten her, disappoint her.

A part of him was fiercely glad he'd taken her virginity. He felt a surge of savage satisfaction that this, at least, was one thing that could never be taken from him, never be undone. He wanted be the first, the last, the *only* man she ever slept with for the rest her life. But that couldn't happen. There would be no question of a repeat performance. That one night would have to be enough to last a lifetime.

She was up and dressed when he returned to the clearing, helping the women. His chest tightened with a fierce possessiveness. Mine. Except she wasn't, and never could be. He forced himself to stroll over to her, even as he memorized every nuance of her appearance. "I'm going for Kit now."

She stiffened then turned, a slight blush staining her cheeks. "Where's the exchange taking place?"

"An abandoned church, over in the next valley. Alejandro knows the place. If all goes well, we'll be back here with Kit before sunset. He'll probably need medical attention, so be ready to help the women if you're needed."

She nodded, uncharacteristically meek and obedient. He narrowed his eyes. "You know you can't come with me, Hellcat."

"I know."

"Swear to me you're not planning something. This is not the time for an adventure."

"I'm not planning anything. I intend to stay right here until you get back."

He blinked and feigned astonishment. "Are you feeling quite well? Did Alejandro give you some of his 'special' sangria?"

"No, why?"

"I'm just a little suspicious of this docility, that's all."

She pursed her lips. "I'm not a complete idiot, Ravenwood. I'm not about to purposely endanger either myself or you by ignoring your advice this time. I had quite enough excitement at the caves, thank you very much."

"Well, good. It's a relief to see you repress the habit of a lifetime and be sensible for once."

She didn't rise to the bait. He drew one of his pistols from his waistband and offered it to her. She shook her head. "You might need it."

"No, I won't. I can't take them with me. I need to maintain the illusion of being a prisoner."

"Isn't that a little risky?"

He shrugged and pressed the gun into her hand. "I'll have my knives and I'll feel better if you're armed. There are sentries posted all around the camp, but that sniper might still be out there."

She tilted her head, her brow furrowed. "This could be a trap. What if the French have discovered the Baker is dead? Won't they kill whoever's sent to deal with them?"

"It's a chance I have to take. Kit would do the same for me." He held her gaze. There was so much he wanted to say, but now was not the time. There might never be a right time. "If something goes wrong—" he cleared his throat "—Alejandro will take you straight back to Scovell. Take my ship back to England."

"Don't you dare get yourself killed, William Ravenwood."

He gave her an elegant ballroom bow. "Of course not, my lady."

She stepped up close and put her hand on his cheek, cutting through his flippancy.

He couldn't stop himself from leaning into the touch, trying to absorb some of her softness, her goodness. Without a word, he took her into his arms and felt her lean against him. It wasn't even a sexual embrace. He simply held her, offering mute comfort, willing the warmth of his body into hers, barely aware of what he was doing.

After an endless time the tension flowed from her limbs and her shoulders relaxed. He drew back reluctantly and paused, hovering over her mouth as if waiting for permission to kiss her.

She closed the distance between them. It was a brief, hard kiss, tasting of sweetness, regret, and despair, and he had to force himself to step back.

He pushed her from his mind as he rode out of camp with Alejandro and Carlos, both of whom were wearing the distinct bright red uniforms of officers in His Majesty's armed forces, provided by Major Scovell.

They reached the ruins around midday and made certain they were the only ones there. The exchange had been set for one o'clock, so they took up a position inside the church and waited.

The ruins had been a good choice. The French border was just over the next pass, and the remoteness of the location ensured there would be no accidental interruptions. The little church had been abandoned for some time, and had obviously been the site of various wartime skirmishes. The blinding white stucco was pitted and pockmarked with shot; inside, the wooden pews had been toppled like dominoes and lay strewn and dusty under the arched roof.

Anything of value had already been looted; empty niches and the bare altar showed gaps where statues and ecclesiastical plate had once sat, and the leaded windows were riddled with bullet holes. Intense rays of sunlight shone through the jagged glass, and the shards that littered the floor crunched beneath his feet.

Raven had just checked all the doors when Carlos's whistle came. A horse-drawn cart was trundling along the valley floor, flanked by four men on foot and one man, clearly the leader, on horseback.

Raven squinted, trying to make out the features of the sixth, a huddled figure, lying prone in the back of the cart, but they were still too far away to confirm his identity.

Alejandro fastened a pair of metal cuffs around his wrists. The deception was necessary to maintain the illusion that he was a prisoner, but Raven's stomach still churned at the feel of them

binding him. Now was not the time to remember his imprisonment. He needed to do this for Kit.

He felt naked and horribly vulnerable without his pistols, but
at least he had his knife, hidden under his shirt. If things went
wrong it would be three men against five. He'd survived worse.

The cart rolled closer.

* * *

HELOISE HAD WATCHED Raven ride out of camp with a sinking
feeling.

The thought of him facing his enemy almost completely
unarmed made her stomach churn. She didn't doubt his ability
with a knife, but what good would that be against a loaded pistol?
And surely there would be more than just three Frenchmen at the
exchange. He'd undoubtedly be outnumbered.

She resisted the urge to follow him for a good ten or fifteen
minutes. But then a flock of birds darkened the sky overhead,
cawing and screeching, and she'd taken it as an ominous sign.
The man she loved was out there, facing the enemy. If he thought
she could just sit here and sew something pretty while she
awaited his return, then he didn't know her at all.

She beckoned Rafael over and began drawing in her sketch-
book. It took quite a few scribbles for him to understand where
she wanted to go, mainly because she had no idea what the
ruined church looked like, and the concept of "the next valley
over" was surprisingly difficult to convey.

Her English churches with pointed spires met with blank
stares. And then she remembered the little church she and Raven
had passed outside Santander. She drew a simple box with a bell
in a niche at the top and a cross on the door.

Rafael nodded enthusiastically. "Ah! *Quieres ir a la iglesia en las
collinas! No esta lejos. Vamos.*"

"*Sí.* Raven. You must take me to Raven. Now! This instant."

237

Worried that she might be under a polite form of armed guard, Heloise decided not to risk informing the others. She didn't want an escort. If the men Raven was meeting heard a large party approaching, they would no doubt assume they were being attacked and react badly.

She managed to persuade Rafael to take their two horses and ride a little way up the track while she slipped out of the camp under the pretense of going to the stream.

At Heloise's urging they kept away from the road that led into the valley and made their way through the forested slopes until Rafa pointed out a tiny whitewashed church in a clearing. He seemed perfectly content to remain with their horses while Heloise crept forward to the edge of the trees, keeping as quiet as possible.

She couldn't see anyone outside the church, but the flock of birds had perched on the roof and sat, as if waiting for something. Heloise shivered with a strange sense of foreboding. The clearing was eerily quiet. And then came the sound of a rattling cart, horses, and marching boots

She ducked down to watch.

CHAPTER 38

"*H*ere they come," Alejandro murmured. "I don't recognize the leader."

Raven grunted, and then his heart stopped in his chest as he caught a movement across the valley and spied a tumble of pale hair. Heloise's face poked up from behind a bush. His temples pounded. *Against his express orders.* He was going to wring her neck. He sent her his most fearsome glare. She was about a hundred yards away, on her stomach under some low scrub, directly across the clearing. The cart was too close for him to risk shouting at her—he'd betray her presence to the approaching Spaniards.

Bloody hell.

Stay there! he mouthed, then schooled his face into an impassive blank as the entourage rolled up the hill and came to a stop in front of the church. Alejandro stepped out from underneath the porch.

"Alvarez?"

The Spaniard nodded warily and dismounted. "Yes."

"It's about bloody time. Step to it, my man."

Raven almost laughed aloud at Alejandro's impeccable

239

English accent. When he'd taught him the language, lazing around the campfire all those years ago, Alejandro had been merciless in mimicking his upper-class vowels. Now the wily old devil sounded as though he'd just stepped out of White's. Raven gave him a mental salute.

"You have our man?" Alvarez grunted.

Alejandro pulled Raven from the shadows of the porch and gave him an unfriendly shove forward. "Indeed. Here's your damned 'Butcher.' "

Raven shuffled forward. Now was the moment. If Alvarez knew what the Butcher looked like, he'd cry foul and all hell would break loose. But the Spaniard merely looked Raven up and down and grunted, apparently satisfied. Raven's heart thumped hard in relief.

"Now let's see our man," Alejandro said.

Alvarez nodded. Two of his men let down the back of the cart and hauled their prisoner out. He fell to the floor, clearly too weak to stand, then groaned and rolled over in the dirt, exposing a face that had been beaten to a bloody pulp and a shock of blond hair, matted with dried blood.

Relief and fury welled up in Raven's chest. Kit had been given the code name Apollo, god of the sun, for his guinea-gold mane. Raven and Richard used to tease him about it mercilessly. It was Kit. Alive, but only just.

Kit shielded his eyes from the sun, as if he'd spent too long in the dark. Every one of his ribs was visible on his too-thin frame. His once-muscular physique was little more than a skeleton. Even worse, when he rolled over, Raven could see that his back was a mass of stripes, from where he'd been repeatedly whipped. A murderous rage burned through his veins like acid.

Alvarez's soldiers lifted Kit by the arms, half dragged him to the center of the clearing, and dropped him at Raven's feet. Raven glanced down and caught his friend's eye.

Kit blinked and his eyes widened in sudden recognition.

Raven held his breath, fearful Kit might expose him, but he needn't have worried. Kit was an agent to the core, no matter that he was half dead. His lips twitched in a tiny smile, even as he closed his eyes and feigned oblivion.

Alejandro unlocked Raven's manacles with every evidence of loathing. They dropped to the ground with a dusty *thud* and Raven heaved an inward sigh of relief.

"Thanks for the hospitality," Raven said sweetly in French. He shot Alejandro a taunting smirk, stepped over Kit's body, and sauntered forward. "Seems I've fared better than this one, eh?"

Alvarez sneered, apparently having no difficulty following his French. "Couple more days and we wouldn't have had him to exchange," he chuckled in the same language. "On death's doorstep, that one. He'll be lucky to make it back to England." He slapped Raven on the back and shook his hand. "Come on, my friend. Let's go."

"One moment!"

Every head snapped toward the new voice and Raven's blood froze as he recognized the man who emerged from behind the church, a gloating smile on his thin face: Georges Lavalle.

Raven did some swift mental calculation. Had Lavalle followed Heloise? No, that was impossible. The only reason for a French agent to be here would be to corroborate the Baker's identity.

Shit.

Lavalle's left arm was bandaged over his coat, tied at the bicep with a piece of cloth. So it had been him, up there in the hills.

Lavalle trained his rifle at Raven's chest. "You're being deceived, Monsieur Alvarez. That man," he nodded at Raven, "is an impostor. Another British spy."

"And who the hell are you?" Alvarez said.

"Lavalle. The Barber. Savary sent me here himself."

Alvarez glared at Raven as if for confirmation of his perfidy.

Raven shrugged. "I don't know what he's talking about," he

said. "I just want to get away from these pig-sucking bastards." He tilted his head at Alejandro and Carlos, who made a fine show of pretending not to understand his French.

Alvarez's guards were clearly confused. Two of them trained their rifles at Lavalle, the other two aimed them at Raven and Alejandro.

"Stop right there," Alvarez told Lavalle as he drew closer. "And put down your weapon."

Lavalle ignored him and continued walking. "You idiot. Seize him and you'll have two English spies to execute instead of one. Savary will be delighted. And when the emperor returns, as he did from Elba, we'll both be rewarded in his glorious new republic."

Raven curled his lip and edged closer to Alvarez.

"There's not going to be any bloody republic," he drawled in English. "And your precious Baker is dead."

* * *

HELOISE COULDN'T UNDERSTAND what was going on. Everyone in the clearing seemed tense, their movements deliberately slow. Raven conversed with the leader of the Spanish group and a body —presumably Kit—was dragged out of the cart and deposited on the ground.

When Alejandro released Raven's manacles she exhaled a shaky breath. His identity as the Baker hadn't been questioned.

She blew a strand of hair from her eye. Did Raven plan to leave with the five soldiers? He said plans were for people with no imagination, but he must have some idea of how he was going to extract himself from their company. She had a horrible feeling that whatever he planned wasn't going to include handshakes and pats on the back.

She tightened her grip on his pistol. A crow perched on the arch above the bell on the crumbling roof and cawed insistently as a thin man sauntered out from behind the church. His gun was trained at Raven's chest.

Oh dear.

Words were exchanged, and while she was too far away to hear what was being said, the look on Raven's face and the sudden tightening of his shoulders suggested the newcomer was both unexpected and unwelcome.

Heloise was more used to decoding written languages than human reactions, but she had no doubt that that things had just gone very wrong. What could she do? She bit her lip. Every instinct she possessed rebelled against shooting one of the men in the clearing, but the situation clearly called for a distraction. And then it came to her. She steadied the pistol against a rock, took aim, and fired.

The church bell tolled wildly on its wooden axle. The sound echoed around the valley and the startled ravens took flight in a great, screeching black cloud.

CHAPTER 39

*R*aven was the first to recover.

Alvarez reached for his pistol as the nearest guard stepped forward to seize Raven's arms. Raven barged his shoulder into Alvarez and sent him sprawling to the ground, grabbed the guard's pistol, and shot the man at point blank range.

The man fell back, clutching his chest as his comrade attacked. Raven used the spent pistol to whip him across the face then threw the gun aside and launched himself at his attacker, pounding his fists into his kidneys, earning an agonized grunt. They fell to the ground in a jumble of limbs.

The two remaining guards dived for cover behind the wagon, firing as they did so. Alejandro shot one, but not before a bullet caught him in the shoulder. He dropped to the ground and cursed in agony, but managed to drag himself into the cover of the porch.

Carlos, emerging from the church, killed the other guard with a bullet to the heart as Raven dealt his opponent a final punch that rendered him unconscious.

But Lavalle had closed the distance. As Raven staggered to his knees he saw the Frenchman's triumphant expression and raised gun and threw himself to the side just as Lavalle fired. A stinging pain exploded in his thigh and he collapsed on the ground, gasping; his leg felt as if it were on fire.

Carlos leaped forward to intercept Lavalle, but the Frenchman hit him with the butt of his rifle and broke his nose. Blood sprayed everywhere and Carlos doubled over, howling and clutching his nose.

Lavalle withdrew a pistol from his coat. "It's going to give me a great deal of satisfaction killing you, Hades." He smiled. "Let's see how you like meeting your namesake, shall we?"

"Hey!"

Raven's blood ran cold as he saw Heloise running from the tree line, waving her arms like a demented windmill. Lavalle turned. "But how perfect. Now I kill two birds with one stone, as you English say, no?" With a sick grin he turned the barrel of his pistol toward Heloise instead.

Raven felt the last of his humanity slipping away. There was a time and a place for mercy. This was not it. Anyone who threatened Heloise died. It was as simple as that.

He roared her name and launched himself at Lavalle, reaching for the knife at his back as he did so. He made a grab for the pistol and turned it upward at the same time as he stabbed his blade hilt-deep into Lavalle's arm.

Lavalle screamed.

There was a deafening crack and a searing agony assaulted Raven's skull. Pain exploded in a bright arc of light, and a rush of liquid, both hot and icy cold at once, poured down his neck. His vision wavered and he staggered back, and Lavalle took full advantage, wrapping his hands around his throat in a crushing grip.

Raven grasped the dagger still in Lavalle's arm and twisted it. Lavalle roared with pain and swore, his face a rictus of fury and hatred. As the pressure on his throat eased, Raven pulled the blade free.

"English bastard," Lavalle hissed through his teeth. He dug his thumbs under Raven's jaw, forcing his head back as if he meant to snap his neck. With a strength born of desperation, Raven thrust the blade upward. It slid between Lavalle's ribs in a sickening give of muscle and bone and plunged directly into his heart.

Lavalle fell backward onto the sandy ground. He gasped once, clutching at his side as if to somehow seal the wound, but it was too late. He gave one last, rattling choke, and stilled.

Raven dropped his head and rested his hands on his knees, panting and nauseous. He could feel his strength slipping away. A steady stream of blood dripped from his head onto the ground, thick and surprisingly bright red. Without warning his injured leg buckled beneath him. He fell to the floor, and the world blurred as he tried to stay conscious.

He turned his head and saw Heloise racing across the clearing toward him, her face pale and terrified. His heart gave an irregular kick. Safe. At least she was safe.

A ripple of movement came from his left. Alvarez was advancing on him, a look of evil triumph on his face. The sneaky bastard had been biding his time, waiting for the chance to strike. Sunlight glinted off the knife in his fist.

Raven shook his head to clear the winking lights that flashed across his vision. He tried to rise but his strength had deserted him. Shit. His limbs refused to obey his commands. He heard Heloise cry out and realized with a sense of disbelief that he was too weak to fight Alvarez.

Heloise was going to watch him die.

He ground his teeth and lunged to his feet just as a shot rang out. Raven glanced down instinctively at his chest. There was no pain, but maybe the agony in his skull and his leg had disguised the fatal hit.

But then Alvarez fell backward, the side of his head blown

away. Raven turned in time to see Kit slump against the wall of the church. A pistol slid from his limp grip.

"I've been dreaming of killing that sadistic bastard for months," Kit rasped. He sent Raven a mocking, exhausted salute. "You're welcome."

His cocky grin was a welcome echo of his former self and Raven managed a weak smile in return. "Good to see you, too, Carlisle." He glanced over at Carlos and Alejandro, both bloody, but alive, and grinned. "Well, that was exciting, eh?"

And then Heloise was on her knees in front of him, crying his name, a flurry of skirts and rose-scented woman. "Oh God, you're hurt! Let me see."

Raven forced himself to stand, bracing himself against the side of the wagon, even though it made his stomach heave. Sweat broke out on his upper lip as he ducked away from her questing hands. "Don't fuss, woman. It's nothing. Head wounds always bleed like the devil. I'm just a bit dizzy, that's all."

He groped his way to the back of the cart and sat down heavily on the backboard. His injured leg was in agony, a throbbing fiery pain in his thigh that burned with every step.

Heloise frowned at him. "Stop being so stupid. You've been shot. Twice. Now is not the time to play the hero. Lie back."

Raven sighed in defeat and complied. It did feel good to lie down. The clouds were spinning and his words seemed slow, his brain sluggish. He experienced an odd sense of detachment, as if he were floating distant, apart from it all. Sounds came and went in waves, distinct then dull, like he was underwater. His head throbbed but through the pain came a weary relief, a relaxing of tension inside him. Safe. She was safe. That was all that mattered. Even if he died, he'd done his job. Contentment washed over him in a calming wave of acceptance.

Heloise climbed up into the cart and used her wadded skirts to staunch the bleeding from his head. She probed his hair, and he hissed in pain, half sitting up. The sense of peace receded sharply.

"Jesus, woman, be careful!"

She slapped his hand away. "I can't help unless I can see what I'm doing. For once in your life you're going to have to let someone else take charge."

Raven subsided with little grace.

* * *

HELOISE TRIED to disguise her panic at the sheer amount of blood streaming from Raven's head. Lavalle's bullet had grazed his temple, in the hair just above his ear.

She shuddered as she realized how close to death he'd been. Another inch to the left and he'd have been a corpse. A wave of nausea rose in her throat. "That was such a stupid thing to do!" she scolded.

Raven shrugged and moved his shoulders so his head was cradled in her lap, shamelessly taking advantage. "It was all going swimmingly until Lavalle showed up."

She stroked the hair from his forehead as she continued to keep pressure on his wound. The bleeding seemed to be slowing, but it was hard to tell. Her skirts were soaked with blood. So much blood.

Raven turned his face into her palm and pressed his lips to the delicate skin on the inside of her wrist and her pulse fluttered. He caught her hand in his and held her palm against his face.

He smiled. "Enough of an adventure for you, Hellcat?"

Heloise frowned. His speech was slurred and his pupils seemed huge. He closed his eyes.

"You idiot," she said fiercely, but her voice wavered and tears blurred her eyes. She pressed her lips together to contain a sob and stroked his cheek. The drying blood was sticky on her fingers. He seemed to be slipping in and out of consciousness.

She shook him, slapped his cheek. "Hey! Don't you dare die on me, Ravenwood!" Her voice was shrill, reedy with panic. His eyes rolled back in his head.

Rafael appeared from the trees, leading the horses, and Heloise experienced a moment of guilty horror that he should witness the aftermath of yet another massacre, but the youth merely glanced at the bodies littering the ground and shrugged.

"Bad men," he said, as if that explained everything. He tied the horses to the backboard, clambered up onto the cart, and took the reins.

Carlos helped Alejandro and Kit into the cart and they set off down the road.

The journey back to the camp seemed endless. Heloise tried to hold Raven's head steady, but every jolt made it loll and she winced in sympathy, even though he was unconscious.

Their arrival caused a flurry of activity. Alejandro barked out orders and within minutes both Kit and Alejandro had been dealt with by Maria and Raven had been carried into Elvira's caravan. Heloise followed in his wake, knowing it made sense to allow the more experienced healer do the work.

She sank down on the caravan steps and stared numbly at her lap. Raven's blood covered everything: her hands, her skirts. The world dimmed and chilled, as if an icy fog twisted round her heart. She squeezed her eyes shut. Oh God. He couldn't die.

It seemed hours later when the old woman came out, wiping her hands on the front of her blood-spattered apron.

Heloise leaped upright. "Is he all right? Please tell me he's alive."

When Elvira nodded, a wave of relief washed over her, so great she staggered and had to sit back down on the step.

"He'll live. Head as hard as granite, that one. I've removed the bullet from his leg, too. You can go in and see him, but I've given him something for the pain so he might not make much sense."

Heloise practically pushed her out of the way.

Raven smiled woozily up at her from the bed and her terror ebbed as she saw that he was indeed still among the living.

"Hellcat."

Heloise sank down on the side of the bunk because her legs threatened to give way again. Her hands were shaking, too, so she hid them in her lap and nodded at the bandage around his head. "You'll have a scar."

He blinked and gave her a slow, lopsided grin. Whatever Elvira had given him had clearly produced a sensation similar to intoxication. "We'll match."

Heloise bit her lip. "Not really. Yours will be hidden by your hair."

Her stomach clenched as she recalled his words the night they'd made love. Only a lover would know about *his* scar. "Are you angry I disobeyed your orders?"

"No. You saved my life with that distraction."

"Shooting a bell isn't terribly heroic," she said wryly.

His eyes darkened. "Real heroism isn't public and showy. Countless examples go unremarked and unrewarded every day. Kit's alive because of you. That's amazing, Hellcat. Don't ever forget it."

Her face warmed but he'd already closed his eyes in exhaustion. Heloise succumbed to temptation and cupped his cheek with her palm. Love and despair gripped her as she realized how close she'd been to losing him. She'd experienced this same, pervasive dread when he'd been kidnapped, morbidly certain that every message that came to the house would be the one that told them of his death.

She took a deep breath and forced herself to draw back. Raven was strong. He'd survived his kidnap. He'd survive this, too. But at what cost?

He frowned as she leaned over and pressed a gentle kiss against his lips. "I'll see you later," she whispered.

CHAPTER 40

*T*he journey back to England was a blur.

Raven and Kit both improved under Elvira's watchful eye but the closer they got to Santander, the more distant Raven became. It was hard to define exactly, but she could sense him withdrawing into himself. He was his usual teasing, charming self, always glad to see her, but his wall of reserve had returned. He made absolutely no references to their one night of intimacy.

Heloise hid her dismay. In her weakest moments she'd imagined never going home, traveling with Raven in this tiny caravan forever, seeing the world, the two of them having adventures. But that had always been an impossible dream. The adventure was decidedly over.

They parted from Alejandro's band at Santander. The wound on Raven's thigh prevented him from stomping around and giving orders, but Kit had improved so much with the gypsy's good food and attention that he assumed command of the *Hope* almost as soon as he walked up the gangplank. Raven was installed in his cabin, and Heloise spent most of the crossing staring out at waters that changed from a welcoming turquoise to an angry, choppy gray.

After the excitement and freedom of the past weeks her life in England loomed ahead like a monstrous gilded cage. She didn't want to reprise the role society had allotted her, that of brilliant-but-wounded-eccentric. Even the attentions of her well-meaning family would feel suffocating.

She had only herself to blame. Raven had never made any secret of the fact that he wouldn't be tied down with one woman forever. Marriage for him was a prison as sure as the one in which he'd been held, except the bars were invisible, and the wounds to the heart instead of the flesh.

The idea of reverting to their almost-friendship made her feel hollow inside. Raven would throw himself into his next adventure, while she'd be stuck at home, getting older and more bitter, trapped in a society that expected so little of her. To marry and settle down and have babies. To think of nothing more frivolous than the style of her hat or the number of ruffles on her gown. She would go mad.

And she'd live in constant fear that one day he'd never come back at all, and she'd hear that he'd been killed, like Tony, in some faraway field miles from those who loved him.

When it finally got too cold on deck she went below, took a deep breath, and knocked on the cabin door. Raven was sitting up in bed, shirt open at the throat, looking as attractively disreputable as usual. Her heart contracted and she glanced quickly away, certain he'd read the yearning in her eyes. "Kit says we'll be back home within the hour."

He nodded. "That's good."

"He's going to stay with you at Ravenwood until you can walk again."

"Oh. Right. Good."

Heloise glanced at him. He was looking down, engrossed in pleating the sheet at his waist.

"I'll go straight home, then, shall I?" she prompted.

"That would probably be best. With Lavalle dead I doubt the French will send another agent after you, but I'm in no state to defend you if they do. Richard will make sure you're well enough protected."

A spark of annoyance kindled in her chest. Nothing had changed, had it? She was still just an irksome responsibility to be handed over to the next available protector. But what had she expected him to say? *Don't go, Heloise. You've ruined me for any other woman. Come home with me and stay forever. Marry me.* She might as well expect the moon to burst into flame. She pinned a bright smile on her face. "I completed another item on my list."

That got his attention. His head snapped up. "I hope it wasn't swim naked or take a bath with somebody."

"Those were your additions, not mine."

"What was left?"

"Play cards for money. I owe Kit Carrington seventeen hundred pounds and my first three legitimate children."

Raven frowned. "You don't have to pay him. He cheats."

"So do I. Unfortunately, he's better than me."

His eyes caught hers, his expression intent. "I'll play cards with you."

She swallowed the sudden tightness in her throat. "I've nothing left to play with."

How true that was. With Raven she'd gambled and lost. It was time to withdraw from the game with what little dignity she had left.

He cleared his throat. "I'm sorry if this embarrasses you, but there's something I need to ask. Have you had your monthly courses yet?"

Her cheeks flamed. "Uh, yes . . . I . . . they . . . yesterday, actually."

He nodded, apparently relieved. "That's good."

"Yes."

The chasm of things unsaid yawned between them, vast and unbridgeable. Heloise groped for the door handle and her throat ached with unshed tears. "Well, goodbye, then."

He made no move to stop her and her heart shriveled a little more. This was dying by degrees.

"Goodbye, Hellcat," he said softly.

* * *

RAVEN GAZED at Heloise for a long time, trying to impress her image onto his brain, to memorize every subtle nuance of her face and body. This would probably be the last time they'd be alone together. He knew it, and he suspected she did, too. As soon as they got home they'd be surrounded by a tumult of family and servants, thrust back into their appointed roles of sometimes friendly enemies.

He knew what she wanted him to say, what he ought to say. He could see the expectation in her eyes, the hope, still, that he would offer for her because he'd ruined her. Or because it would be expected of him.

He ought to do it, wanted to, but the words stuck in his throat, refused to form on his tongue. He couldn't be so selfish. He was meant to be alone. And she deserved far better.

His throat ached and his breath caught as he watched defeat and desolation creep into her expression. With a heartbreaking curl of her lips that he supposed was meant to be a smile, she turned and left.

Raven listened to her footfalls fade away and bit the inside of his cheek to stop himself from calling her back. He was crumbling inside. This was how he'd felt in prison, watching the pale glow of his jailor's lantern disappear down the corridor: filled with longing, anger and regret.

She was the one infinitely precious thing in his existence. The rest of his life stretched bleakly ahead of him, no light, no Hellcat, no sunshine. Without her he'd be banished to darkness, the torture a thousand times worse than before because now he knew exactly what he was missing.

But maintaining his distance was vital. Sometimes you needed to amputate a limb, however painful, for the person to survive. True, they'd always be missing a part of themselves, but they'd be alive. Heloise would survive without him. There was no other alternative.

He dropped his head back against the wall and winced as he aggravated his wound. He might never be whole again, but at least he'd set her free.

* * *

RICHARD WAS WAITING on the jetty as they pulled into the cove, the tails of his greatcoat blowing in the wind. Heloise endured his smothering hug as she disembarked, but there was no time for talk. Kit raced down the gangplank and the two men embraced with gleeful exclamations, and then all was bustle as they organized Raven's transfer from the ship. Two burly footmen formed a chair with their linked arms and carried him, complaining, up the steep path.

Heloise clutched her yellow gypsy shawl around her shoulders to ward off the damp chill and followed the procession up the steps cut in the cliff. Had it really been only three weeks since Raven's ball? An eternity had passed since then.

A gray drizzle permeated the air as they started down the hill toward Ravenwood, and Richard turned to her with a smile. "There's no need for you to come, Helly. I'll see Kit and Raven settled. You go on home and see Maman and Father."

Heloise bit her lip. Of course. She couldn't go with Raven. She wasn't one of the boys. She was back in the land of propriety and censure, where an unmarried woman could no more tend to a male friend in his home than she could fly to the moon. She wanted to shout and scream, but lacked even the energy for that. What was the point?

She turned and trudged toward the border of their lands, deliberately averting her gaze from the crumbling seashell folly in the distance. As if she needed more reminders of Raven's history of rejecting her.

It was strange and jarring, being home. Her parents were overjoyed to have her back and she felt a twinge of guilt that she'd caused them so much worry. She gave them a highly expurgated version of her adventures, ignored their concerned questions, pleaded exhaustion, and fled to her room.

Everything here looked exactly the same, but she experienced an awful sense of disconnection, homesick even though she was home. Her room had always been a sanctuary, but it offered scant comfort now; Raven was everywhere she looked. Heloise screwed her eyes shut tight, but the afterimage of him was burned into her brain. Her chest felt hollow, like she'd left a vital part of herself in Spain, but already the whole adventure wavered in her mind, fading, as if it had happened to someone else.

She curled up in the center of the bed, drew the covers over herself, and prayed she wouldn't dream.

CHAPTER 41

"You've a visitor," Richard said, by way of greeting. He closed Raven's bedroom door and sauntered over to the side of the bed with his usual languid grace.

Raven frowned, instantly suspicious of his casual tone. "Other than you? If it's your sister, tell her to go away. I don't want to see her."

Richard made himself comfortable on the chair next to the bed and stretched out his long legs. "It's not my sister, although you really ought to see her. She's asked after you every day for the past week."

Raven sat up, managing to hide a wince at the pain that lanced through his thigh. Doctor Gilbert had checked the wound a week ago and declared it fine, but the damn thing was taking a frustratingly long time to heal. He was going out of his mind with boredom.

"Tell her I'm fine. Tell her I'm considering her reputation, even if she's not. She shouldn't be allowed anywhere near a man's bedroom, invalid or not."

Richard shot him an amused glance. "Since when did you care

about proprieties? Especially when it comes to inviting women into your boudoir?"

"I've *always* cared about reputation when it comes to your sister, you know that. And besides, she's not 'women,' she's . . ." Raven floundered for a suitable adjective and settled for "Something else entirely."

Richard grinned. "Well, *that's* true. I can't believe you spent so long in her company without strangling her. You have my undying respect." He leaned over and poured two glasses of brandy from the decanter on the nightstand. "Here you go. Drink up. Doctor's orders."

Raven accepted the tumbler and took a grateful sip, then stared moodily at the amber liquid. "How is she, by the way?" He tried to match Richard's casual tone, but suspected he failed miserably.

"Miserable," Richard said, echoing his thoughts with uncanny accuracy. Raven schooled his face into a blank mask.

"She talks and laughs, but there's no spark."

Raven swirled the liquid in the glass. His gut knotted unpleasantly. He shouldn't drink brandy on an empty stomach.

"She's like Mother's Swiss music box. When you wind it up the top opens and a little bird automaton pops out and sings a tune." Richard took a slow sip of brandy. "It's beautiful. But completely unnatural."

Raven took another drink. His friend was too perceptive for his own good. "I kissed her," he muttered.

Richard raised his brows.

Raven raised his eyes to heaven. "I did a lot more than bloody kiss her, all right?" God, this was harder than he'd imagined. "I seduced her." He tensed and waited for the explosion, but it never came. "Go on, hit me. I deserve it."

Richard put down his glass. "I thought something like that must have happened."

Raven shot him a wary glance. "You don't seem surprised."

"I'm not. This has been on the horizon for years. The only surprise is that you held out for as long as you did. Everyone knows the way you look at each other. The temperature goes up a hundred degrees whenever you're both in the same room. It was only a matter of time before one of you snapped. And besides, knowing Heloise, I'm pretty sure it wouldn't have been entirely one-sided."

Raven's heart was racing. "Does your father know?"

"He probably suspects."

"Will he expect me to offer for her?" He held his breath, like a man hanging from a ledge by his fingertips.

"No."

Raven exhaled. The sinking feeling in his stomach was not disappointment. Of course it wasn't. He didn't want to get married. It was the brandy. Guilty conscience. Relief at being let off the proverbial hook. All of the above. He cleared his throat. "Well, that's good."

"He does want her to marry, of course. He's wanted that for years."

"Of course."

"She could still accept Wilton."

Brandy splashed onto his wrist. He set the tumbler down and wiped his hand on the covers. "Really?"

She couldn't marry Wilton. Wilton was dull and worthy, comfortable and kind. Everything he was not. Wilton would crush her soul with respectability. Wilton wouldn't take her adventuring. Wilton wouldn't help her cross out a single item on her list. He'd frown and disapprove. Except for the one about the stupid feminine skills like knitting and crocheting. That one he'd like, the sanctimonious sod. Raven clamped his lips together. Heloise Hampden was Not. His. Problem.

Wilton wouldn't cherish her. He'd belittle her achievements. *He'd never make her come.*

The idea of another man even touching her was enough to

have him take another swig of brandy. He savored the burn in his throat and tamped down the urge to cut off Wilton's hands.

"Father wouldn't agree to it, anyway," Richard said, pouring them both a second drink.

"Why not? He's been telling her to marry someone exactly like Wilton for years. The boring old fart's an earl, isn't he?"

"It's not about titles or money. Father would let Heloise marry the tinker if she loved him. But only if the tinker loved her back."

"Ah," Raven managed.

"She doesn't want Wilton, and he couldn't handle her, in any case. She'd walk all over him. God knows, the girl would try the patience of a saint."

Raven raised his glass in a mocking toast. "Amen to that."

Richard met his eyes, his gaze direct and shrewd. "You're no saint. But it's you she wants."

For half a heartbeat Raven stilled. And then he forced his glass to his lips and took a deep swallow. "I'm not the man for her."

Richard shrugged. "I think you're exactly the man for her. Who else should she have? A drunken wastrel like Collingham? A fortune-hunting fop who cares more about the fit of his coat than about her?"

"I'm not offering for her. I'm doing her a favor. She can do much better than me."

"That's true. Besides, if you offered for her, she'd probably just think you were asking out of a misplaced sense of duty."

"I don't want to get married. Ever."

Richard's eyes twinkled in amusement. "That's exactly what Heloise said the other day, so you're undoubtedly safe. As far as I'm aware, no one's ever persuaded her to do anything she doesn't want to."

Raven narrowed his eyes. "Forget it, Richard. Now go away."

"Don't you want to know who your visitor is?"

Raven bit back a curse. He'd forgotten all about that. "If it's not Hellcat, who is it?"

Richard's smile widened. "Your esteemed grandfather."

Raven sank back into the pillows with a groan. "Oh bloody hell. What does he want?"

That was just typical of the sneaky old buzzard, taking advantage of the only moment of weakness he'd had in the last few years. Raven was in no physical shape to either physically eject him from the house, or to escape himself.

"The same thing he's wanted for the past six years, I expect," Richard said. "Your forgiveness. A reconciliation. Although I quite understand why you hate him so much. The bastard does want you give you thousands of pounds and the title of marquis." His mouth curled at his own sarcasm. "How utterly unreasonable."

"It's not as simple as that and you know it."

"I know he's a wily old devil, just like you. And I think he's doing whatever he can to make amends for past mistakes."

Raven closed his eyes, suddenly exhausted. He knew exactly what Heloise would say about the matter. She'd tell him to let go of the past and forgive his grandfather. But then, she was so much more merciful than Raven was.

Richard smiled an evil smile. "I'll tell him to come up, shall I?"

CHAPTER 42

"Your grandfather, sir," a footman intoned.

Raven didn't bother to bite back a curse. Instead he took the opportunity to study the figure that entered the room. There was no doubt that they were related. It was like looking at an older image of himself; the same green eyes, same straight nose. The duke's hair was gray now, but still, the similarities were undeniable.

"To what do I owe the pleasure of your esteemed company, sir?"

The Duke of Avondale's mouth curved into a cynical smile that Raven had seen reflected in his own mirror a thousand times. "My doctor recently suggested that bracing coastal weather might be beneficial to my health."

"Ah. The condition of your health is always a subject that interests me greatly."

His grandfather acknowledged the acidic double-edged politeness with an inclination of the head. "Indeed. I heard you were indisposed from my good friend Castlereagh."

He seemed supremely indifferent to the animosity rolling off Raven.

"I've no need of a nursemaid. It's too late to act concerned about my welfare now."

The old man crossed the room, leaning heavily on his gold-topped cane. He sat next to the bed, in the chair Richard had vacated. His eyes met Raven's. "I am sorry for what happened, William. More than you will ever know."

Raven turned his head away and stared blankly out the window. "I don't care. I don't want your apology, I want you to leave."

"Have you never done something in the heat of the moment that you bitterly regretted afterward?" the duke asked softly. "Something you'd do anything in your power to take back, if you could."

Raven squeezed his eyes shut. He wished he could close his ears, too, to block out the patient, reasonable words. Damn him. He thought of Heloise, of the way he'd treated her. Shame rolled through him, so acute he winced. He'd acted in anger and jealousy and fear, and hurt the one person he'd sworn to protect. Even worse, unlike his grandfather, he'd done it with full knowledge of the pain he was inflicting.

"Go away."

His grandfather ignored the command. "I've had six years to regret what happened when you were kidnapped, William. I was proud and stubborn and I didn't want some criminal bastard to have the upper hand over me. So instead of agreeing to his demands I hired my own men to find you. But they took too long. I should have just paid the ransom and had you back again, and to hell with the money and my pride. I'm sorry."

Raven couldn't bring himself to speak. He stared at the clouds scudding across the sky beyond the wavy panes of glass.

The duke sighed. "I have something for you."

From the corner of his eye Raven saw him rest his cane against the bed and remove a gold signet ring from his left hand.

He placed it on the coverlet by Raven's hip, careful not to touch him.

"That was your father's. He gave it to your mother as an engagement ring. Every Marquis of Ormonde has worn it, for over three hundred years. It's yours. Even if you still refuse to accept the title." A hint of humor warmed his voice. "Perhaps you'll have need of it, too."

That startled Raven enough to turn his head. "How so, sir?"

The duke regarded him shrewdly. "Lord Hampden once told me that he'd accept nothing less than a royal duke for his brilliant daughter. But royal dukes are so thin on the ground these days. I do believe he'd settle for a mere marquis. However disreputable." The green eyes twinkled. "Provided the marquis loved his daughter, of course."

Raven met the old man's gaze squarely. "I have no plans to marry, Your Grace."

The old man rose stiffly to his feet and made his way to the door. "Don't be as great a fool as I was, William."

Raven closed his eyes as the door clicked shut. He and his grandfather were so alike, much as it galled him to admit it. He'd sworn never to feel sympathy, compassion, or understanding for the old man. But Heloise's damned altruism must have been rubbing off on him. His grandfather was only human. He'd made a mistake, just as Raven had.

A knock at the door interrupted such dangerously merciful thoughts. Manvers, Raven's inscrutable valet, entered with his customary lack of fuss.

"I have located that poem you requested, my lord. It took a little time, but I have it here." He handed Raven a slim leather-bound volume.

"Thank you, Manvers. That will be all."

Raven settled himself more comfortably against the pillows and inspected the cover. It was a collection of poems by the Civil War poet and soldier Richard Lovelace. He flicked to the page marked with a ribbon. Ah, there it was. He'd recalled snatches of this damn poem the entire time he'd been imprisoned. It was entitled, aptly enough, 'To Althea from prison.' He read the last stanza. The poem had been written over two hundred years ago, but the poet's thoughts had mirrored his own exactly.

Stone Walls do not a Prison make,
Nor Iron bars a Cage;
Minds innocent and quiet take
That for an Hermitage.
If I have freedom in my Love,
And in my soul am free,
Angels alone, that soar above,
Enjoy such Liberty.

Raven gazed at the printed lines until they blurred before his eyes and the truth hit him with the force of a blow. Loving Heloise wasn't bondage. Loving her was freedom.

The blood rushed in his ears. He'd always left women before they had the chance to leave him, before he became attached to them. It avoided the risk of being hurt, or disappointed, as he'd been with his grandfather. The idea of permanence, of being tied down to one place and one person was utterly terrifying. But if that person was Heloise, and the place was by her side? That was another matter entirely.

He'd been such a coward, afraid to reach for her. Afraid to willingly accept the ties of love and give his heart over to her keeping. He shook his head. She was his. No other man would put his hands on her. He'd been her first, dammit. He was going to be her last. Her *only.*

The rightness of that sank deep into his bones and Raven let out a choked laugh. He wasn't good enough for her, but God, people in life never got what they deserved, did they? Sinners won the lottery, and good, kind men like Tony died young.

Heloise was stubborn, infuriating, and altogether too

provocative for his peace of mind. Damned if he was going to let her make *someone else's* life miserable.

His grandfather was right. She deserved to be a wife of a marquis, not a disreputable smuggler spy. He'd accused her of cowardice for shutting herself away with her translations and codes, but wasn't that exactly what he'd been doing, too? He'd used his drive for justice as an excuse for never staying in one place too long, a way of avoiding roots and responsibilities. To reject his father's titles and position was an insult to the memory of his parents, an insult to everything he could be.

He felt the weight of it all then, the responsibilities of his position, and realized with a start of surprise that he *wanted* those claims upon his heart. Heloise was his anchor, the kite string that kept him tethered. He shook his head again. Perhaps that bullet really had disordered his brain. Who'd have thought he'd ever choose bonds? But for her? Anything. He'd dedicate the rest of his life to trying to be worthy of her.

He sat up straighter, ignoring the pain in his thigh, and rang the bell. Manvers appeared almost immediately.

"Yes, my lord?"

"I need paper, pen, and ink. And tell my grandfather to stay. He's going to help me host a ball. In two weeks time."

Manvers's inscrutable expression showed no hint of what was undoubtedly his inner turmoil at hearing such news. "Another ball, my lord? So soon after the last?"

Raven smiled at the subtle reprimand. "Not a masked ball this time, Manvers. This will be an entirely more sedate affair."

Manvers bowed, his patrician features softening ever-so-slightly. "I am relieved to hear it, my lord. It shall be done."

CHAPTER 43

The company of Miss Heloise Hampden is requested by his Grace the Duke of Avondale and his grandson, the Marquis of Ormonde, at a ball to honor of the wounded heroes of Waterloo.

Heloise snagged a flute of champagne from a passing servant and took a deep swallow. Parties were no fun if you'd been invited.

She squeezed herself behind a marble pillar and tried to block out the buzz of conversation all around. Coming here had been a mistake of epic proportions; she was in no mood to socialize. She wanted to hit things. Break things. Moreover, she was sick and tired of hearing how bloody *wonderful* Lord Ravenwood was.

Ravenwood had set up a charitable trust to support wounded veterans.

Ravenwood had healed the rift with his grandfather.

Ravenwood was the matrimonial catch of the decade.

Heloise gave a derisive snort. For years the ton had given him up as a lost cause. But apparently a little philanthropy and a lavish cold buffet was all that was needed to forgive a decade's worth of scandal and neglect. The hypocrisy made her ill.

This joint ball with his grandfather was as clear a public

declaration of their rapprochement as an advertisement in the *Times*. And despite the ridiculously late notice, the cream of society had flocked to attend, all desperate to see it for themselves.

Heaven only knew why Raven had suddenly decided to forgive his grandfather now, after all this time. She doubted it had anything to do with her lectures on the subject.

She took another long swig of champagne. And speaking of neglect, why hadn't he—? No. She wasn't going to think about him. It hurt her chest. She was ice. Marble. Other neutral, inert things. Ravenwood could go to the devil.

For the past few weeks she'd managed to retreat into a blissful isolation, a muffled cocoon where nothing could touch her. She'd been numb and protected; no pain or strong emotions. But it hadn't lasted. Anger had crept through her defenses, catching her out when she least expected it.

The rational part of her brain reasoned that she should be grateful to Raven for showing her an adventure, for giving her the opportunity to prove herself. She'd vanquished her fear of water, was proud that she'd risen to the challenge.

But he'd also shown her the heights of pleasure her body could achieve, and it would have been better not to know. She would have preferred to exist in blissful ignorance. She couldn't imagine any other man touching her as Raven had. The idea brought a wave of disgust.

And then his summons to this ball had come, and her heart had kicked back into painful, pulsing life. She'd missed him the past three weeks, missed him with an ache in her chest: his lazy smile, his company, his teasing. His presence. The way he only had to look at her to make her hot and shivery.

The crowd here tonight was very different from that at the masquerade. Heloise was pleased to see a goodly number of elderly matrons, dowagers, and wallflowers present. She *liked* wallflowers. After she'd received her scar she'd made a point of talking to girls she'd barely noticed before. Not the beautiful ones. The shy ones, the plain ones. And she'd discovered that they generally had far more interesting things to say than the beautiful girls. Ugly girls couldn't rely on their looks to snare a husband; they had to cultivate humor, wit, and intelligence instead. She was glad Raven had invited them.

She cast her gaze up at the ceiling and found Hades and Persephone among the painted throng. She narrowed her eyes. Traitorous Persephone didn't seem to be struggling all that hard. Heloise sighed. Perhaps she was tired of living with her mother. Perhaps she, too, craved a little darkness in which to hide.

Richard sidled up, champagne glass in hand. "A penny for your thoughts?"

Heloise lowered her eyes from the ceiling. "Lord Wilton just proposed again. I'm debating whether to accept him."

Richard sipped his drink. "No you're not. You'd be bored to tears within days."

Heloise bit her lip. It was hard to argue with facts.

"Besides," Richard continued, "how can you consider marrying Wilton when you're in love with Raven?"

All the blood leeched from her face.

"You've been in love with him for years," he said gently. "We've all known it."

Heloise ignored the aching tightness in her throat and raised her chin. "So? Raven doesn't even want to *see* me, let alone marry me."

"He doesn't want you to see him laid low with injury. Male pride."

"That's ridiculous. I saw him right after he'd been shot in the head. You can't get much lower than that."

Richard shrugged. "That's men for you."

Heloise let out a deep huff and scanned the room. "Have you even seen him tonight? Am I the only one who thinks it odd that the host isn't here?" She waved her hand in a dismissing gesture.

"No, of course not. It's Raven. He can do whatever he likes—even fail to attend his own party."

Richard slanted her an amused glance.

Heloise raised her shoulder. "It's of no interest to me what he does in his own house."

"Of course not," Richard echoed dryly. "So what do you think of his plans to open a hospital for veterans, then?"

Heloise wholeheartedly approved the principle. Just not the scheme's author. There had been a huge influx of ex-soldiers following Waterloo, men like Sergeant Mullaney who'd defended their country, for whom no provision had been made. They should be honored, not treated like vermin and left to beg on the streets. At least Raven was using his unwanted inheritance for something worthwhile. Still, one good act was not enough to blot out a lifetime of sin.

"The man's a paragon of virtue. I don't want to talk about him. What are you up to? Still trying to track down Philippe Lacorte?"

Richard clenched his jaw. His inability to locate the brilliant French forger had been bothering him for months.

"The man's as elusive as smoke. But don't worry, I'll get him. Sooner or later."

His determined look made Heloise smile. Richard was as stubborn as she. She had no doubt he'd get his man eventually.

She turned and for a split second her heart stopped beating. An older version of Raven was crossing the room toward her, leaning slightly on a gold-topped cane.

Richard nodded in welcome. "Raven's grandfather, the Duke of Avondale."

Heloise sank into a deep, automatic curtsy as the man stopped in front of her. "Your Grace."

The duke raised his quizzing glass and studied her as she straightened. His hair was gray beneath his wig, and his clothes, though unadorned, were of the highest quality. Next to Richard's broad-shouldered frame, he seemed slight, but he studied her with eyes as startlingly green and shrewd as his grandson's.

"Miss Hampden." He smiled with a slight bow. "It is an honor to make your acquaintance at last. I have heard a great deal about you from my good friend Castlereagh. He says you are invaluable."

Heloise flushed. "Thank you."

He nodded, as if he approved of what he saw. "And you survived three whole weeks in the company of my grandson. You have both my congratulations and my condolences. Knowing his temperament as I do, I can only assume it must have been an extremely trying time for you." The hint of a smile twitched the corner of his mouth and a wicked twinkle entered his eye. "And yet you appear to have emerged remarkably unscathed."

Heloise's mouth curved in an answering smile. "I endured it, my lord," she said demurely. "It was certainly . . . an adventure."

"I am delighted to hear it. My grandson is very fond of adventures. Do enjoy the evening, Miss Hampden."

He bowed and stalked off just as Raven's valet, Manvers, appeared at her shoulder with a small silver tray. He offered it forward to her with a slight cough.

"From Lord Ravenwood, ma'am."

Heloise glanced down. On the tray sat a single, ripe pomegranate.

Her heart slammed against her ribs. What did he mean by this? The swine had ignored her for the past three weeks. Was it a challenge? A summons? Trust Raven to be both provocative and frustratingly enigmatic at the same time.

"Did Lord Ravenwood wish you to convey any message with this?"

"No, ma'am."

Manvers's face was as impassive as ever, but Heloise thought she could detect the faintest hint of a mischievous twinkle in his slate gray eyes. "I do believe he expressed an intention to retire to his chamber."

Her face heated, but she exchanged her empty champagne glass for the fruit and managed to nod, as if she'd been expecting just such a bizarre gift in the middle of a ballroom. "Thank you, Manvers."

Richard raised his eyebrows and Heloise felt her skin flush even more. She glanced up at the balcony, sure she'd find Raven watching her, but he was nowhere to be seen.

"And I thought ladies liked *flowers*," Richard said. "Remind me to stock up on exotic produce the next time I want to get a girl's attention." He nudged her shoulder with his own. "Looks like he's willing to see you now."

Heloise swallowed a sudden flurry of panic. "I suppose so."

Richard gave her another nudge and his eyes crinkled at the corners. "So what are you waiting for?"

Heloise pushed through the overcrowded rooms, dodging servants and guests. Her whole body tingled with a sense of urgency, of anticipation. Raven, the beast, knew she could be summoned by such a tantalizing lure. She *had* to know what he meant by it. The possibilities and connotations made her heart pound.

She reached the main staircase, ran lightly up the stairs, and raced down the hallway, toward Raven's private suite, glad she didn't encounter anyone else. The noise of the party grew dimmer as she ventured deeper into the house and the thick runner muffled the sounds of her slippers. By the time she skidded to a stop in front of his door she was out of breath. Her hair was coming down from its pins and the hand that clutched the pomegranate was clammy.

She paused, suddenly unsure. No strip of light showed beneath the door. What if Manvers had been wrong? She tried the handle, expecting it to be locked, but it swung open. She stepped inside.

The room was in shadow. No candles had been lit; only the embers of a fire glowed in the grate. Her spirits dipped in anticlimax. He wasn't here. She turned, suddenly desperate to get away, but a movement in the shadows stopped her dead.

"Stay."

Raven stood at the window, looking out at the dark gardens. He'd removed his jacket; the pale moonlight outlined his broad shoulders and slim waist and when he turned to her the fire glow laved the angle of his cheek and the straight line of his jaw.

Heloise let her hand drop from the doorknob and just stood there, tongue-tied and stupid. He stalked forward and reached past without touching her, just a faint disturbance in the air, then closed the door and turned the key in the lock.

He took the pomegranate from her nerveless fingers and placed it gently on the bedside table, then casually unbuttoned the silver studs at his wrists. He placed them on the side table then loosened his cravat, tugged it off, and laid it carefully over the back of the armchair by the fire. Then he shrugged out of his shirt.

He still hadn't looked at her.

Heloise couldn't look away. Her eyes drank in the sight of him, roving his body to ensure his injuries had healed. The bandage was gone from his head, and there had been no sign of a limp when he'd crossed the room. Her pulse beat strongly in her throat as he withdrew a pistol and a knife from the small of his back and laid them next to the pomegranate. He sat on the edge of the bed. There was a metallic clatter as he picked something up and Heloise drew in a shocked breath as she recognized the handcuffs.

His eyes caught hers.

CHAPTER 44

*R*aven's heart was racing as if he'd just mounted the steps to the guillotine.

He snapped one end of the cuffs around his wrist and pushed down the spurt of panic that assailed him. The *snick* as they snapped shut sounded like the slam of a prison door; he kept his eyes fixed on her for courage. If he looked away from her he'd be lost.

Without breaking eye contact he attached the other end to the bedpost and leaned back against the headboard, forcing his reluctant muscles to obey. His skin felt too tight, every sinew screamed with tension. He'd rather swim naked across an alligator-infested swamp than do this, but it had to be done. He had to prove the depth of his love.

Heloise found her voice. "What are you doing?"

He managed to summon a faint, self-mocking smile. "Proving you're the only thing I've never wanted to escape from."

* * *

Heloise couldn't breathe.

What did he mean by that? Just because he didn't want to escape from her didn't mean he wanted her forever. But at least he was admitting he cared for her, which was more than he'd ever done before. Raven hated being trapped. And yet he'd voluntarily placed himself in the worst situation he could devise. For her.

A reluctant smile curved her lips. A normal man would have used soft words and flowers. Raven sent her strange fruit, locked them together in a darkened room, placed his weapons out of reach, and chained himself to a bed. Lunatic.

She swallowed the sudden tightness in her throat and aimed for a wry tone. "The fact that you need to attach yourself to a heavy piece of furniture to endure my presence is hardly flattering."

"I thought you might appreciate the gesture."

She adopted a pitying, superior expression. "I can't believe you actually trust me to release you. After all you did to me?" She glanced at his pistol on the nightstand. "I should shoot you right now and have done with it."

"I trust you," he said solemnly. "With my life."

Oh goodness.

Heloise took a step toward the bed. "This isn't the same situation at all, you know."

Raven's lips quirked. "You're right. I'm a *willing* prisoner." A hint of his usual wickedness returned as he raised his cuffed wrist a fraction for emphasis.

"Where's the key?"

He motioned across the room. "Over there, on the desk."

She nodded, but made no move to retrieve it. She'd spent the past three weeks moping around, alternating between righteous fury and abject misery. She wasn't letting him go until she'd made him suffer, just a little bit.

As if sensing her resolve, Raven eyed her warily as she approached the bed. When her knees hit the side she reached out and traced the veins on the inside of his exposed wrist with her fingertips. He hissed through his teeth and gave an involuntary jerk.

She traced up his arm to his shoulder, enjoying the way his muscles leaped and twitched under her gentle touch. She glanced at him from under her lashes. "I hate to say it, Ravenwood, but it sounds as if you can't live without me."

"I could live without you," he said. "I just wouldn't want to."

The room wavered and dimmed. She'd waited six long years to hear him say something like that, but now, after everything that had happened, it wasn't enough. She wanted more than a temporary carte blanche. Nothing less than complete surrender would do. He didn't have to live without her. He had to want to live *with* her. Permanently.

Heloise's pulse hammered in her throat. She'd spent the past few weeks trying to resign herself to a future that didn't include Raven. Now, suddenly, an entirely different possibility was within her grasp. Like that card in Elvira's tarot, she held the power to influence her own destiny. She just had to be brave enough to wield it.

She plucked the pomegranate from the side table and brandished it in front of his nose. "Why did you send me this?"

Raven glanced at it, then back up at her. "When Persephone's in the underworld it's winter up on the earth, right?"

She nodded. "It's not spring until she returns."

He gave a defiant shrug. "That's how it is with me. When you go, all the light goes, too."

A warm glow started deep within her body and expanded to fill her with a piercing joy. He loved her.

With shaking hands she broke open the pomegranate and tipped some of the jewel red seeds into the palm of her hand. She placed one between her lips. Raven's gaze fastened on her mouth and the naked hunger in his expression made her skin tingle. He raised his eyes to hers and she caught the challenge in his look.

"If you eat that you'll be stuck with me forever," he said softly.

She took the seed from her lips and pressed it between his own. "You first."

Heloise held her breath as Raven parted his lips and took both the seed and her finger into his mouth. She snatched her hand back with a gasp, and he bit down with an audible *crunch* and swallowed.

He raised his brows in unmistakable challenge. "Your turn."

She swallowed her own seed with an air of defiance. They were bound together now. This wordless communion sealed a covenant as solemn and sacred as vows spoken in church. God help him if he didn't mean it. She'd shoot him with his own pistols if he abandoned her.

"Hey, come back," Raven protested as she suddenly stepped away from the bed. He reached for her with his free hand but she skipped out of range.

"You're in no position to be making demands," she chided.

He shot her a mock-furious glare and she took a moment to study him in the dim light. He lay stretched out on the bed, long and lithe and powerful. Temptation in the flesh. A heady thrum of joy pulsed through her veins.

Raven's eyes widened as she kicked off her dancing slippers and reached round to undo the row of buttons at the back of her dress. "What are you doing?"

"What do you think I'm doing? I'm taking advantage of you, of course."

Her amber dress had only three buttons. She undid them, pushed the short puff sleeves down her arms, and let the dress fall to the ground in a graceful collapse. She undid the front lacing of her short stays, taking a relieved breath as the constriction on her ribs eased, then untied her petticoats and let them drop, too. She was left in just a scandalous rose silk chemise, and her stockings.

Raven hadn't said a word.

Heloise glanced down at herself, suddenly self-conscious. In the firelight the silk shimmered over the contours of her body like the petals of a rose.

Raven let out an unsteady breath, half laugh, half groan. "Christ, Hellcat. You're killing me." He eyed her approvingly. "Have I ever told you how much I appreciate your taste in undergarments?"

"Several times, I believe. You have my mother to thank."

He sent her a questioning look.

"She says one should always wear nice underwear because you never know when you might get run over by a carriage." Heloise smiled. "I'd have thought if you'd have more to worry about than whether your underwear was matching, but still." Heloise ground to a halt, uncomfortably aware she was babbling.

"I love your mother."

"She *is* French," she said, as if that were sufficient explanation. Which, to a man like Raven, a connoisseur of the European female, it probably was.

His gaze roved over her, as intimate as a caress. "Come here."

The mattress dipped with her weight as she crawled up it toward him.

"Be gentle," he teased.

She gave him an arch smile. "I promise not to torture you *too* much."

It was kiss like no other they'd shared. Heloise threw her arms around his neck and kissed him with all the ardor and enthusiasm in her heart. What started as a sweet exploration soon metamorphosed into an urgent mating of mouths. She couldn't get enough of the taste of him, the wicked swirl of his tongue, the passionate press of his lips. She offered herself unashamedly, teasing him, thrusting deep then retreating in passionate surrender.

He pulled back, panting. "Vixen."

Her hair had been arranged in an elaborate coil. Heloise sat back on her heels as he raised his free hand and gently pulled out a pin. A curl fell down against her neck. Another pin. Another. He worked slowly, methodically, until her hair fell down around her shoulders in a soft cloud. He threaded his fingers through it and combed it forward to cover her breasts. She shivered.

Heloise ran her palms over his shoulders, enjoying the reflexive leap of his muscles, luxuriating in the feel of him. She nibbled kisses on his collarbone, teethed the muscle on the side of his neck, and felt the racing pulse beneath his skin, heavy and erotic against her lips.

The metal cuff forced Raven's right arm out at an awkward angle, but he used his left hand to stroke down her back and squeeze her bottom and she let out a groan of encouragement. She stroked his biceps, his chest, petting him like a giant house cat. Instinct told her that whatever had felt good to her surely felt good to him, too. He bared his teeth when she circled his flat male nipples with her fingers and when she flicked her tongue over them he hissed in a breath and curled up toward her.

The muscles of his stomach tensed one by one as she slid her hand downward and ran a finger from his navel to the top of his waistband.

She smiled against his skin.

CHAPTER 45

*R*aven swallowed, his throat tight with excitement.

She was so beautiful; her brow furrowed in concentration as she explored his body, as immersed in the sensations as if she were studying a new, mystifying code.

He couldn't ask for more.

She toyed with the waistband of his breeches, then brushed her hand over the hard shape of him. His hips bucked off the bed. She lifted her eyes to his.

"Don't stop there," he rasped.

She popped open the buttons of his breeches. His cock sprang free and he raised his hips from the bed to help her as she drew down his breeches over his thighs and threw them to the floor. He lay naked in front of her, more vulnerable than he'd ever been in his life. He reached up with his free hand and caught her nape.

"Touch me," he ordered.

She obeyed. She closed her fingers around his shaft and the exquisite pressure made his eyes roll back in his head. He throbbed beneath her palm and groaned as she made a tentative slide, up and down. He arched up into her touch.

And then she leaned forward and took him in her mouth.

The sight of her lips closing around him had him bowing off the bed. Sweet heaven. Her untutored exploration was the most erotic thing he'd ever experienced in his life. Raven threaded his free hand through her hair and smoothed his thumb over the scar at her temple. She tensed, an almost imperceptible pause, then turned her face into his hand, accepting the caress.

She glanced up at him with a wicked, sparkling look from beneath her lashes.

"You're the expert," she whispered. "Now what shall I do?"

He lost himself in her thunderstorm eyes. "Take me," he whispered, breathing hard. "Do it, Hellcat. If you want me, take me now."

She placed her hands on his shoulders and straddled him. Her skin was flushed, her lips parted, as he used his free hand to position himself at the entrance to her body. She lowered herself down and her wet heat closed over him, barely an inch.

"More." He panted. He could hardly choke out the words, the sensation of her was so incredible. "Slowly. That's it."

He moved his hand to her hip to steady her, guide her, and watched her face as she bit her lip in concentration. She slid down further, and he saw stars. His hips arched upward automatically and he captured her mouth with his own, kissing her hard, merging his soul with hers. He caught her gasp as he filled her with a deep, swift stroke that slid him fully home.

He paused, afraid he'd hurt her, but she rose up and slid down on him again with a moan of delight.

Light filled him, seeping through his veins, banishing the darkness and leaving only glowing pleasure in its wake. His heart was beating as if he'd run a race. Need pounded through his bloodstream, roaring in his ears, demanding he take. And take and take. He wanted to roll her over and get on top, but the metal cuff prevented him. He concentrated on her instead. Her breasts on his chest, hard-tipped and perfect, her lips on his, her hands clutching his shoulders, her legs tight around his hips as he drove into her again with a guttural cry.

She threw her head back in abandon. Her long hair brushed his thighs. His mind went blank. She wiped his soul clean, burned him away until they were nothing but bodies, his and hers, hot and sliding, pumping deep. Nothing but the feel of her all around him, inside him, as he was inside her. She filled his heart, his soul. So deep there was no getting her out.

He heard her gasp in pleasure and began to quicken the rhythm of his strokes. She rocked her hips, drawing him deeper; he felt her inner muscles clutching him and her climax triggered his own. He surrendered to it, felt the pulse of him flowing into her, and he cried out, savage and triumphant, falling, dissolving and being reborn.

Heloise collapsed onto him, panting and limp. After a few moments she let out a shaky laugh and rolled onto the bed next to him.

Raven sat up, the handcuffs clinking against the wooden post. He'd lost all feeling in his right arm and had nearly pulled his shoulder out of its socket, but it had been worth it.

He jiggled his arm. "Let me out of these. Please."

Heloise slipped out of bed and padded across the room to the desk. "Is this what you're after?" she teased, holding up the key.

Raven eyed the slim perfection of her naked body, pale and sleek in the fireglow. "It's *exactly* what I'm after," he growled.

She came back to him and slid the key into the lock. The metal fell away and he rubbed his wrist. His fingers tingled with returning circulation and there were raw red marks on his skin, but he didn't care. He'd never imagined he could give himself so completely to another person. But surrendering control to Heloise was a pleasure, not a punishment.

He gathered her into his arms, tucked her head beneath his chin, and drew the covers over them both. She let out a long, contented sigh.

CHAPTER 46

"*C*ome on, get up. We're going."

Heloise blinked at the pale light filtering in the window and stifled a groan.

Raven slid out of bed and she took a moment to appreciate the sight of him naked as he crossed the room. It was still barely dawn, but she could see broad shoulders, narrow hips, muscled thighs. She could have looked at him forever. She added an extra line to her list. "Make love to Raven in full daylight." Her pulse quickened.

She bit back a sigh of disappointment as he shrugged into his breeches.

"Get dressed," he urged impatiently. He tossed her dress at her and she caught it with a huff of indignation.

"Where are we going?"

"It's a surprise."

There was something extremely intimate about having a man help one dress, Heloise decided. Raven's long fingers tied tapes and fastened buttons with deft speed and she smiled as he dropped playful kisses on the nape of her neck.

Then he caught her hand and led her out into the corridor,

down the grand staircase, through the deserted ballroom, and to the hall. Heloise gave a choked sound of protest as he opened the front door and pulled her outside, but he simply tugged on her hand and stalked across the dew-wet grass.

Her silk ball slippers became instantly soaked but Heloise laughed aloud at the mad, thrilling chase. She followed him across the gardens, skirts blowing, out of breath, heart singing with joy. "What are you doing, you madman?" she panted.

He guided her down the steps cut into the cliff and Heloise followed him up the gangplank of the ship with a smile. "I can't help noticing that you've kidnapped me again, William Raven-wood," she scolded.

"This is the last time, I swear. Come here."

Raven drew her over to the rail and positioned himself behind her, looking out to sea. He pulled her back against his chest.

Heloise caught her breath as the sun broke free of the horizon in a blaze of peach and gold. Raven rested his chin on the top of her head and pointed into the distance. "Africa's over there. Egypt. The Nile. Cairo and Alexandria and all those dusty tombs and ghastly pyramids you seem to be so in love with."

"I know that."

"Do you want to go?"

Heloise tilted her head so she could look at him, her pulse beating hard in her throat. "To Egypt? With you?"

He frowned. "Of course with me. Who else?"

She hid a smile at his exasperation, even as her heart swelled. She furrowed her brow and feigned indecision. "I don't know. You'll probably try to sell me to a band of pirates or swap me for a herd of camels and a nice Heriz rug . . ."

"Do you want to go?" he repeated, his tone subtly threatening.

A gust of wind caught the sails behind them. The impatient snap of sailcloth and rattle of brass fittings were a siren's call, impossible to resist. Her stomach fluttered in anticipation.

"I might get seasick."

"I've had a whole crate of pink gin put in the cabin already."

"I hear it's terribly hot."

She could swear he was grinding his teeth.

"I'll buy you a hat. And a fan."

She adopted her most prim and proper expression. "Just think of the scandal."

"I don't give a damn about the scandal, and neither do you."

"That's because you have no reputation to lose," she admonished sternly.

"The way I see it, you have two options. I can either kill you . . ."

"Or—?" she prompted.

"Or you can marry me."

His offhand declaration was hardly the gushing proposal she'd dreamed of as a girl, but she could feel his tension in the tightness of his muscled forearms around her.

He honestly thought she might refuse him. He was such an idiot.

She tossed her head. He deserved to suffer just a little bit. "Death it is, then. I'm sure you can make it quick and painless."

He glanced at her and away. "Marriage to me would be neither quick nor painless, you know." A muscle ticked in his jaw. "I can't promise not to hurt you. In fact, I'm sure I will. I won't mean to, but it's inevitable. And you'll hurt me." He sighed. "But that's what bloody love is, isn't it? It's giving someone the power to hurt you and trusting in your heart that they won't."

Heloise studied the profile of his half-turned face. The molten glow of sunrise touched his hair and illuminated the fine grain of his jaw and her heart swelled with love for such an impossible, wonderful man.

"Well?" he said gruffly. "Is it yes or no?"

She waited until he finally plucked up the courage to look at her. "That would depend."

"On what?"

"On whether you love me." Her voice trembled as she gazed up at him. "Because I've loved you for so long I couldn't bear it if you didn't love me back."

He closed his eyes and she couldn't tell if it was exasperation or relief.

"Do I love you?" he growled. "Of course I bloody love you! I love you when you tease, and when you're brave, and when you cry. I even loved you when you ate that stupid carob, and when you nearly got me killed."

He turned her in his arms, caught her chin, and stared deeply into her eyes. "I want your light. Your goodness. Your warmth. I want everything that you are. I will love you until the day I die, and probably long after that. Only an idiot would even have to ask."

"I'm not an idiot," she said.

"So you'll marry me." He made it a statement, not a question.

Heloise sighed, as if it were an enormous imposition. "Well, if I *must*. But only to avert a scandal. And because I want to get my hands on your enormously impressive . . . library."

All the tension drained out of him and his eyes took on a teasing glint. "Of course. What woman could resist something so monumental?"

Heloise was laughing as he lowered his lips to hers.

When they finally pulled apart Raven chuckled. "You're doing my home a grave disservice, you know. Ravenwood has plenty of other rooms, in addition to the impressive library."

"How many?"

"Sixty-eight, give or take a closet or two." He nuzzled her neck. "I'm going to make love to you in every one of them."

She smiled against his shoulder. "That's an awful lot."

"It is. We'll start as soon as we get back from Egypt. If we can manage two per day we should be finished by March next year."

"You are a rogue and a scoundrel."

"Yes," he said unrepentantly. "But I'm yours."

EPILOGUE

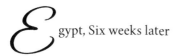 gypt, Six weeks later

"Time for a break, Lady Ravenwood."

Heloise sighed as her husband of exactly three weeks came up behind her and nuzzled her neck.

"Five more minutes," she murmured, blowing sand from a hieroglyphic fragment. "I really think I'm—"

Her protest was cut off as he slipped his hand into the front of her loose bodice. She gave a yelp of surprise then softened against him as a sweep of languid heat suffused her.

He smiled against her nape. "Have I told you how much I approve of these loose-fitting clothes? They allow such wonderful access."

He spun her around, lowered his head, and kissed the top curve of her breast. They both groaned in pleasure. Heloise attempted a token protest as he lifted her up to sit on the sun-warmed block of granite and settled himself between her thighs.

She leaned back as he tugged the linen shirt from the waistband of her loose trousers and ran his hands up her ribs.

"Raven, we can't! Anyone one might come along!"

He dropped a leisurely kiss on her collarbone. "I've sent all the servants back to the ship."

"Someone else might come!"

"I don't care. You can blame these trousers you're wearing. They're worse than breeches. While you've been scrambling around, I've been forced to watch your bottom wriggling about in a most provocative manner."

Heloise let her head fall back. The past few weeks had been a revelation. He'd taught her so much. About her body, and pleasure. And love.

They'd left straight after their hastily planned wedding and in the past week alone Heloise had crossed off every remaining item on her original list. Raven had taken advantage of a deserted beach on one of the Greek islands to take her swimming in the ocean at midnight. Naked. It had been the most extraordinary, wickedly liberating sensation imaginable. And when her list had been exhausted, her outrageous husband had formulated an entirely new, decidedly more scandalous, one. He was coming up with new additions daily.

Egypt had been everything she'd imagined, and more. She'd seen Bedouins and Tuaregs, snake charmers and souks, spices and dates. She'd held her nose at the stink of the tanneries, covered her ears against the din of metalworkers hammering brassware in the streets, and punched Raven in the kidneys for pretending to exchange her for a nice Heriz rug.

Even the wonderful illustrations in the *Description de l'Égypte* hadn't done justice to the still-bright colors of wall paintings and temples over two thousand years old. Heloise was in love with everything, even the reluctant camels—which were more woolly, like a lamb, than hairy like a horse—and were always grumbling and sneezing and spitting. The flies were a constant nuisance, the sand scoured her face, and the midday sun was unbearably hot, but she wouldn't have changed it for the world. The discomfort was more than a fair exchange for freedom.

"You know we're going to have to go home eventually, don't you?" she murmured.

Raven paused in the act of pushing down her bodice. "Yes. But not just yet."

"That sounds as if you have a plan."

His grin made her stomach somersault, as usual, and she wondered if she'd ever grow immune to his charm. She hoped not.

"I never make plans. Plans are for people—"

"—with no imagination," she finished. "Yes, I know."

"I have an *excellent* imagination, Lady Ravenwood." He kissed her, long and deep. When he resurfaced he said, "I'm going to retire from field work, now that I have a wife."

She smiled. "I should hope so. I'd be extremely cross if you went and got yourself killed now you've finally realized you love me. You've endured more than enough injuries on behalf of King and Country. Besides, scrabbling around in back alleyways is undignified and no suitable position for a man who will one day be a duke."

He made a disgruntled face. "Castlereagh wants to retire. He's looking for someone to take over as head of the network . . ."

She patted his chest. "There you go, then."

"It's not going to be easy, accepting the responsibilities of a dukedom, either," he said, kissing her ear.

"I know. That's the thing about power. It's a poisoned chalice. The Ancient Egyptians had a riddle about it."

"Of course they did," he groaned.

" 'What's sweeter than honey and more bitter than bile? The office of vizier.' " Heloise put her hand up to his face and stroked his cheek. "But we'll do it together. You're not alone. Not anymore."

He turned his face and kissed the inside of her wrist. "I think our first official party when we get back home should be a masked ball. What do you think?"

"If you wish. We already have the masks."

He looked at her in feigned amazement. "What's this? Acquiescence? Actual obedience? I think I need to sit down!"

Heloise shot him a demure smile. "I'm extremely agreeable when it comes to doing things I *want* to do."

"Let's test that theory, shall we? Kiss me again, Lady Ravenwood."

"Yes, my lord. With pleasure."

ABOUT THE AUTHOR

Kate Bateman, also writing as K. C. Bateman, is the #1 Amazon bestselling author of Regency and Renaissance historical romances, including *To Steal a Heart, A Raven's Heart and A Counterfeit Heart*. Her Renaissance romp, *The Devil To Pay* was a 2019 RITA award finalist.

She's also an auctioneer and fine art appraiser, the co-founder and director of Bateman's Auctioneers, a fine art and antiques auction house in the UK. She currently lives in Illinois with her husband and three inexhaustible children, but returns to England regularly to appear as an antiques expert on several popular BBC television shows, each of which reach up to 2.5 million viewers.

Kate loves to hear from readers. Contact her via her website: www.kcbateman.com and sign up for her newsletter to receive regular updates on new releases, giveaways and exclusive excerpts.

ALSO BY K. C. BATEMAN / KATE BATEMAN

Secrets & Spies Series:
To Steal a Heart
A Raven's Heart
A Counterfeit Heart

The Devil To Pay

Bow Street Bachelors Series:
This Earl Of Mine
To Catch An Earl
The Princess & The Rogue (Coming December 2020)

Novellas:
The Promise of A Kiss
A Midnight Clear

FOLLOW

Follow Kate online for the latest new releases, giveaways, exclusive sneak peeks, and more! You can find her at:

Amazon
Barnes & Noble
Apple Ibooks
Kobo
Google Play

Join Kate's FB group: Badasses in Bodices

Sign ip for Kate's monthly-ish newsletter via her website for news, exclusive excerpts and giveaways.

Follow both K.C. Bateman and Kate Bateman on Bookbub for new releases and sales.

Add Kate's books to your Goodreads lists, or leave a review!

SNEAK PEEK

Read on for a sneak peek of the next exhilarating historical
romance in K. C. Bateman's Secrets and Spies series
A Counterfeit Heart . . .

A COUNTERFEIT HEART

hapter 1

Bois de Vincennes, Paris, March 1816.

It didn't take long to burn a fortune.

"Don't throw it on like that! Fan the paper out. You need to let the air get to it."

Sabine de la Tour sent her best friend Anton Carnaud an exasperated glance and tossed another bundle of banknotes onto the fire. It smoldered then caught with a bright flare, curling and charring to nothing in an instant. "That's all the francs. Pass me some rubles."

Another fat wad joined the conflagration. Little spurts of green and blue jumped up as the flames consumed the ink. The intensity of the fire heated her cheeks so she stepped back and tilted her head to watch the glowing embers float up into the night sky.

It was a fitting end, really. Almost like a funeral pyre, the most damning evidence of Philippe Lacorte, notorious French counterfeiter, going up in smoke. Sabine quelled the faintest twinge of regret and glanced over at Anton. "It feels strange, don't you think? Doing the right thing for once."

He shook his head. "It feels wrong." He poked a pile of Austrian gulden into the fire with a stick. "Who in their right mind burns money? It's like taking a penknife to a Rembrandt."

Sabine nudged his shoulder, well used to his grumbling. "You know I'm right. If we spend it, we'll be no better than Napoleon. This is our chance to turn over a new leaf."

Anton added another sheaf of banknotes to the blaze with a pained expression. "I happen to like being a criminal," he grumbled. "Besides, we made all this money. Seems only fair we should get to spend it. No one would know. Your fakes are so good nobody can tell the difference. What's a few million francs in the grand scheme of things?"

"We'd know," Sabine frowned at him. "'Truth is the highest thing that man may keep.'"

Anton rolled his eyes. "Don't start quoting dead Greeks at me."

"That's a dead Englishman," she smiled wryly. "Geoffrey Chaucer."

Anton sniffed, unimpressed by anything that came from the opposite—and therefore wrong—side of the channel. He sprinkled a handful of assignats onto the flames. "You appreciate the irony of trying to be an honest forger, don't you?"

It was Sabine's turn to roll her eyes.

Anton shot her a teasing, pitying glance. "It's because you're half-Anglais. Everyone knows the English are mad. The French half of you knows what fun we could have. Think of it, chérie—ballgowns, diamonds, banquets!" His eyes took on a dreamy, faraway glow. "Women, wine, song!" He gave a magnificent Gallic shrug. "Mais, non. You listen to the English half. The half that is boring and dull and—"

"—law-abiding?" Sabine suggested tartly. "Sensible? The half that wants to keep my neck firmly attached to my shoulders instead of in a basket in front of the guillotine?"

She bit her lip as a wave of guilt assailed her. Anton was only in danger of losing his head because of her. For years he'd protected her identity by acting as Philippe Lacorte's public representative. He'd dealt with all the unsavory characters who'd wanted her forger's skills while she'd remained blissfully anonymous. Even the man who'd overseen the Emperor's own counterfeiting operation, General Jean Malet, hadn't known the real name of the elusive forger he'd employed. He'd never seen Sabine as anything more than an attractive assistant at the print shop in Rue Pélican.

Now, with Napoleon exiled on St Helena and Savary, head of the Secret Police, also banished, General Malet was the only one who knew about the existence of the fake fortune the Emperor had amassed to fill his coffers.

The fortune Sabine had just 'liberated'.

Anton frowned into the flames. The pink glow highlighted his chiseled features and Sabine studied him dispassionately. She knew him too well to harbor any romantic feelings about him, but there was no doubt he had a very handsome profile. Unfortunately, it was a profile that General Malet could recognize all too easily.

As if reading her mind he said, "Speaking of guillotines, Malet would gladly see me in a tumbril. He's out for blood. And I'm his prime suspect."

"Which is why we're getting you out of here," Sabine said briskly. "The boat to England leaves at dawn. We have enough money to get us as far as London."

Anton gave a frustrated huff and pointed at the fire. "In case you hadn't noticed, we have a pile of money right—"

She shot him a warning scowl. "No. We are not using the fakes. It's high time we started doing things legally. This English lord's been trying to engage Lacorte's services for months. One job for him and we'll be able to pay for your passage to Boston. You'll be safe from Malet forever."

"It could be a trap," Anton murmured darkly. "This Lovell says he wants to employ Lacorte, but we've been on opposite sides of the war for the past ten years. The English can't be trusted."

Sabine let out a faint, frustrated sigh. It was a risk, to deliver herself into the arms of the enemy, to seek out the one man she'd spent months avoiding. Her heart beat in her throat at the thought of him. Richard Hampden, Viscount Lovell. She'd only seen him once, weeks ago, but the memory was seared upon her brain.

He, of anyone, had come closest to unmasking her. He'd followed Lacorte's trail right to her doorstep, like a bloodhound after a fox. She'd barely had time to hide behind the back-room door and press her eye to a gap in the wood before the bell above the entrance had tinkled and he'd entered the print shop.

It had been dark outside; the flickering street lamps had cast long shadows along Rue Pélican. Sabine had squinted, trying to make out his features, but all she could see was that he was tall; he ducked to enter the low doorway. She raised her eyebrows. So this was the relentless Lord Lovell.

Not for the first time she cursed her short-sightedness. Too many hours of close-work meant that anything over ten feet was frustratingly blurry. He moved closer, further into the shop—and into knee-weakening, stomach-flipping focus.

Sabine caught her breath. All the information she'd gleaned about her foe from Anton's vague, typically male attempts at description had in no way prepared her for the heart-stopping, visceral reality.

Technically, Anton had been correct. Richard Hampden was over six feet tall with mid-brown hair. But those basic facts failed to convey the sheer magnetic presence of his lean, broad-shouldered frame. There was no spare fat around his lean hips, no unhealthy pallor to his skin. He moved like water, with a liquid grace that suggested quietly restrained power, an animal at the very peak of fitness.

Anton had guessed his age as between twenty-eight and thirty-five. Certainly, Hampden was no young puppy; his face held the hard lines and sharp angles of experience rather than the rounded look of boyhood.

Sabine studied the elegant severity of his dark blue coat, the pale knee breeches outlining long, muscular legs. There was nothing remarkable in the clothes themselves to make him stand out in a crowd, and yet there was something about him that commanded attention. That drew the eye, and held it.

Her life often hinged on the ability to correctly identify dangerous men. Every sense she possessed told her that the man talking with Anton was very dangerous indeed.

Sabine pressed her forehead to the rough planks and swore softly. The Englishman turned, almost as if he sensed her lurking behind the door, and everything inside her stilled. Something—an instant of awareness, almost of recognition—shot through her as she saw his face in full. Of all the things she'd been prepared for, she hadn't envisaged this: Viscount Lovell was magnificent.

And then he'd turned his attention back to Anton, and she'd let out a shaky breath of relief.

She'd dreamed of him ever since. Disturbing, jumbled dreams in which she was always running, he pursuing. She'd wake the very instant she was caught, her heart pounding in a curious mix of panic and knotted desire.

Sabine shook her head at her own foolishness. It was just her luck to conceive an instant attraction to the least suitable man in Europe. The thought of facing him again made her shiver with equal parts anticipation and dread, but he was the obvious answer to her current dilemma. He had money; she needed funds. Voilà tout.

At least now she was prepared. One of the basic tenets of warfare was 'know thine enemy,' after all. Sabine drew her cloak more securely around her shoulders and watched Anton feed the rest of the money to the flames. The embers fluttered upwards like a cloud of glowing butterflies.

When this was all over she would be like a phoenix. Philippe Lacorte would disappear and Sabine de la Tour would emerge from the ashes to reclaim the identity she'd abandoned eight years ago. She would live a normal life.

But not yet. There was still too much to do.

Sabine brushed off her skirts and picked up the bag she'd packed for traveling. There was something rather pathetic in the fact that her whole life fit into one single valise, but she squared her shoulders and glanced over at Anton. "Come on, let's go. Before someone sees the smoke and decides to investigate."

They couldn't go home, to the print shop on Rue Pélican. Malet had already ripped the place apart looking for 'his' money. Her stomach had given a sickening lurch as she'd taken in the carnage. Books pulled from the shelves, paintings ripped from the walls, canvases torn. Old maps shredded, drawers pulled out and upended. Their home, her sanctuary for the past eight years, had been utterly ransacked.

But there had been triumph amid the loss. Malet had found neither Anton nor the money. And if Sabine had anything to do with it, he never would.

Anton hefted the two bags of English banknotes that had been spared the flames as Sabine turned her back on Paris. For the first time in eight long years she was free.

It was time to track down Lord Lovell.

Chapter 2

THREE DAYS LATER. London. 10.45pm.

SABINE PRESSED her hand to her stomach in a vain attempt to quell her nerves. She couldn't back out now; she'd come to this imposing townhouse for the sole purpose of propositioning the man inside. She straightened her shoulders and took a calming breath. She was Europe's greatest forger. She could fake anything. Even a confidence she was far from feeling.

Number five Upper Brook Street was located in the exclusive, aristocratic enclave of Mayfair. To the east loomed the tree-lined railings of Grosvenor Square. To the west carriages rattled past on Park Lane, and beyond that spread the expansive darkness of Hyde Park.

Even at this late hour the streets were busy. Link-boys, with flaming torches of pitch and tow, ran alongside sedan chairs conveying people to and from their evening's entertainments or followed pedestrians to light their way home in exchange for a farthing.

Sabine mounted the shallow flight of steps in front of the house. The knocker was so shiny she could see her own face reflected in it; the snarling lion's nose distorted her features so she appeared no more than a blur of dark hair and dark eyes. The heavy brass fell against the black wood with a crack that sounded like gunfire.

An elderly male servant answered, dressed in dark livery. If he was surprised to see a lone woman on his master's doorstep at almost eleven o'clock in the evening he gave no outward sign. Clearly he was both well-trained and discreet. Or perhaps it was not such an unusual occurrence, Sabine thought wryly.

He raised bushy grey brows. "May I help you, madam?"

Sabine suppressed a smile. Apparently twenty-four was too ancient to still be addressed as 'mademoiselle.' She strove to recall her mother's polite, English tones. "You can indeed. I am here to see Viscount Lovell."

"And who might I inform him is calling?" The butler's impassive countenance gave nothing away.

Sabine tilted her head. "Someone whose acquaintance he has been seeking for a very long time. Please give him this." She pulled the letter she'd prepared from her cloak.

The butler took it and she waited to see if he would usher her inside or make her wait upon the doorstep. Perhaps he would send her around the back to the servants' entrance. For some reason the thought made her smile.

Instead he opened the door and indicated for her to step inside. "If you would care to wait here, madam, I will inform his lordship of your visit."

Sabine gave an imperious nod, as if it was no more than she expected. "Please do. I am quite certain he will want to see me."

She glanced around the hallway as the butler strode away. It was suitably grand for the residence of a viscount, with a black and white tiled floor and an imposing staircase curving upwards to the upper levels. The dark mahogany doors leading off the hallway were all closed. She had not been anywhere so elegant in years, but she would not be overawed. She had lived in a house as grand as this herself, once.

A thin under-footman, emerging from below stairs, regarded her suspiciously, as if she might be thinking of stealing something. Sabine watched in amusement as he took in her appearance, silently assessing her net worth and social position with one glance.

The dismissive curl of his lip told her his conclusion. No doubt her accent pronounced her as one of the hated French, and he clearly supposed her mistress material, a female of the *canaille*. His eyes flicked insultingly to her stomach and she suppressed another smile. Did he suppose she was *enceinte*? Come to inform his lordship of her delicate condition? Ha. Sabine caught his eye and returned his insolent glance with one of her own.

He dropped his eyes first.

* * *

"You have a visitor, my lord."

Richard Hampden, Viscount Lovell, glanced at the ornate gilt clock on the mantelpiece and raised one dark eyebrow at his major-domo.

"At this hour?" The clock showed five minutes to eleven. He and Raven had only stopped into the library for a glass of brandy before heading out to White's.

The elderly servant bowed. "A female, my lord."

Richard narrowed his eyes at his butler's studied lack of intonation—and careful choice of noun. "What kind of female? A lady? Or a woman? Because it's an important distinction, as you well know."

The servant drew himself up, his impassive countenance belied by the amused twinkle in his eye. "It's not for me to say, sir. I wouldn't dare to be so bold as to venture an opinion. Suffice to say that she is unaccompanied."

A smile twitched Richard's lips. "Hodges, you are the model of diplomacy. Castlereagh could have done with you at the Congress of Vienna. Say no more. No *lady* would visit a gentleman's house alone—which makes it all the more interesting."

His best friend, William Ravenwood, Marquis of Ormonde, frowned. "If you're expecting a tart, Richard, I'm off."

"I'm not expecting anyone." Richard took a sip of his excellent brandy. "I ended things with Caro Williams a fortnight ago. And even if I hadn't, I never entertain my mistresses here."

Hodges was still loitering by the door. He cleared his throat and offered forth a folded missive. "She seemed confident that you would see her. She asked me to give you this."

Richard set down his glass and took the paper just as Hodges spoke again. "And though she speaks English, my lord, her accent is decidedly French."

Raven raised his brows at the butler's disapproving tones. "French, eh?" He leaned forward and tried to read over Richard's shoulder. "What does it say? Is it a love letter?"

Richard opened the paper and froze.

"What is it?" Raven asked.

Richard gave a disbelieving chuckle. "It's an invitation. To call here tonight, at eleven o'clock. From myself, apparently."

He turned the paper around so Raven could inspect the perfect copy of Richard's own signature at the bottom of the page.

Raven grinned. "How enterprising. I'll say this, Richard, the lengths to which women will go to get your attention is extraordinary."

Richard half laughed, half groaned. The subject of his popularity was one he found alternately amusing and distasteful.

"I suppose word's got out about you giving Caro her congé." Raven chuckled with all the smug satisfaction of a happily married man blissfully un-pursued by a monstrous regiment of women.

Richard scowled at him. "I had to—you know my rules. Three months, no longer. No virgins. No wives. No exceptions."

As a system it had worked exceptionally well for the past few years. None of the women with whom he consorted harbored any false expectation of marriage. Both sides entered into the dalliance knowing it was based on mutual exclusivity and enjoyment, and when it was over they parted ways as friends. He'd never met a woman he couldn't walk away from.

The only problem was, whenever he finished with one woman there was a mad, undignified scramble to be the next in line. It had become even worse since his father had inherited the Earldom. Richard had been elevated to Viscount Lovell, heir to the Earl of Lindsey, and the women had become even more attentive. The lack of a decent challenge was downright depressing. And despite his very publicly expressed preferences, every last one of them seemed convinced they'd be the exception he'd cave in and marry.

He glanced over at Raven. "Is this your idea of a joke?"

Raven held up his hands. "It's nothing to do with me, I swear. I've no idea who she is."

Richard studied the handwriting closely. If he didn't know better he'd have sworn it really was his own signature. Who on earth would have the audacity to present him with what was quite obviously a forged note?

His pulse accelerated in anticipation. Nothing like a new challenge to liven things up.

Hodges was still hovering, awaiting instruction.

"Did she say anything else?" Richard asked.

"She did not, sir."

Richard rose to his feet with a smile. He'd been so bored recently. Perhaps his mystery guest could cure his current state of ennui. "Well, then. Let's see what she wants."

WANT TO READ MORE? Check out A Counterfeit Heart on Amazon, Barnes & Noble, Kobo, Apple iBooks & Google Play.

Printed in Great Britain
by Amazon

41692411R00179